high lonesome road

also by

betsy thornton

THE COWBOY RIDES AWAY

high lonesome road

BETSY THORNTON

THOMAS DUNNE BOOKS
ST. MARTIN'S MINOTAUR
❧ NEW YORK

TO ALIX

THOMAS DUNNE BOOKS.
An imprint of St. Martin's Press

HIGH LONESOME ROAD. Copyright © 2001 by Betsy
Thornton. All rights reserved. Printed in the United
States of America. No part of this book may be used or
reproduced in any manner whatsoever without written
permission except in the case of brief quotations embod-
ied in critical articles or reviews. For information,
address St. Martin's Press, 175 Fifth Avenue, New York,
N.Y. 10010.

www.minotaurbooks.com

Designed by Lorelle Graffeo

ISBN 0-312-26861-0

First Edition: February 2001

10 9 8 7 6 5 4 3 2 1

127236

MYSTERY

acknowledgments

I would like to thank Elizabeth Atwood Taylor for her superb editing skills, Nancy Tunks for telling me about ropers, and Bob Pomeroy for driving me all over the place in search of material.

prelude

IN ARIZONA LATE ONE NIGHT IN ABOUT
*mid-September, a man got into his '78 sea green Cadillac Eldorado
and drove out to Highway 80. The two-lane blacktop cut through
the Sulphur Springs Valley from the Mexican border to Interstate
10, through farmlands and ranches, a little town or two—cows,
horses, sheep, cotton, chilies, and a whole lot of pecans. The man
was a drinking man, but that night he was sober. He'd driven this
highway all his life, knew when it twisted and when it stretched
out long and straight, knew the big dangerous curve where the
road reached the hilly parts as you approached the interstate.*

*Just before the curve, the speed limit sign said 35, but anyone
who knew the road knew how to gauge their speed to hit the curve
just right. The man was going maybe seventy-five miles an hour
when his headlights hit the sign. He accelerated heavily, going
dead straight for the curve at ninety miles an hour. When the car
left the road, it sailed free through the grasslands, flying in the
dark, until, with a loud crunch, it hit the big rocks at the base of
a hill.*

*The impact jerked the man's head backward, breaking his
neck as the front end of the car crumpled, forcing the steering
column through his body. His vital signs continued, maybe ten,
fifteen minutes, but he was certainly dead when the sheriff's deputy found him forty-five minutes later.*

1

Things like this had a way of happening out in the valley, but still, all the deputies talked about it afterward, for a couple of weeks, until something more exciting came along. Talked about how fast he had to have been going, talked about how, cold sober, he had never, even at the end, hit the brakes.

The bookmobile driver was nervous. She squirted Evian water from a plastic bottle on the dash into her mouth as she drove the stretch of Highway 80 between Dot Stone's and the Olander Meadow stop, but her mouth still felt dry. At Dot's stop, an old man and his wife had shown up, but Dot hadn't even been there.

"She's over to the Baptist church," the old man had told the driver. He wore paint-stained jeans and a straw cowboy hat. "Helping with the rummage sale," he'd added, looking at the driver, at her long pink dress and her black cowboy boots, at her wonderful thick hair, coppery bright in the sunshine. Almost too wonderful, unreal.

For a moment, he'd looked sad; then he'd rallied. "I swear, you got to be the prettiest driver in the history of the bookmobile," he'd said admiringly.

The wife, in jeans and plain roping boots, not fancy ones like the driver wore, had stood stoically by, holding a stack of books.

The driver had smiled at the wife, so she wouldn't take offense, but the wife wouldn't meet her eyes. Most of the women were guarded out here in the valley, suspicious of strangers.

"You drive careful now," the old man had said in parting. "There was a real bad accident, few miles past Olander's, not two weeks ago."

The driver had looked serious. "So I heard," she'd said.

Now the driver was thinking about the Olanders. They were old-time ranchers, Andy had told her; there would be three or four rowdy kids and a grandma at the Olander Meadow stop. People around, so why be nervous? But she was. I shouldn't have made that call, she thought, passing the old billboard Andy had mentioned. The billboard was moored in a sea of sunflowers, a Baptist billboard, something about Jesus. She swallowed, took another swig of Evian.

What did Baptists think of suicide, because suicide is what it must have been. Not an accident. Was he barred from the Kingdom? She'd met people who told her they'd seen Jesus, that He'd appeared in a warm glow, or in a dream that was more than a dream. Lucas, for one. Lucas had been saved. Jesus had spoken to him, and he was saved.

Well, hallelujah, she thought. And how long had it lasted? Still, she could use a little help from Jesus now. Or somebody. What if no one believes me?

She tried to concentrate on driving, the big van swaying and clattering clumsily down the narrow, empty road—so empty out here, it was hard not to think, so she switched her mind to her son, her golden boy. With this new library job, she could get him some good running shoes, get his teeth fixed. Maybe next summer drive him to some art classes at the museum in Tucson.

But summer was far away. The job was mostly boring, but if she hadn't been so nervous, she would have enjoyed this part. The wind rippled the desert grass, pale gold in the sunshine, dotted with dark green mesquite, rimmed with hazy mountains. Fall was beautiful in the high desert, a blaze of golden light clear to Thanksgiving.

Then it will be winter, she thought as she approached the old abandoned house, half-hidden by enormous oaks, just before the dirt road where Andy's directions said she was supposed to turn. Winter, the leaves here would be gone from the sheltering trees and the house left exposed—empty and desolate. Wait, though—a flash of chrome—was that a car, parked among the trees?

She peered in the rearview mirror, saw only the big oaks, a cluster of white prickle poppies. In a nearby field, a trio of black crows floated down for a landing, vivid against the pale grass, somehow ominous. She tightened her hands on the steering wheel, slowed the clumsy van to ten miles an hour, and turned at the dirt road, concentrating, trying to shake her sense of something out of kilter, something seriously wrong. Don't think; don't think.

She pulled up past the stand of tamarisk at the edge of Olander Meadow in a cloud of dust, expecting to see Olanders, all lined up, the rowdy kids and grandma, but instead—*unbelievable*—the meadow was full of skeletons. Skeletons, some fallen, some still erect, eight, nine, ten feet tall. She blinked and saw they were only yuccas the long stems bleached white by the sun, the waxy spears of white flowers dried, turned to hard, clattering pods.

Where were the Olanders?

She parked the van on the edge of the broad meadow at the end of the road. The singing of cicadas filled the air, a mechanical whirring sound winding up to a peak, then receding. They muted the voice in her head, the one that kept telling her, Don't think; don't think. She took a deep breath, then climbed down the steps, her cowboy boots noisy on the metal.

Gathering up the skirts of her long pink dress, she walked through the crowd of yuccas and ankle-high grass to the center of the meadow, where thistle grew, and prickle poppies and sunflowers. From here, she could see a long way down the road, see the Olander ranch—an adobe house, a couple of trailers, and a collection of out-buildings. That was where they'd be walking from. I have time, she thought.

She reached into her pocket, pulled out a joint, and lit up. Took a drag, coughed, dragged again. The cicadas wound down; birds were chirping in the tamarisk. The mountains in the distance, purple now, seemed to float above a gold sea, the air fragrant with the drying grasses. Lucas had once taught her some of the names. She could hear his voice again: "Careless weed, Gramma, love grass, you pretty thing."

Relaxed finally, she fell into a dream of Venice, California, where she had lived many years ago. Sitting on a bench on Ocean Front, by the Cadillac Hotel, as the evening sun softened the pastel fronts of the buildings, drums throbbing out on the beach, someone playing a flute, a guitar. She wore an antique dress, old soft black velvet, and silver bells round her ankles. "You look like a goddess in that dress," her friend James was telling her. Thinking of him brought tears to her eyes. She thought of his sister, polite, smiling, distant.

She shrugged, took one more toke, then wet her fingers, pinched the end. Slipping the roach in her pocket, in a half dream, she walked slowly back to the van and clattered up the metal steps. Inside, it was muggy and smelled like someone's attic.

Neva was right, It was a mess in here, but she was a little spacey now, didn't feel like sweeping. If Neva wanted the van to be clean, she could drive it herself. But Neva was too scared. They all were except Andy. They would rather sit at a desk, drink coffee, watch the clock. She walked to the back of the van, looking for something to read while she waited for the Olanders, a book with beautiful pictures. It was hard to decide . . . so many books.

She pulled one out, *The Houses of Santa Fe,* places to live, photographed so they looked like houses you would see in a dream, hermetic and beautiful. It could have been five minutes, ten, when she heard the noise. Not so near, but distinct. She froze, then looked out through the dusty windows, hoping to see Olanders, but she saw nothing but the yuccas. They'd be noisy anyway, talking. Where were they anyway? She listened hard and heard only cicadas, and the wind; it was rising now, gusting a little.

Coyotes, deer, javelina live out here, she thought to reassure herself. Hadn't Andy told her that only a month ago he'd seen a mountain lion loping across the road in front of the van? It's just an animal. But her hands were cold, every sense alert, so she heard the whisper, like grass parting.

She set down the book carefully, her heart fluttering in her chest. The door, she thought, there's only one. I'm trapped in here; I've got to get out. She took a step forward.

And then suddenly, she heard a hollow metallic thump—and saw a figure at the bookmobile door, silhouetted against the light coming in through the front windshield, dark, no details except the shape of the cowboy hat.

Cowboy hat. Oh God. Oh please. Not *again.*

The sun glinted off something, just for a second, a metallic glint about chest level.

"No," she screamed. "Get out of here! Get out!"

She half-turned, frantic but there was no way out, just a wall of books, more books to either side. She grabbed at the books on the shelf that held the Arizona Collection and began to throw them. Screaming and throwing. *The High-Desert Landscape, Life on a Ranch, The Copper Odyssey, Ghost Towns of Arizona.*

The desert took her screams and dissolved them in the wind—they melted into the landscape, signifying nothing. Adrenaline pumping, she was on her own. She grabbed some more books, held them in front of her like a shield, moved forward determinedly toward the only way out. Terrified but moving.

The first bullet hit her left shoulder, but she kept going, shielded by books. The second hit her in the chest, between *Cowboy Cookery* and *My Life as a Cowboy,* and she stumbled, but she didn't fall. She thought of her son then, saw his face, so bright, so innocent, and it gave her strength. The bullets kept coming—*bam, bam, bam.*

Miraculously, she reached the front door, and the shooter backed away. Did she see Him then, if only for a second, as she fell, plummeting down the steps?

She lay motionless at the bottom, facedown in the meadow, the spiky grasses mingling with her bright hair. Still clutching two books, *Cattle Ranching in the Old West* and *A Beautiful Cruel Country.*

Well, maybe she deserved it.

We had an exercise we always used at the end of the first class of the Victim Witness Program's volunteer training, called "the Married Woman Exercise." It went like this:

THE MARRIED WOMAN EXERCISE

Once upon a time, a husband and wife lived together in a part of the city separated by a river from their places of employment, shopping and entertainment. The husband had to work nights. Each evening, he left his wife and took the ferry to work, returning in the morning.

The wife soon tired of this arrangement. Restless and lonely, she would take the next ferry into town each evening and develop relationships with a series of lovers. Anxious to preserve her marriage, she always returned home before her husband. In fact, her relationships were always limited. When they threatened to become too intense, she would precipitate a quarrel with her current lover and begin a new relationship.

One night, she caused a quarrel with a man we will call Lover One. He slammed the door in her face, and she started back to the ferry. Suddenly, she realized that she had forgotten to bring money for her return fare. She swallowed her pride and returned to Lover One's apartment to borrow the fare. But Lover One was vindictive and angry because of the quarrel. He slammed the door in her face, leaving her with no money. She remembered that a previous lover, whom we will call Lover Two, lived just a few doors away. Surely he would give her the ferry fare. But Lover Two was still so hurt from their old quarrel that he, too, refused her the money.

Now the hour was late and the woman was getting desperate. She rushed down to the ferry and pleaded with the ferryboat captain. He knew her as a regular customer. She asked if he could let her ride free and if she could pay the next night. But the captain insisted that rules were rules and he could not let her ride without paying.

Dawn would soon be breaking and her husband would be returning home from work. The woman remembered that there was a free bridge about a mile farther on. But the road to the bridge was a dangerous one, known to be frequented by highwaymen. But she had to get home, so she took the road. On the way, a highwayman stepped out of the bushes and demanded her money. She told him she had none. He seized her. In the ensuing tussle, the highwayman stabbed the woman, and she died. Thus our story ends. There have been six characters: husband, wife, Lover One, Lover Two, ferryboat captain, and the highwayman. We would like you to list the characters you feel are responsible for the woman's death.

chapter one

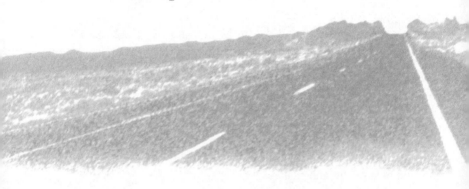

SHORTLY AFTER A FRIEND OF MINE, SHERIFF'S
Department detective Kyle Barnett, killed a man and was transferred
up to the Willcox area, I switched jobs from victim-compensation advocate to victim advocate. I'd moved to Dudley, Arizona, from New
York City a couple of years before, and it was about time to get a
little more financial security. The new job was only twenty hours a
week, but it paid better; plus, I got full benefits. It was one of those
part-time jobs that could easily stretch to thirty, forty hours, but I
was supposed to keep track, and not work more, so I couldn't come
back and sue the county.

I was fighting depression, and the job was just what I needed.
And when I worked more, I didn't write it down. I worked as hard as
I could so I could go home and fall asleep, exhausted. But sometimes
I still woke up at three in the morning to think about Kyle and the
things I knew about him that no one else did and the things he knew
about me.

No one had even questioned me during the investigation, an investigation that had not made it to a grand jury. No one had questioned me, though I was the last person, before Kyle, to see the man
he'd killed alive.

Bobbie, Kyle's sister, didn't question me, either, but I thought if
anyone would know something she would. She volunteered for the
Victim Witness Program, and we were pretty good friends, but we

never spoke about what had happened. What would be the point?
He'd been a bad man, deserved to die. "Don't wimp out on me, Chloe,"
Bobbie would have said.

One of the things I did in my new job was teach the nine-week
training course for volunteers in the northern, sparsely populated
part of the county, where Kyle had been transferred. When I drove
through the little towns and down the long, empty roads through the
fertile fields and grasslands of the valley to Willcox, where I taught
the class, I looked for Kyle, looked for him straight ahead and in my
rearview mirror, looked for him when I passed the sheriff's substation
as I drove into Willcox, but I never saw him. Maybe that was because
he always saw me first.

Then after he separated from his wife, resigned from the Sheriff's
Department, and left the county, I still looked for him, not on the
long high-desert roads, but late at night, three o'clock in the morning,
when I woke in my house in Old Dudley and heard my heart going
tick, tick, tick.

I grew up with two brothers, Danny and James. Danny, the youngest,
was a wild boy, and he now lives in a Buddhist colony in Vermont.
The eldest of us, James, is dead.

Years ago, I visited James when he lived in Venice, California. He
was strong and happy and healthy then. He rented the downstairs
half of a shabby frame house on one of the streets by Venice Beach.
We'd get up every morning, my favorite brother and I and walk down
to Ocean Front Walk, past the old Jewish people sitting on the
benches, past the palm trees and the young hippies playing drums
and guitars, and panhandling. We would walk across the sand to the
sparkling water, then along the water's edge.

Sometimes, Erica came along. Erica Hill. She lived upstairs, a
beautiful woman with thick dark hair that fell nearly to the small of
her back. She and I were about the same age, but she seemed ageless,
born wise and confident, and I was in awe of her. She wore silver
bells and Indian prints and old soft velvets, and to me, she was the

quintessential hippie, back when the word meant something new and different and free.

The polluted California air had been dense and dreamy sweet in Venice. Erica, James, and I burned patchouli incense, and ate rice and vegetables with delicious sauces our mothers had never heard of. I knew that James loved Erica, in his way, but they were never lovers. Back then, I wondered, Why not? Now, of course, I know.

James died of AIDS a few years ago, in L.A. His lover, Hal, nursed him through his last terrible year. It's because of Hal that I moved from New York to Old Dudley. After James's death, Hal left L.A., bought the house in Old Dudley where I live. Hal is dead now, too, and he willed the house to me.

Dudley is composed of two towns, Old Dudley and New Dudley. New Dudley is out on the flats and not much different from the way it was thirty years ago, but Old Dudley is like no other place in Cochise County. A tiny, quaint mining town in the mountains, colonized, when the mines closed down, by hippies. They moved here in droves in the late seventies, opened up galleries, crafts stores, the Natural Food Co-op.

Sometimes when I walk around the streets here, I am reminded of Venice—the wood houses, the music coming up from the Gulch, the hippies. It fills me with nostalgia for who I once was, back in Venice, back in New York, too, for a while. After a brief marriage, I'd left my husband, moved to the East Village. But hippies didn't survive for long in New York City.

I tried odd jobs—waitressing, social work—left the city, went back; then I saw the ad for Friendly Investigations, Friendly being the name of the owner and not the tone of the organization, and applied for a job there. I'd worked for two years as an investigator, mostly a skip tracer; then I'd gotten my license. It had been an accident really, a profession by default for someone who'd majored in literature. It satisfied my morbid curiosity about people's secret lives, just as literature had. Mostly, I worked for professional women who wanted to know about the financial situations of their boyfriends, or their fiancés. A feminist sort of job, I told myself, but after awhile, I felt as though I were working for a bunch of greedy females whose hearts were stamped with dollar signs.

But the hippies make me impatient, too—survivors clinging to this last outpost. They don't get involved beyond their own little world, don't do things like take the Victim Witness Program volunteer training. Victim Witness volunteers mostly come from New Dudley, a couple of miles past the old mining pit, where the true locals live, the ones who've lived here all their lives. They own the established businesses and support law enforcement.

I didn't usually do the Dudley trainings, but the Dudley trainer got bronchitis and I took over her first class. Just luck—or maybe *karma*'s a better word—that after all those years, the most unlikely person showed up there: Erica Hill.

The class was held at night, in a room in the Health Department, maybe fifteen pleasant, unassuming people, more women than men, crammed into uncomfortable metal desks. We'd already finished the first get-acquainted exercise, and I was about to launch into the training, when Erica walked in.

I didn't recognize her, barely glanced her way, saw a mass of hair, crinkly rose silk, silver jewelry, glinting under the fluorescent lights.

"Hi," I said brightly. "Have a seat. I'm Chloe Newcombe, the trainer for tonight."

She didn't move, stood there, her mouth open. *"Chloe?"*

I looked at her then. She smiled. "Chloe, it's Erica. Remember? From Venice. Erica Hill."

"Erica." For a second, I was stunned, thrown off balance. "My God, of course. I wasn't expecting . . . But you look just the same."

She almost did. Her hair. It had always been beautiful; she'd told me once she conditioned it with olive oil, wrapped . . .

In front of me, fifteen people sat with polite smiles on their faces. I had a training to do. Suddenly, everything in the room seemed too bright, exposing me in its glare.

"Well!" I said even more brightly. "It's *great* to see you again. Have a seat. We can talk after class."

I spoke to the class about what the training would cover, talked about taking risks and learning to grow. The fluorescent lights shone down, reflecting back off the beige tile floor as I hung up newsprint with masking tape on the walls, my points printed on them. I talked and talked myself hoarse, my voice droning on, drowning out the sound of my thoughts.

After that, we broke into little groups and did a few exercises designed to get people to trust one another, to reveal themselves. I was supposed to circulate, offering encouragement, but I stood at the board in front, my back to the class, and carefully erased some notes I'd written there in marker.

Thinking of Erica, Venice, *James*. I no longer thought of James the way I used to; months could go by without my really remembering. But now Erica had brought him back, full-blown and vivid. Distantly, I watched my arm moving up and down as I erased my name, my title.

By the end of the class, I'd pulled myself together, Chloe Newcombe, trainer for Victim Witness Program volunteers, and I handed out the Married Woman Exercise. When everyone was done reading it, I made a chart on the board, with all the characters listed and the order of their responsibility for the woman's death from most to least. No one had been asked to list them in order of responsibility, but we cheated and drew the graph that way, so they'd be encouraged to blame everyone.

And they did. They gave every person on the list a share of the blame—the husband for being insensitive and leaving her alone, the ferryboat captain for his cold "Rules are rules" policy, the lovers for not helping out. Of course, the highwayman got some of the blame, but most of it centered on the married woman, whose wicked life had led to her death.

Then Erica spoke up, her voice impatient. "What's wrong with everyone? Can't you all see that *no one*'s responsible for her death but the highwayman? How can she be responsible when he's the one who *killed* her?"

The class fell silent, looking at Erica.

"Everyone in this class is entitled to their *opinion*," I said, lying.

"But I happen to agree with Erica." I paused significantly. "We have to be careful about *blaming the victim.*"

Lights went on in the faces of the class, tricked into betraying their own image of themselves as good, thoughtful people. I probably had a smug little smile on my face. I don't remember. Don't remember much about the class except for Erica and what she said. I am still haunted by that.

After class, Erica stuck around, being helpful. She dumped the coffeepot and rinsed it out while I rolled up the newsprint. We walked out together to the parking lot, me with the newsprint portfolio and one box, Erica with the coffee makings in the other.

Outside, it was balmy, late summer in the desert, and smelled of rain.

"How long have you lived here?" Erica asked.

"A couple of years or so," I said.

"I can't believe it. That we never *saw* each other till now. Of course, people here—they get in their own little enclaves, don't they?"

"Yes." Looking at Erica, I wanted to say, I *work;* I don't hang out. But it would have sounded so priggish, so right-wing.

"I bet we've passed on the street and we . . . we weren't *looking.* I don't think I would have recognized you right away, if you hadn't told me your name." She tilted her head. "You look so . . ." She paused.

"Straight," I said. I was wearing a white linen jacket, a short black-and-white-print dress, little heels.

She laughed. "How did you end up here anyway?"

I shifted the newsprint portfolio to my other arm. "I inherited Hal's house."

"Oh, of course," she said. "It makes sense. I heard he'd moved here. I was in Nicaragua that summer."

We paused while I locked the outer door. I was tired from the class and wanted to go home. I knew her, and yet I didn't. Years stood between us and the faraway summer when I'd known her. I felt shy and artificial.

"And you," I said politely, "what are you doing here? Are you working?"

She sighed. "Well, I've been waitressing."

Waitressing. She could have been anything, done anything. But none of us was the sum of her job. And she still looked . . . well, magnificent, standing there in her fantasy crinkled rose clothes, silver jewelry, her hair gleaming under the lights of the parking lot. Aging, yes, but becomingly.

"Actually, I may be getting a new job. A pretty good one. But jobs . . ." She shrugged. "They don't matter. I've lived here almost twenty years now, and it's been good for me." Her face lit up. "For one thing, I'm a mother."

"Oh," I said, "you have *children*?"

"One. He's sixteen now. Troy." It was just a boy's name, but she said it so proudly, as if the name alone had some cosmic meaning. Troy. The famous Troy. Then she added her, eyes shining, "He's such a good boy, funny and loving and creative. He was born on my birthday, so we're both Scorpios. I'm a single mother."

She smiled at me as she played with a silver cross hanging around her neck. Cool teenage boys wore crosses dangling from one pierced ear; rock stars wore big heavy crosses on cords. Actual Christians probably wore them, too. "Oh," she added, "and we have a dog, too, Krishna."

It figured. I turned the key and tested the door to make sure it was secure. Busying myself with the little details because I didn't know what to say.

"Do you ever think about Venice?" she asked as we walked to my car. "Wasn't it heavenly? Sometimes I think I'd like to go back, but by now, they've probably wrecked it. And anyway, it would be myself I'd be looking for, you know?"

Her voice was the way I remembered it, animated and compelling. I opened the hatchback of my car and put my box inside. "Yes, I do know."

"I have to get home now," she said, handing me the box with the coffee stuff. Her face lit up again. "I promised Troy I'd get right home. He's got some project. . . ." She laughed and shrugged. "*Anyway,* let's get together sometime and talk. I'd really like to do that."

I had a little image then of me, Erica, and James, sitting on Venice Beach. Seagulls plunged, skimming the water; the sun was going down. James was listening intently, smiling as Erica told him a story. I sat to one side, drawing little pictures in the wet sand.

"Definitely," I said.

"You've got my number, from when I signed in."

I could have given her my card, written my home phone number on it, but I didn't.

"My car's right here." She began to walk away, toward a pumpkin-colored car of indeterminate make and vintage. Then she hesitated, looking back at me. "James," she said softly. "I miss him even now. I'm so so sorry."

I felt as though she'd pierced my heart. "I am, too," I said, more coldly than I intended.

I drove home that night, biting my lip to keep from crying, stumbling over Big Foot, my cat, as I walked into my house, Hal's house, in the dark. I switched on lights and went to the filing cabinet in the little room I used as an office, off the living room. I reached way back in the second drawer and pulled out James's letters, tied together with a bit of black yarn. I hadn't looked at them in years.

I sat on the floor of the room, reading the letters and crying, long after bedtime.

"One of the things I hate most about this premature dying thing," he'd written, "is not knowing what will happen to people. I guess it's just my gossipy old self. Erica Hill, for one. How I regret that I won't be able to know how she turns out. Will she end up enlightened at the feet of some guru, or maybe just be swept away by a rich man to hang out on the beaches at Cannes? Who knows, maybe there's a link between the living and the dead, a wavelength—if you and I ever connect, you'll let me know what happens to Erica, won't you?"

And I hadn't even given her my card.

Maybe that was why she never called me. I didn't call her. She never came to another class. The trainer told me Erica had left a message that she'd gotten a job and didn't have the time. I promised myself I would call her eventually. But I kept putting it off.

One afternoon, two or three weeks later, I saw her as I was sitting in the new juice bar that had just opened up on the second floor above the Natural Foods Co-op. My neighbor Lourdes and I had stopped in to try it out. We were both drinking raspberry smoothies, and I looked out the window, and there was Erica, floating down Main Street in a red-and-black gauze dress, black boots. Beside her, then in front, then behind was a young teenager in black-and-white-striped pants, black T-shirt, big running shoes. It had to be Troy. The famous Troy. He had the only dreadlocks I'd ever seen on a blond and he wandered, rather than walked, down the streets like a young puppy, sniffing at all the shops along the way.

When he reached the Co-op, he sniffed there. He never looked up to the second floor, so he didn't see me looking down on him. Black-frame glasses, childish face. With his Raggedy Andy hair, his big feet, he was clownish, charming, and dazzling all at once. I wanted to smile, just looking at him.

And Erica looked happy. Once, we'd both been in Venice, California, living with careless faith, the way she seemed to live now still. In her forties, single, a child to support. I imagined she had accumulated nothing in the way of financial security, probably didn't even have health insurance. Thinking that, through an act of sheer will and a mainly vegetable diet, she would never grow old, would live forever. A life of no security at all.

I could have run down, stopped her, but I didn't want to abandon Lourdes. I watched Erica in her gauze dress and her elaborate jewelry and sensed a life I could have been leading myself but for various things, accidental possibly, that had happened to me. My job was still part-time, but I had full benefits. One of us had taken the easy way in life, one the hard. You had to think a long time to figure out which was which.

chapter two

ON THE DAY OF THE MURDER, I SPENT THE
morning in Division Two, Judge Collins's court, with Rita, a tough-
talking, wiry divorcée of twenty-five. She'd been the night clerk at a
Circle K over in Sierra Vista when an eighteen-year-old kid named
Victor Wilson, cranked up on methamphetamine, came in with a gun
and held her up for a couple of six-packs of beer and twenty candy
bars.

Victor's lawyer was deputy public defender Stuart Ross, fashion-
able black wire-rimmed glasses, gold hoop glittering in one ear, thinning blond hair in a ponytail. Stuart was new in Cochise County, had
done mostly juvie drug cases so far, but they were pushing him up
the ladder. He stood there, one hand protectively on the shoulder of
his scraggly client, while Rita, visibly shaking, came up to give her
victim impact statement. What the gun held to her head and, later,
the sound of the shot fired wildly into the air had done to her life.
The nightmares, the slow-motion flashbacks, the hypervigilance; what
it cost her still to get up the nerve to pick up a carton of milk at a
Circle K.

The armed robbery had cost plenty, and would for a long time
to come. Real violence makes everyone around it pay and pay, no
credits rolling at the end.

The judge gave Victor the max, seven to ten. Rita dissolved into
tears.

Stuart Ross swooshed by me afterward, giving me a cold, lawyerly stare. My eyes froze right back at him.

In the afternoon, I had to drive to Willcox for a volunteer meeting, and as I was walking to my car in the parking lot behind the county attorney's offices, Stuart Ross hurried out of the drug unit. He'd loosened his necktie, lost his jacket. Though it was fall, it was probably in the nineties, and the wind, a breeze that morning, had reached the discomfort level almost of a sirocco.

"Hold on!" Stuart called to me.

I got into my car, to signify haste. I was still wearing my court clothes, and the seat was burning hot, blistering my thighs through my sheer black panty hose. My black skirt was fashionably, uncomfortably too short. I tugged it down and looked at Stuart out the window.

He ambled over, not hurrying now, Mr. Cool, his cowboy boots noisy on the parking lot's blacktop, a red disclosure file under his arm. Resting one hand on top of my car, he leaned in toward the window and grinned down at me.

"Pecan?" he said, holding one out to me, already cracked.

I took it.

"Well," he said, "we got Victor taken care of—eighteen years old, and now he's on the fast track to career criminal. I guess you think he got what he deserved?"

"It's the victim you should ask," I said. He smelled like tobacco and, I thought, Brut.

"But I'm not. I'm asking you."

"I'm just a conduit for the victim," I said glibly. "That's my job." I reached for my purse and got out my keys. "What do *you* think?"

He looked at his watch. "You got an hour?"

"I don't even have the time we're taking now." I turned the key in the ignition, but Stuart didn't move away. Or maybe Old Spice. Did they still sell Old Spice?

"Besides seeing you in court," he said, "I've also seen you at the post office. You live in that corner house up on Ocotillo. I live around here, too. Alone?"

"What?"

"You live alone?"

"Yes."

The wind, which was already gusting, whipped at the sleeve of his wash-and-wear blue dress shirt. "I'd like to take you out to dinner," he said. "We could talk about Old Dudley."

Whoopee. His lawyer's voice was melodious, persuasive. His cranked-up client had actually fired the gun, but the jury hadn't gone for the charge of attempted murder.

I glanced over his shoulder at the offices of the county attorney. The sun glittered on the windows, and I imagined everyone, everyone watching us. "I don't know."

"Sure you do." He glanced back, too. "We're not going to talk about *cases.* "

"Look," I said, "why don't you call me. I've got a meeting in Willcox. I have to go."

"When do you get back?"

"Seven-fifteen or so." I revved up the engine.

"Perfect," said Stuart. "I'm always hungry after meetings, aren't you? Ever been to that Mexican restaurant, Chez Ramon, on Main Street?"

"Not yet," I said impatiently.

"Tell you what. I'll meet you there at seven-thirty." He backed away.

"Wait!" I said.

"Bye." He kept on backing. The wind played with his tie, throwing it over his shoulder. He waved. "If you argue, you'll be late."

My parents are academics, with a string of published articles about the conduct of business in the Roman Empire. I have been weaned from them for many years, but the first sick thought that came to mind as I drove off was how happy my mother would be if I wrote and told her I was going out with a lawyer.

I didn't know it, but by then they must have already found the body, every sheriff's deputy's car within fifty miles pulling up to Olander Meadow. The yellow tape with CRIME SCENE—DO NOT CROSS was probably being strung up about then, and the lab van on its way.

I ate Stuart's pecan as I sped through the valley, going seventy-five miles an hour on the two-lane blacktop to make up for the five minutes I'd lost; feeling smug, having this lawyer work so hard to get me to go out with him. The music on my stereo was turned up loud, Gram Parsons singing "A Song for You" "Oh, my land is like a wild goose." I was going through a Gram Parsons period and I loved this song—couldn't get enough of it.

Somehow, the terrain outside looked just like the song described—bordered with sunflowers and vast, empty; the wind tugging at the mesquite, churning the grasses into a gold sea. The valley was only a twenty-minute drive from Old Dudley, but you might as well have taken a spaceship to another planet. I'd spent most of my adult life in New York City, and the valley never failed to fascinate me, its many faces changing hour by hour as the sun rode through the sky—burned out and dry in the noon sun but ethereal and mysterious by sunset.

Cowboys lived here, farmers, ranchers, and people who still caught small animals and sold the pelts. There were plenty of animals to catch—coyote, javelina, porcupines, bunny rabbits and jackrabbits, deer, mountain lions. Everyone owned a gun; someone was always getting shot in bar fights. Harsh and violent and beautiful, the valley was like a remnant of an older America, or maybe not a remnant at all, but the secret that lay at America's heart.

To my right was the faded old billboard:

JESUS IS THE LIVING WORD
THE BIBLE IS THE WRITTEN WORD

Was that what sustained the people who lived out here in the valley? And like magic, Gram Parsons was singing—"Jesus built a ship to sing a song to—"

Suddenly, it occurred to me, came to me like shock: Right now, I thought, I'm *happy*.

I pushed the rewind button and the song started again as I approached Kansas Settlement Road. An old gray pickup was parked on the side at the stop sign, and it began honking at me.

"Fuck you, too," I said out loud. Alone in a car, I lose my manners. As I made the turn, I turned the stereo louder to drown out the honking. I was headed a way down the road before I realized it was Frankie, one of the Willcox volunteers, honking at me. I hit the brakes, backed up.

The wind slammed at the car door as I opened it and got out, my black silk jacket flapping around me. The waistband of my skirt dug into my flesh.

Frankie leaped out of her truck. "Damn!" she said. In the wind, her bright red hair, usually arranged in a careful gypsy shag, stood straight up. Frankie was close to sixty. She was wearing skintight jeans and a pink sweatshirt with a black cowboy boot appliquéd on with fuchsia thread and gold studs. "I knew I'd catch you if I just waited here. We got a call-out, and not a damn person's around."

"What about the damn meeting?"

"I left a note in case I caught you; told 'em call-out, no meeting. You ain't gonna believe this. Somebody shot the *bookmobile lady*."

"No *kidding*."

"Shot her dead. Every deputy around's tore out there as fast as they could go." Frankie worked for the Sheriff's Department, so she was in on everything from the start. "That's where we're going, too. It's not far. We can take my truck. Get in."

The truck smelled like a cigarette warehouse would smell if it burned down. Springs popped out of the seat everywhere. On the floor was a baseball bat and a cardboard box of pecans, hardly room for my feet. Frankie lit a cigarette from one burning in the ashtray as we tore down the road.

"So this is a death notification?" I asked, clinging to my seat.

"No. We got to help out the bookmobile patron that found her. Dot Stone. She went home and called nine one one, then drove right back to the scene, and now she won't leave. That's why Ed called us. Only reason he *would* call us."

"Oh shit," I said. "*Ed Masters* is the investigator?"

"Yep." Frankie clicked her tongue. "Why'd they make him detective anyway? Everybody knows he blew that stabbing over at Cochise Stronghold, and this is gonna be a big one. Kind of thing like this, makes me sick Kyle up and quit like that."

She glanced at me. Her gold cat's eyes were accented with midnight blue mascara. "You knew Kyle, of course."

We whizzed down the two-lane blacktop, empty ranchland on either side, mountains far away. Going from nowhere to nowhere. "Umm," I said.

"Dot used to be a schoolteacher," Frankie went on. "She had two of my boys, third grade. Her husband died last April, dropped dead out in the pecan orchard. She's had her share."

"Who's going to notify the relatives, then?"

"If the victim's got kin, which I guess she must, they should be calling Dudley Victim Witness. That's where she's from. Jesus Christ, it just occurred to me; you live there. I hope it ain't someone you know."

"I don't know any bookmobile ladies," I said. "That's the county library; Dudley people use the city library."

We passed a house on the left, abandoned, falling down, obscured by trees. Just after the house, Frankie turned onto a dirt road.

"What's the victim's name, though?" I asked. "Just in case." I watched the tamarisk that grew along the edge of the road as it blew in the wind.

"Elsie . . . Elsie," said Frankie. "Damn. Not Elsie. Last name's Hill."

Tamarisk has another name, salt cedar. It grows in arid land, and suddenly my throat felt parched, as dried-up as the land. I swallowed. "Hill?"

"Yeah."

"*Erica?*" I said. "Could it be *Erica* Hill?"

"That's it," said Frankie. "Erica Hill. Shit, you *do* know her."

Little goose bumps rose on my arms and I had the sensation of sweat drying instantly on my body. For a second, my mind went blank, numbed out. I clutched the edge of the seat, digging my nails into the musty upholstery.

"You okay? Chloe, you look about as white as a ghost."

I should have called her. Suddenly, I had a terrible sense of being swept away by things, caught up in the little details of my own self-ishness, while everything that really mattered passed me by. *Why didn't I call her?* And I'd trained Frankie, taught her how to be a volunteer. I was a fraud.

"I'm okay," I said, lying.

chapter three

THE DIRT ROAD TURNED, BORDERING A
broad meadow full of yuccas, then finally stopped abruptly at a stand
of tamarisk. There was crime-scene tape everywhere, coming loose
and fluttering in the breeze, and a slew of cars—two sheriff's deputies', a white Geo, an old gray station wagon, and the bookmobile
van—big and beige, COCHISE COUNTY LIBRARY DISTRICT in black
letters on its side.

Frankie pulled in next to a deputy's car and suddenly drew in
her breath. "There's the victim."

I looked, saw Erica. She was sprawled in the pale, spiky grass,
boneless and inert by the bookmobile door, a book clutched in her
right hand. One cowboy boot was twisted oddly on the first step up,
her long pink skirt bunched at her knees. Her brown hair, streaked
with bright copper in the sun, fanned out over a dark blouse. Then
with a shock, I realized that it wasn't a blouse at all; it was the dark
stain of blood. I looked away.

"Poor thing," Frankie said.

My heart thud-thudded in my chest, and my hands were cold as
ice. I swallowed and rubbed my arms briskly as if to up my circula-
tion.

"I don't know, Chloe," Frankie said from somewhere far away.
"You don't look too good. I can handle Dot by myself, if you want to
sit a minute."

"Dot," I said. My voice sounded far away, too, a dim roar in my ears.

"Dot Stone." Frankie pointed. "Over there."

I looked, saw a woman, white-haired, substantial, by the edge of the field, near an old gray station wagon. She wore a man's blue work shirt, jeans, and cowboy boots, her arms folded across her chest.

"Maybe I *will* sit," I said. "Just for a minute."

Frankie opened her door and got out.

I sat, eyes closed, but, behind the lids, I still saw Erica lying there. I couldn't stand it. I got out of the truck, too, and walked to a point where the bookmobile hid her body. The wind had died down and dried grasses pricked at my panty hose, their smell pungent in my nose.

Out in the field, Ed Masters paced slowly up and down among the yuccas. A couple of deputies, standing near the road, alert and tense, nodded at me. I took a deep breath, trying to breathe from the diaphragm, the way they teach in yoga classes, then another.

My mind started to clear. Frankie was talking to Dot Stone. Traumatized by finding the body. A victim. I was a victim advocate. I walked toward them.

". . . except for Lucas," Dot was saying. Her face was ruddy and sunburned, nose thick like a man's, blue eyes blank with shock behind pink plastic-rimmed glasses. "He was real close to her once."

Lucas? Who was Lucas? Someone close to Erica? For the first time, I remembered Troy. The famous Troy. I felt sick. Erica was a single mother, but he had to have a father, didn't he? Could Lucas . . .

"That a fact," Frankie was saying. "That man gets around more than—" She saw me then and stopped. "But here's Chloe; she's the advocate from the county attorney's, Dot. She knew her, too. Didn't you, Chloe?"

"We'd sort of lost touch," I said. The euphemism rang in my mind, lost touch, lost touch. From where we stood, I couldn't see Erica's body, but I saw her, hair gleaming under the lights of the parking lot at the Health Department, offering friendship as I stood by and held back, a polite stranger.

In the next field over, a dust devil whirled. The sky was a hard, impenetrable blue, like plastic.

"It's an awful shame," said Dot. "She was so pretty. No blood at all on her face, I recognized her right away." She put her hand over her mouth. "Her face. I never will forget the look on her pretty face as long as I live."

"Sure you don't want to go home now?" Frankie said. "We'll come, too, sit with you."

Dot shook her head stubbornly. "Not until I know she's all right."

"Honey," said Frankie gently. "She's not going to be all right. I talked to the deputy before we even got here. She's dead, Dot."

Dot's eyes sharpened for a second. "I'm not a dope, Frankie. I know she's *dead*." She wrapped her arms around her body. "I want to be here till the mortuary van comes and they take her away is all. I *told* Ed Masters that. He was a student of mine."

"Is that the truth," said Frankie.

Dot nodded. "Ate crayons, paste, you name it."

Frankie and I looked across the meadow at Ed, big and beefy, carefully stepping over a fallen yucca in the middle of the meadow. Yuccas were everywhere, dry, skeletal—some tilted down, some towering over Ed. Sunflowers, too, brown and dazzling gold. From down the road behind us came the sound of a vehicle.

Frankie turned. "Look," she said. "Here comes the mortuary van now, thank God."

We watched it pull in, cream-colored and discreet. Two medics got out, their faces blank, serious.

Dot looked at me. "I missed her 'cause of the church rummage sale. Looked at the schedule and tore over here. I was pretty close before I saw her, and the first thing I thought was, She's taking a nap, right there by the bookmobile. But it wasn't right, and I knew it. Funny how you know something but you don't."

"Shock," said Frankie.

Dot sniffed. "You can call it what you want. Anyway, I got out of my car and went over to her." She sighed, hyperventilating a little. "I keep thinking if I'd come just a little sooner, maybe I coulda saved her. I keep thinking he mighta changed his mind, seeing me pull up. He was still around when I got here. I saw him."

"What?" I asked. "You *saw* him?"

Dot nodded. "In the rearview mirror as I was leaving. Must have been there the whole time, watching me." She pointed at the meadow. "Over there standing in those yuccas."

A long silence followed. Frankie and I stared out at the meadow, as if someone besides Ed might still be there. An ominous dark shape, a murderer, standing in the yuccas.

Frankie's eyes met mine. I knew we were thinking the same thing. Dot was lucky to be alive.

"Dot, you told Ed that, didn't you?" said Frankie.

"Course I did. Why do you think Ed's out there now?"

"And you could identify him? If you saw him again?"

"I never said that. It was just a glimpse, in that little bitty mirror. Couldn't make out any features. When I saw him, I spun out of there fast as I could. Wasn't an animal, 'cause it was big enough and the right shape to be human. Besides, I saw the cowboy hat."

I shuddered, looked around, feeling as if eyes were boring into my back. Nothing to see but the meadow, the blank fields, the light sharp and glittery. The medics came around the bookmobile, carrying a stretcher. I averted my eyes.

And then suddenly, I remembered Troy again, that day I'd seen him through the window of the juice bar, blond dreadlocks, big feet, zigzagging down the street, clownish and dazzling. Saw the pride shining on Erica's face as she talked about him—the wunderkind, the famous Troy. Saw all that dazzle wiped out in an instant.

"Frankie," I said urgently. "Erica has a *son*. The death notification. Who's going to do it? I've got to talk to Ed."

The last time I'd seen Ed, he'd been in uniform; now he wore an ugly brown polyester suit, inelegant, tight at the shoulders, the sleeves too short. Had it been his court suit when he was a deputy? Had Kyle recommended Ed's promotion, before he left? I didn't think so.

"Hi there, Chloe." He reminded me of a big steer, blunt-nosed, placid. Now he was sweating, beads of water dotting his red forehead. "Dot okay?"

"As good as can be expected," I said. "Ed, who's doing the death notification? Have you called Dudley Victim Witness?"

"This is a *homicide*," said Ed. "We ain't called nobody."

"Then I want to do it. I knew the victim. She has a son—Troy. I can—"

"Hold on," Ed interrupted. "How old?"

"Sixteen, I think."

"He ever been in trouble?"

"Not that I know of. He's just a kid, Ed," I pleaded. "This is going to be terrible for him." I could hear the strain in my voice, needing to make him understand. *"Please."*

Deliberately, Ed reached into his pocket, took out a pecan, and cracked it with his teeth. He looked at me intently. "How'd you know the victim?"

"We were friends back when I used to live in California. I didn't even know she lived here until about a month ago. She took a Victim Witness training class," I said. "Then she dropped out. She got a job— this job, I guess. I don't know anything else about her life."

James's words went through my mind: ". . . if you and I ever connect you'll let me know what happens to Erica, won't you?" What *had* happened to her really? I had no idea.

A fly landed on Ed's forehead. He swatted at it, his eyes facing inward. "I'll do it myself. This is a homicide investigation." His face was stolid. "I got to go by the book here."

"There's no reason why I can't follow you there and do the notification. It'll get him calmed down."

Ed stood, hands on hips, looking down at me. "You folks are fine, as far as you go, but I got the say here. It's law enforcement that calls you out. I make the determination, and I decided I'll do it myself."

"That's ridiculous." I could feel the anger rising, and I kept my voice low, fighting it. "Kyle used us all the time, for everything. And Kyle was—" I stopped, bit off the words I'd meant to say: a *good* cop. "Kyle never had a problem with us."

I might as well have said it. Ed's eyes turned from neutral to hostile.

"Well, I'm not Kyle," he said. "You just go back and take care of your business." His voice rose. "I called you to get that schoolteacher off the crime scene, damn it, and she's still standing there."

Someone touched my arm. "Chloe?"

"What?"

Frankie was beside me. "Come on, let's go say bye to Dot." She glanced at Ed. "She's ready to go home now."

Ed turned his back, strode away, and got into a white Geo. Frustration washed over me. I couldn't have handled it worse if I'd tried.

"Shit," I said.

"Never you mind," Frankie said. "You got to let it go. Ed's a stubborn old goat. The mortuary van's gone and Dot's going home to read her Bible. She don't need us anymore. But Chloe?"

"What?"

She grinned, looking down at my hands. "Victim Witness people ain't supposed to assault police officers."

I looked down, too. My fists were so tightly clenched, my fingers ached. I hadn't even been aware of it.

chapter four

STUART AND I EMERGED FROM CHEZ RAMON.
It had been a mistake meeting him for dinner. All I wanted to talk about was Erica's murder, and it wouldn't be kosher to discuss being at a crime scene with a defense attorney. Above us, the 1940s red neon sign of a Mexican slumbering under a giant sombrero blinked on and off, like the lights of a sheriff's deputy's car when it stops in front of a house and everyone in the residence gets chest pains. I was numb from the events that afternoon, so tired that I tripped on the step going out and bumped into the blackboard with the day's special chalked on it: jalapeño ravioli.

"Whoops." Stuart took my arm.

The words formed a mantra in my mind. Jalapeño ravioli. Jalapeño ravioli. Had I ordered it? I couldn't remember.

Then I realized Stuart was still holding my arm. "Sorry." I removed his hand.

Stuart stepped away from me. He was still wearing his court clothes. His tie was printed with the Statue of Liberty. The neon light blinked on his trendy black wire-rimmed glasses; his gold earring glittered. "What's to be sorry about?"

"I shouldn't have accepted your dinner invitation," I said as we began to walk down Main Street, past the shops selling ethnic clothes, beaded earrings, three pair for ten dollars, posters of scenic Old Dudley. "I'm totally exhausted."

"Accepted?" Stuart said. "You didn't *accept;* I bulldozed you. I know what I'm like." He lit a cigarette. "Besides, it's been relaxing not having to maintain a conversation. I think it's great, and now we're *talking* about it."

I couldn't think of anything further to say as we crossed over to the grassy park in front of the Mining Museum. The temperature had dropped maybe twenty or thirty degrees since afternoon. My feet were leaden. Two kids in baseball caps, holding skateboards, were sitting in the dark on the iron bench to our right. The sweet smell of marijuana wafted over as we passed. Stuart nodded at them—former clients?—then glanced at his watch.

"I have to be somewhere at nine," he said, breaking the silence. "One of the prosecutors wants me to be present when they question someone. Homicide case. I didn't know when we set this up."

He hadn't known that afternoon. Nine o'clock at night was a pretty urgent time to be questioning someone. A suspect in Erica's murder? That might be it. A dark shape, the right size to be human, wearing a cowboy hat.

"Oh?" I said. "Which prosecutor?"

"It doesn't matter."

I didn't see why that would be especially confidential, but I didn't press it.

"I'm a victim myself," Stuart said suddenly, "if you can believe that." His voice had changed, taken on an injured air, as if he had a slew of voices and brought them out as the occasion demanded.

No. I didn't want to hear it, whatever it was. My reserves were drained and I had nothing left.

But he plunged on. "Domestic violence. I'm serious. My ex-wife and I were drinkers. I've been sober for four years now, and I still go to AA meetings. As far as I know, she hasn't even quit. She got violent when she was drunk, but I never realized it till she smashed up my computer with a ball-peen hammer. I was going to court every day drunk, too scared of what would happen when I sobered up."

"Well," I said. "Wow."

Was it just me who attracted drunks, or did every man in America drink too much? Why had I let him pressure me into having dinner with him? Why had I shown up at the restaurant thinking it would give me a break, distract me? I had too much unfinished business to take care of. That's why I never called Erica, too, wasn't it?

Silently, we climbed the steps up from the park and walked by the hotel. A few late diners were sitting out on the porch, sipping wine and trying to look warm.

"Here." Stuart reached into his pocket. He pulled out a plastic disk. "It's my sober for four years chip. It's legit; I'm not the guy I was just talking about anymore."

I said nothing. What could I say? If he wasn't the guy he was just talking about, then who was he? Who was Erica? Who was Kyle? Who was anybody? I stumbled then, tripped on a pothole in the badly maintained street.

Stuart caught my arm. "That's the second time you almost fell. It's lucky for you I'm here."

I shrugged him off.

"Anyway," he went on, "I apologize for my behavior so far. I can understand why you wouldn't want to talk to me."

"That's just paranoia," I said. "I'm tired, really."

"I know I operate too fast. I drank so much, I never learned about how to be a normal human being, I guess. All I can do is prepare briefs, plea-bargain, all that shit. I know I shouldn't be telling you this stuff about me, especially since you don't even know what a charming guy I can be. I mean, I think I could be a charming guy, if I ever got the chance. If I could just stop doing things so fast." He tossed his cigarette and and lit up another.

I buttoned my silk jacket, my fingers fumbling, and turned the collar up. "That's okay," I said.

"I want it to be over with," Stuart went on, his voice a little desperate, doggedly pleading his case in front of a jury he suspected had already decided against him. "I want to be sitting in front of the TV watching an old movie with someone I already know. Isn't that what everybody wants?"

Probably. For a while now, I had not trusted my instincts about men. Kyle, his clear gray Boy Scout eyes. Flowering privet grew through the iron railings as we passed the Presbyterian church, its familiar sweet scent reminding me somehow of life when I was young and trusting. Reminding me but not taking me there. On the sign in front, big black letters on a white background proclaimed SUNDAY SERMON: FEAR OR FAITH?

I thought of the Bible billboard out in the valley. Not far from the crime scene. And all of a sudden, things came together. Like the prosecutor Stuart wouldn't name—it would be a juvenile prosecutor was why. We started up the long set of steps to the street that ended in my driveway. I clutched the iron railing and pulled myself up step by step. A *juvenile* prosecutor.

"I—don't—know—how it is with—you," Stuart said, panting when we finally reached the top, "but when you're sitting—across from a stranger, the person's face starts to look really—*big*. He paused, took a deep breath. "My hands always get in the way, and you can't even smoke anymore in these New Age restaurants."

So it would be a juvenile they would be questioning at nine o'clock at night. A juvenile who would need a defense attorney present. A *suspect.* Ed hadn't wanted me to give Troy the death notification. Surely it wasn't because *Troy* was a suspect. Maybe I was just overwrought, jumping to conclusions.

We reached my driveway, walked past my car. The carport light reflected on the windshield, which was covered with squashed bugs. There had to be more bugs in the valley than maybe anywhere else in the world. Maybe even some of the bugs on my windshield had seen it all happen. I was giddy with fatigue. We stopped at my door, facing each other in the carport.

For a second, I ignored my fatigue and looked at Stuart. A marriage full of drunken scenes, the humiliations of showing up drunk in court, then four years in AA. In spite of the dash of his gold earring, his face under the carport light looked battered, vulnerable. I wanted to feel scorn, exasperation—keep my edge; instead, I thought, It couldn't have been easy, learning how to rejoin the human race.

"So," he said, backing away, as if he'd read my thoughts and they terrified him. "I got to run. How about tomorrow night?"

"Tomorrow night?"

"Dinner. Or something."

"Too soon," I said.

"Thursday, then," he said, his voice suddenly efficient. "Dinner. I could cook at my house. I'm over on Clawson, only a couple of blocks away. Four oh nine Clawson, right side of the street, white house. Got that?"

"Got it." My voice sounded feeble.

He began to walk back to the street. "I'll be home early that day. Come around five," he called over his shoulder.

Juveniles commit crimes all the time. Why not ask, so I wouldn't have to worry about it? "Stuart," I said. "Wait."

He stopped at the edge of the driveway.

"The suspect," I said. "It's . . . it's not *Troy,* is it?"

"Troy?" Suddenly, his voice was alert. "Do you know Troy?"

"Not exactly, but . . ."

"Hey." He held his hands out from his sides, palms up. "I didn't say suspect, did I? I don't know what you're talking about."

I walked into my house, closed the door, stood there in the kitchen for a moment. It couldn't be Troy. In the dark, I saw her again, lying by the door of the bookmobile, one cowboy boot on the bookmobile step, her pink dress, dark red from the waist up, her bright hair fanned about her. *No.* She was so proud of Troy. Kids don't kill parents who are proud of them.

Time spun backward and I saw her yet again, sitting on the beach, talking to James while I sat to one side, drawing little—

Suddenly, I was dizzy, dizzy with time travel and fatigue, dizzy with fighting off my thoughts. I clutched the edge of the counter and took some deep breaths.

"Too *much,*" I said out loud.

The sound of my own voice calmed me. I flicked on the kitchen light. Pens, loose change, used Kleenex, notebook, my address book, several shopping lists, receipts from the Safeway, and a pack of Butter Rum Life Savers were scattered about on the floor. Big Foot meowed at me from the counter, where he lay draped over my big purse, which I'd left behind, having traded it for a trendy little wallet-sized one. It must have been quite a battle, but he'd subdued it.

"You shithead." I picked him up, hugged him tightly, whispered in his ear as he squirmed. "You're no better than a *dog.*"

My cat. My house. I locked the door behind me. My life. What there was of it. Erica's life—gone, thrown away, when she probably had thirty more good years ahead of her.

One of the things I had to learn as a victim advocate was that you can't be responsible for everyone. Maybe not everyone, but you have to be responsible for some people. How easily I could have picked up the phone, met Erica for lunch, sat out on the terrace of the hotel, talked about Venice. So easy. Now that it was impossible, I was astonished I hadn't done it. If there was anything—*anything*—I could do for her now, I would, to make up to her, to James, to myself. I promised myself this, and it felt good, like an absolution.

Which was absurd. Erica was dead.

By now, I'd reached my second wind; wired, speeding on adrenaline.

The house looked dusty, and lately the refrigerator had taken to running continually, emitting odd chirps. My lips felt stretched; I must have been smiling at Stuart more than I'd realized. Good girl, trying to please. How sick. That was probably why he'd decided to bare his soul to me. I don't trust soul barers. They tell you everything till you get to know them; then it's all dark secrets.

I scraped together the stuff on the floor and put everything back in my purse in a jumble. *Why* would Troy be a suspect? Well, initially, family members always are. So was it just Ed Masters, going by the book?

Had Ed found something incriminating at the scene, before I got there? Like *what*? There wouldn't have been time yet to check out fingerprints. They hadn't given Stuart any homicide cases yet. Why would he be there, instead of some other attorney? I knew that for a while he'd handled juvenile drug cases. And, of course, Erica had probably smoked a little grass from time to time. Could Troy have gotten busted for possession at some point and Stuart had been his attorney?

I checked the French doors to make sure they were locked. Not that someone couldn't just break a pane and reach in, like Jeff Bridges in *Jagged Edge*. Everything secure, I sat down at the kitchen counter, drank a glass of water, and ate a banana. Both good for stress, as I taught in my crisis intervention classes.

Normal kids grew up in Old Dudley with parents who smoked dope. Two-parent families, where the adults ate meals with the children and helped them with their schoolwork, except that daddy and mommy smoked a joint instead of drinking a beer. Hadn't I heard once that Ed had done a stint as a DARE officer at the schools? Would that turn him against Troy automatically? Ed was as straight and gung ho as they come. To someone like Ed, Troy's appearance—the dreadlocks, the hippie clothes—would be more than a little bizarre. Maybe to someone like Ed, he *looked* like a criminal.

But I was obsessing. I knew nothing, would have to wait till the next day to find out. I got up and took two Advil, in case I was going to get a headache during the night. The water I kept in the refrigerator wasn't as cold as it should have been. Cold enough, though. I went to bed and lay stiffly for what seemed like hours, willing myself to sleep.

When I awoke sometime in the very early morning, it wasn't Erica I thought of, or Troy, but Kyle. Maybe it was my talk with Ed that had triggered it; it had been three weeks since I'd last awakened like this. I'd thought I was getting better.

But now it was as clear in my mind as if it had happened only hours ago. Kyle asking me to help with the investigation, just this once, showing me how to put on the wire, the Nagra reel-to-reel, so I would be taping what the man, the man who almost trusted me, said to me as we talked in the café. A bad man, a man who killed people. A man Kyle wanted to get, not just because Kyle was a cop but for personal reasons, as well.

The man had left before me, and as I'd excited the café and walked out into the balmy desert night, I'd heard the shots. Kyle was a good cop, had never killed anyone in his twenty years in law enforcement, but this was personal. So when I heard the shots, I knew, knew what had happened. I drove directly to where the shots had come from. Kyle's vehicle was parked by the side of the road, and so was the other one, blocking my view of the dead man. I took off the wire, gave it to Kyle.

"Leave," he said then. "Go home and stay there. Now."

Later, when they had the investigation, I thought they might call me, question me about it, but no one ever did, because no one knew about the tape. If they had, they might have dug deeper; after all, Smith & Wesson juries are not legal in the state of Arizona. Resisting arrest, that was what they finally decided. The scene had been set when Kyle, the A number-one detective, called for backup—the marijuana, the gun beside the dead man.

And I wondered now, as I had so many nights before, What did he do with that tape?

chapter five

THE LEAVES OF THE YOUNG COTTON-
woods that grew among the blackberry bushes in the drainage ditches
twinkled gold in the morning light. Asters bloomed everywhere in
purple drifts, and the little wood houses of Old Dudley seemed still
asleep. The unemployed jogged, walked their dogs down the canyon
as I drove to work. It took me back to another fall, when I used to
go to work hopped up on the expectation of possibly running into
Kyle. I hadn't seen him for months now; maybe I'd never see him
again. Would just carry this picture of clear-eyed Boy Scout Kyle, jaw
tight with tension, long after he was an old man, like some weird
portrait of Dorian Gray.

As I passed the back of the courthouse, Stuart Ross was standing
outside, smoking and talking to a security guard. He looked straight
at me but gave no sign of recognition. I didn't care.

But I remembered that if there was anything Kyle hated most in
the world, it was defense attorneys. "Weasels," he called them.

My office had a separate entrance outside, but I always went in
and swung by Gigi, the receptionist. She looked up when she saw
me. Her dark bangs were curled in a perfect straight line across her
forehead; she wore a hot-pink dress with bright gold buttons marching down the front and looked like someone out of a Danielle Steele
TV movie. She smiled alertly. She was new, and eager to be everyone's
friend.

I paused to pick up my messages, and then, instead of going back out to my office, headed down the hall, past a clutch of prosecutors in the break room discussing *Apollo 13*. I walked over to Marilu and Carol. They were the two legal secretaries for the Criminal Division, and while the attorneys were goofing off and discussing *Apollo 13*, they were mission control.

Carol was standing at Marilu's desk, wearing a green miniskirt, hands held out from her side like a Betty Boop girl. She was a frosted blonde, middle forties and trim.

"That looks darling on you," said Marilu. "But I can't *find* cute things like that for full-figured women." She looked down at her black tunic top. "I had a Big Mac last night and I almost died of ecstasy. Today, I bought a big bag of pecans from the lady here who sells them. What can you make with pecans that's low-fat?"

I stood politely by. Displease Carol and Marilu and you might as well quit your job. After a minute, Marilu looked up at me over her pink-tinted power glasses. Her desk was littered with pictures of her children and a pink fuzzy thing with duck feet.

"Victim Witness had a call-out yesterday," I said. "The homicide in the valley. Erica Hill?"

"That poor woman!" exclaimed Marilu.

"Oh my God," said Carol, big-eyed. "You guys went out on *that*?"

"I was at the scene. To be with the woman who found her. Dot Stone. I thought I'd call and give her an update."

"There isn't any update. They called Victor," said Marilu. "But they don't have anything yet."

Her phone rang then, so I went to Victor's office. He had a bunch of cartoons about lawyers taped on his door, and a quote from James Burke about slime rising to the top. I was glad it was Victor; he was voluble, a talker.

Victor had a youthful face, gray hair. He was at his desk, barricaded behind a stack of disclosure files, eating a bowl of Wheaties. He wore Dockers, a blue shirt, and red suspenders. Except for the suspenders, a clone of Stuart's getup the previous night. They must give lawyers a little book on what to wear when they graduate from law school. But Victor was a prosecutor—no gold earring, and a good haircut.

"Erica Hill," I said. "Any suspects?" I held my breath.

Victor shook his head back and forth. "Zero, zilch, nada."

So they hadn't charged Troy the night before. I was so relieved, I sat down.

"Investigation is ongoing in the competent hands of Ed Masters." Victor looked skeptical. "It's going to be tough. It's not like a house where there's a limited number of occupants. A bookmobile. Shit."

"I knew her," I said. "She was a friend of my brother's."

"No kidding?" Victor leaned back in his chair, put his hands behind his head. "I didn't know you had a brother here."

"I don't. This was back in California, years ago. But I met her again when she took a Victim Witness training class about a month ago."

"She was a *volunteer*?"

I shook my head. "She just took one class."

Victor was looking at me with interest. "So you guys were buddies, huh?"

"Not . . . I didn't know she lived here till I saw her at the class. We were going to get together sometime, but . . ." I shrugged, implying that it was just one of those things. "You've got nothing?"

"Well, she was probably shot with a thirty-eight or a three fifty-seven Magnum, something about that caliber. A revolver anyway. No shell casings. Shot a whole bunch of times."

"You mean like someone kept on shooting till they emptied the gun?"

"Exactly. There's a weird kind of logic there—if you shot her enough times, you wouldn't have to check and make sure she was dead. Wouldn't have to get near her, shedding evidence."

"Victor," I said, "that's a prosecutor's logic, not a murderer's. Emptying a gun sounds more like passion than logic."

He laughed. "Except this looks planned. I mean, you're going to drive out to the middle of nowhere with a loaded gun and then decide to shoot someone in the heat of passion if anyone happens to be there?"

"Passion can stay with you for miles and miles," I said.

Victor snorted. "Not in the eyes of the law it can't."

"A revolver. You'd think out there, it would be a shotgun. A revolver's not a farmer's weapon, or a hunter's."

"Plenty of gun nuts out there," said Victor. "A gun nut could own anything. But I don't think it was someone from out in the valley."

"Why not?"

"Because," said Victor, "who's going to know her out there? She was a Dudley resident. *Old* Dudley. If it had been New Dudley, it might have been different, but Old Dudley people aren't really locals. They don't know anyone outside of their own little barrio." He laughed. "So to speak."

"But Dot Stone knew her. And wouldn't all the bookmobile patrons?"

"She wasn't the regular driver. She drove it only two days, and the first day wasn't even in the valley. The regular guy was on vacation."

"Oh," I said. *"Oh."* I was surprised. "How did Dot know her, then?"

"Hell, maybe she came into Dudley, checked out books there, too."

"There was someone else," I said, trying to remember. "They were talking about someone else who knew her. What was his name?"

Victor shrugged. "Ed hasn't sent in any reports yet. All we can do is speculate. Could have been a stalker, ex-husband, ex-lover, whatever. Stalked her until he found a good opportunity. They post the bookmobile schedule in the newspaper every week. Anyone who wanted to find her could have."

"Why weren't there any patrons at the stop?" I asked suddenly. "The only reason Dot was there was because she'd missed her earlier."

"I asked Ed about that," said Victor. "It was the Olander stop, and they were out of town."

"Isn't that something only a local would know?"

"Whoever it was could have been following her all the way, or even been ahead of her, and when he saw the Olanders weren't home, he grabbed the opportunity." He shrugged. "Who knows?"

"So this is going to be your case?"

"Not necessarily."

I jumped in, hoping to get Victor to show his hand if Troy was in any way involved in the investigation. "Ed's a *jerk*," I said. "He didn't call Victim Witness to do the notification for the victim's son. He did it himself, and the kid's only sixteen."

"You know Ed. He's old school." His voice was glib. "A cop, not a social worker."

"All the more reason for calling us."

Victor picked up a pen and turned it around and around in his fingers. He didn't look at me. "What do you want me to do, Chloe? Take it up with Ed."

"Thanks anyway," I said.

A stalker, I thought as I walked to my office. Ex-husband, ex-lover, what? Erica had described herself as a single mother, but she'd had plenty of men in her life when I knew her. At least they weren't arresting Troy. I unlocked the door and almost tripped on a big box in the hall. Pecans. My boss must have ordered them before she took off on vacation.

I went into in my small, cramped office and sat down, staring at the litter of papers and pamphlets that obscured my desk. Could I do something for Troy? No, it was all in the hands of Ed Masters. Kyle would have gotten the case if he hadn't up and quit. Thinking of Kyle, anxiety burned behind my breastbone.

I spread out my messages on the desk, but I didn't read them. The previous night had brought everything back. Would Kyle have shot the man if I hadn't agreed to the wire? I hadn't known what Kyle was going to do, but I could have figured it out. How many times had I thought this before? How many times was I going to have to think about it again? Suddenly, my head felt light; space was closing in on me. That was all I needed, to have a panic attack right there in my office.

I got up quickly. My heels clicked in the hallway as I walked to the break room. I concentrated on the sound, officious, busy. The room was empty now, thank God. I filled a coffee cup with water and drank it standing by the greasy microwave. A note over the sink read YOUR MOTHER DOESN'T WORK HERE. PLEASE CLEAN UP AFTER YOURSELF.

After a few minutes, I felt a little better, but there was some irony here: me, possibly a criminal, standing in the break room, the heart of the prosecutor's domain. And there *was* something I could do—find out from Frankie who it was that Dot had said knew Erica, out in the valley.

I left the cup in the sink for mom to wash, went back to my office, and called the County Sheriff's Department in Willcox.

"Frankie, Dot said there was some guy out in the valley who knew Erica."

"Lucas." She chuckled. "If there's a good-looking woman within a hundred miles, Lucas'll find her."

"Was he Erica's boyfriend?"

"Dot said not lately. By the way, I called Dot, and she seems to be doing okay. And I asked Ed about Troy—the notification—and Ed said he was fine. He said Troy was going to call some aunt, out in California."

I didn't remember Erica ever mentioning a sister, but back then, so many people had left the banality of family behind, to drift on Venice Beach, unfettered, free.

"But listen to this," Frankie went on, lowering her voice. "I told him Victim Witness could go talk to Troy, do a follow-up. . . ." She paused. "And Ed said no, he wants us to stay away from the kid for now. This is just between you and me." Her words were muffled, as if she had her hand cupped over the receiver. "You know what I think? From the way Ed's acting and all? That *boy's* his suspect."

"How do you know that? No one's saying it here," I protested.

"Well, he's got to make the case first."

"*Damn* it," I said. "Frankie, he's only sixteen. My impression was that Erica had a good relationship with her son."

"You never know what goes on in families. And kids now, they got these drugs. Methamphetamines. It makes them crazy. Anybody could kill when they're on that."

I sighed. "So I have to stay away."

"That's right. I got my job and you got yours. I don't know about you, but I'd like to hang on to mine."

I hung up, thinking about the famous Troy, a stone killer, cranked up on drugs. I didn't think so. What did I know, though? Back in Venice, people did any drug they could get their hands on, speed included—mostly grass, but also downers, hashish, LSD, PCP, angel dust, peyote, mescaline. . . . The list went on and on. It was a wonder anyone had survived.

The phone rang.

"I need a shoemaker for you," said Gigi.

"What?"

Gigi laughed apologetically. "I'll put her through."

"Hello," I said to the phone. "This is Chloe at Victim Witness."

"This is Neva Shumaker." A woman's voice, clear and crisp. "I'm the head librarian for the Cochise County Library District. Detective Masters suggested I call you."

Well, thank you, Ed. A miracle. "Yes?"

"I don't know if you've heard, but, well, one of the employees here was murdered."

I said, "I do know, and I'm glad you called. It must be very difficult for all of you there. Anything we can do to help . . ."

"Detective Masters was here questioning everyone. No one's been fit to work since. He said maybe you could come over and do a—I'm not sure of the word."

"A debriefing?"

"That's it. What is it you do exactly?"

"Well, basically, everyone sits around in a group and we talk. How they're feeling about what happened, that kind of thing."

There was a long pause.

"Oh, no," said Neva dubiously. "I don't think so. We're not *group* people here at the library. Besides, some of my staff members are at a library conference in San Antonio. There's only three, not counting me. Maybe you could just talk to them individually?"

"Whatever's comfortable," I said, "I'll be happy to do."

There was another pause. "One of them," said Neva, "I'm very concerned about. Sally. Sally Smith. She's our reference librarian."

"I could be there within half an hour," I said.

chapter six

THE COUNTY LIBRARY IS LOCATED IN A BIG
old dark brick building fronted with Arizona cypress, situated in the
heart of the residential area of Old Dudley. Carrying my Victim Witness Program bag, a hideous bright plaid tote, I opened one of the
double front doors and went inside to a big empty hall—wood floor,
very high ceiling, some stairs to my right. The plaster on the walls
was water-stained, and farther down the hall, some of it had fallen.
Everything smelled faintly of mold.

A pale, lanky man appeared, slowly sweeping up the plaster with
a push broom, making streaks on the floorboards. When he saw me,
he dropped the broom. It clattered noisily onto the floor.

"Hi there!" he said. "I'm *Myron*. What you name?"

"Chloe," I said. "Can you tell me where the library is?"

"I'm going there now," someone said.

I looked around.

A man stood behind me. He had on mirrored shades, which reflected my own image back at me, all nose, distorted like a hobgoblin.
He wore a red bandanna around his neck, T-shirt, leather vest, jeans,
cowboy boots. His hair was dark, combed back in a pompadour, semi-
Elvis. Older than his image, maybe forty.

Myron gave a kind of whoop. "What you doin' here, Andy? You
on *vacation.*" His voice was slow and he had a slack grin on his face.

Andy waved. "Hey, Myron, what's up?"

"Nothin'. She dead, too. Somebody *kill* her."

"It's pretty sad."

"It is too sad." Myron picked up the broom again. "You two like pecans? Got a whole bunch!"

We both said no thanks.

"Got to work! Bye now!"

"The library's up the stairs," Andy said. "I work there. Myron's Jude's brother—she works in interlibrary loan. Myron's a soft brain, and Neva lets him come here and sweep."

"I know who you are," I said. "The regular bookmobile driver."

He nodded. "Andy Marookian."

"I'm Chloe Newcombe, from Victim Witness at the county attorney's. Neva called and asked me to come over here and talk to people."

"Oh, yeah," he said. "Well, follow me. The library's the only thing in here. This used to be the high school a long time ago. They tried to move us out once into some sort of *office* building, but we fought it." He cleared his throat noisily. "Did they arrest anyone yet?" His voice was strained. He coughed. "Damn allergies."

"No. I'm sorry."

He looked crestfallen. "I'm supposed to be on vacation, but first some cop comes to my house, and then Neva badgered me into coming in for a staff meeting. She's good at badgering."

I looked at Andy directly, but he was hard to read with those two mirrors in front of his eyes. "How are you doing?" I asked. "This must be pretty hard to take."

"Of course I'm upset," he said defensively, "but it's not something I can't deal with on my own. I guess Sally could use some help. She's nuts anyway."

He was thin and the seat of his jeans bagged out, but he hoisted his shoulders as if they were broad and heavy, and then started up some stairs to the right. I followed.

"Andy, how is it that Erica knew Dot Stone? She'd never driven the bookmobile out there before, had she?"

"No." He stared at me from behind the mirrors. "Dot knew Erica?"

"Dot found her," I said gently. "She knew who Erica was right away. Knew her name."

He looked confused. "The last time I saw Dot, I didn't know who would be driving. Dot *found* her? Poor old thing." He stared off into space, his face blank. Then, as if remembering suddenly who he was supposed to be, he started back up the stairs.

He looked lonely, the set of his shoulders tense, as if he was just barely coping.

"I'm glad you're here," I said. "I'm sure you'll be a big help."

On the second floor, we went in through a door into another hall, offices along both sides. I smelled more mold, an undertone of chalk. A book cart was in the center of the hall, books scattered beside it. There was a deadly, expectant quiet, as if people were holding their breath. Andy paused at the door to an office.

"In there," he said in a low voice. "That's Tech Services, where Erica worked."

I looked in the room. Three desks, ferns on the window ledge. "Everyone's at a conference," said Andy. "That's Erica's desk." He pointed at a desk by the window. It held a typewriter and a wild jumble of books, cards and card pockets. "Erica had to type up the card pockets, glue them into the books, stamp them, that kind of thing. She always read the children's picture books all the way through. Neva used to sneak in and catch her."

"Really," I said.

"Neva's like Erica's complete opposite. They didn't get along." He glanced nervously down the hall. "No matter what she says now. Jude—that's who Neva likes. Well, come on."

I followed him to the middle office on the left, big and bare except for an Indian rug on the floor, a few stacks of books, a bookcase along one wall. A thin woman in a navy blue suit, her undoctored salt-and-pepper hair pulled back, was sitting behind a desk.

She got up quickly when she saw us and came across the room. She wore pewter ethnic earrings and Birkenstocks, which contrasted strangely with her suit. What might have been sharp features were numbed with fatigue.

"Chloe? I'm Neva. Thank you for coming." Her voice was clipped, tense her gray eyes oddly flat. She glanced over my shoulder. "Andy. Did you get a chance to talk to Chloe?"

"Oh, sure." He moved away to the door, his boots skittering on the wood floor. "I'm fine. I'll just go see what I can do."

She watched him go, then turned to me. "He could at least *try*," she said in exasperation. "We still have a job to do here, and I don't want my staff falling apart. We have a meeting at eleven-thirty, and I want them reasonably calm for it. Sit down. Coffee?"

"No thanks."

I sat in a metal folding chair while Neva sat at her desk. She sat so straight, she might have been balancing a book on her head.

"Erica was only with us a month and a half, but she was so magnetic," Neva said in a voice that sounded rehearsed. "She blazed like a star. It makes me think of a poem by Edna St. Vincent Millay—'My candle burns at both ends;/It will not last the night . . .' "

" 'But, ah, my' something, 'and, oh, my friends—/It gives a lovely light,' " I said.

Neva half-smiled. " 'Foes,' " she said. " 'But, ah, my foes.' "

She turned her head and stared out the window. The town, bright with autumn colors, meandered sloppily up the hills. Crooked flights of stairs led to small wooden houses, many of them now all spruced up and painted interesting colors. Once, they had belonged to miners, then to the hippies who had aged here and, from the looks of Andy and even Neva, gotten jobs at the county library.

"Yesterday was so surreal." Neva turned her head away from the window. "Some officer, not Detective Masters, came and told me. I said thank you, like a robot, and then I realized that because of the conference, there was no one here to tell. Jude was at home because Myron, her brother, was sick, so I called her and Andy. Sally was out with the minibookmobile, so I waited until she showed up."

"Sally's the one you're worried about," I said.

"She went completely white when I told her. Then she got so calm, it was unnatural. I sent her home to rest up, but today she can hardly function. I can't coddle her, not with this skeleton staff. As it is, I'm going to ask Andy to cut short his vacation."

"How about you?" I asked. "How are you doing?"

Neva looked insulted. "I'm *fine,*" she said. "I'm not a counselor person. So many counselors are twisted themselves in some way, don't you think?" She folded her hands in front of her on the desk, fingers linked, white at the knuckles. "They look at you with their patronizing smiles, like they've already figured you out. When you've been around Old Dudley people as long as I have, you realize *someone* has to be the grown-up."

"Jude's interlibrary loan, and Sally's reference," said Neva as she led me to a room that had two desks, one very neat, with a few big books on it and an African violet. A woman sat behind the other, which overflowed with stacks of books with markers in them, more books stacked on the floor and in a cart beside it.

"Jude," said Neva, "this is Chloe Newcombe, from the Victim Witness Program."

Jude got up slowly, bowing her head piously. In fact, she did resemble an ex-nun. She was a stocky, broad-faced woman, fifty something, and wore maroon knit pants and a colorless, baggy T-shirt.

"I don't see Sally," Neva said. "I hope she's hasn't—"

"Back with the computers," said Jude.

"Well, you can show Chloe where, then," said Neva. "I've already told Sally about Victim Witness coming. And you can maybe talk to Chloe, too." She paused and then, her voice softer, said, "I saw Myron downstairs. He seems much better."

A look passed between them, charged, carrying some baggage, although I didn't know what. Then Jude nodded. "He is."

"Vitamin C," said Neva. "I'm a believer. Well, I've got to get back to work."

Jude watched her go, face impassive.

"I know Neva wants me to speak to you," Jude said to me, "but I really didn't know Erica. She only worked here a few weeks and it was in Tech Services. They're always talking and giggling in Tech Services," she pursed her lips, "but you don't have the time to *socialize* in interlibrary loan."

She looked down at her desk, arranging a stack of books. Her hands were big, fingers blunt, awkward. I thought of her brother, Myron, downstairs sweeping, had a glimpse of her life, dreary, no giggling and talking, dreary and full of work.

"Still," I said, "violent death is hard for all of us."

Jude's eyes veered away from mine. She sat down abruptly, folded her big hands on her desk. "I live over in New Dudley," she said. "Lived there all my life. Old Dudley used to be different. Things have changed a lot since these new people moved in."

"Jude," I said, "Erica was killed out in the *valley.*"

"Cars," said Jude vaguely. "People have *cars.*"

"What people?" I asked.

She looked blank. "It's Sally you should be talking to." She nodded at the other desk—neat, the big books and the African violet. Next to the African violet was a white china cat. "*I'll* be just fine."

"Are you sure there's nothing I can do? Lots of people find it's helpful to talk to counselors. . . ."

Jude looked superior. "I have a pastor for anything like that." She stared past me for a moment. I waited, sensing something further to come. Then she squared her shoulders, as if coming to a decision. "Well, there is one thing. I didn't mention it to the detective. I don't think anyone did."

"Oh?" I said.

"Afterward, I thought about it, and I think it's my duty to tell someone. Maybe you can decide if the detective should know?"

I nodded.

"Erica and Andy? They broke up." Jude paused significantly. "It was only a month ago. You have to wonder how he's taking it."

Yes, you did. "Well," I said to Jude, using a phrase I hated, "thank you for sharing that with me."

* * *

I walked toward the back of the library, where Jude had pointed, passing through a tunnel composed of shelves and shelves of books. A slight blond person, her back to me, sat at a desk in front of a computer. She was wearing a long pale yellow dress with spaghetti straps over a tiny white T-shirt—a childish dress, like that an adolescent might wear.

"Sally?" I said when I got close.

She yelped, turned abruptly, a big book beside her crashing to the floor. In spite of the childish dress, I saw with kind of a shock that she was maybe forty, not a girl at all—fine lines were etched around her mouth and eyes. Her eyes were a pale, pale blue, her bobbed hair white blond.

"I'm so sorry," I said. "I didn't mean to startle you. I'm Chloe Newcombe, from the Victim Witness Program."

Sally held her hand over her heart, as if waiting for it to slow down. She was uncomfortably thin, like a kitten that's been doused with water.

"It's okay," she said breathlessly. "Neva said . . ." She floundered nervously. "She said you were going to talk to us about . . . *Erica.*"

Worried, I pulled a chair over and sat down. Not only was she very nervous; she was both hypervigilant and hyperventilating. All my movements were slow and careful, in deference to her state. "Pretty bad, huh?" I said. "Want to talk about it?"

Behind her, the computer had gone into screen-saver mode, eerie little nightmare faces grinning and vanishing. She sat for a moment, looking down at the floor, trying to compose herself.

Then she looked up, her pale eyes rimmed with pink. "Nobody's acting *right,*" she whispered. "Jude is glad, because she thinks Erica . . . Erica deserved it. Neva, too. Andy . . ."

She stared past me at the books. "It hurts. It hurts to be around them."

"People have different ways of dealing with things," I said. "For their own protection."

She nodded blankly. "And . . . and me," she said, "me, I wake up at night, and I know I'm going to *die.*"

"Sally," I said, "that's not such an unusual reaction considering what's happened, but you might want to think about seeing a counselor."

"I have one," she said. "Here in Dudley. I go to group every Tuesday night. He's *wonderful.*"

"That's great," I said. "You might want to give him a call, maybe see him before next Tuesday." Beyond the shelves of books, I heard people talking, moving chairs. I glanced at my watch—almost eleven-thirty, time for the staff meeting.

I handed her my card. "You can call me anytime," I said, "if you want to talk some more. And promise me that you'll get in touch with your counselor right away?"

Sally stood up. "It would be meaningless," she said. "Don't you see?"

"No, I don't. What do you mean?"

I heard Neva's voice from beyond the shelves, very distinct. "Now where's *Sally?*"

Sally looked past my shoulder, in the direction of the voice. "Because." She leaned over toward me. "What could my counselor *do*? Didn't you understand what I said?" Her voice was plaintive.

"What you said?"

"I'm going to *die.* He's going to kill me, too."

For a second, I was stunned. "Who?"

"The man," said Sally. Her voice trembled. "The man in the *cowboy hat.*"

"Western clothes," a voice said.

I jumped.

Neva stood right behind me. "He was wearing western clothes. Detective Masters asked all of us if we'd ever seen Erica with a man who wore western clothes, a cowboy hat." Her voice was calm, but you could sense impatience just barely reined in. "Half the men in Cochise County wear cowboy hats. Sally, we need you now. Thank you so much, Miss Newcombe, for coming."

chapter seven

THE NEXT DAY I WENT TO STUART'S HOUSE,
a typical one-story miner's shack, narrow front porch, the shiplap
painted a fading white, with green trim. I parked under a chinaberry
tree, behind a dented old blue truck, maybe that of a construction
worker staying late. The weather was mild, yellow leaves drifting
down. Somewhere, violins were lamenting; it sounded like Mozart. I
can't ignore music, the way some people can. Can't have the radio
on at work, with someone singing about being heartbroken as I run
off a few copies on a Xerox machine. I felt a twinge in my heart.

Honeysuckle and roses, possibly pink, now parchment, hung in a
tangled mass over the wire fence surrounding the front yard. When
I opened the gate, I scratched my hand on a long strand of stiff wire.

"Ouch!" Blood welled up and I licked it off the back of my hand.

The yard was just clumps of grass, with patches of vinca; the
cement path leading to the porch was littered with chinaberries, like
wizened little beige marbles. The front door was wide open, the smell
of spicy grease cutting through all that heartbreak. I walked in.

The living room looked like a secondhand store, filled with non-
descript furniture in neutral tones, including two old couches and,
between them, the biggest coffee table I'd ever seen. Ashtrays overflowed everywhere and about two months' worth of newspapers were
stacked on the floor.

"Stuart!" I called.

He emerged through a door in back, a big fork in his hand. He was wearing a voluminous canvas apron stained here and there with red streaks. "I'm barbecuing," he said over the Mozart. "Out back. Ribs. Do you like ribs?"

"Sure."

Violins still whined eloquently and elegantly, and I couldn't connect what they were saying with the man in the big apron, holding a fork. Abruptly, Stuart leaned down and turned off the music. "We're going for a little ride in a minute. What'd you do to your hand?"

I looked down. Blood had welled up again and was running onto my fingers. "Scratched it on your fence. Where are we going?"

"Why don't you go in the john. There's probably some antibiotic cream in the medicine cabinet," he added, pointing at a door.

I went into the bathroom. The sink had a gray film on the white porcelain and a toothbrush lay on the side, a squirt of toothpaste on it. Next to it, a cigarette had burned down to ash. On the back of the toilet, three small books lay open, one on top of the other. The top one said *Meditations for Men Who Do Too Much*. Like Stuart, who read not one but three meditation books? I used to throw the I Ching. I turned the top book over and looked at the open page in front of me; what I read next would define this evening. It was a quote from Groucho Marx: "Either this man is dead or my watch has stopped."

"Chloe?" called Stuart.

Guiltily, I put down the book, opened the medicine cabinet, and found a tube of antibiotic cream with the top off. "Just a second," I called.

When I got back to the living room, Stuart was there. He'd taken off the apron, and he was wearing a denim work shirt that was frayed at the collar. "Grab those containers on the coffee table." He hoisted a bag. "Let's go."

I picked up the containers—one had coleslaw, the other potato salad from the Safeway deli—and followed him out the front door. Outside, we put everything in the back of the old truck.

"Look," I protested once we'd gotten started, heading up the hill and then down. "Would you mind telling me where we're going?"

"Relax." Stuart punched a button and the car filled up with more

Mozart, transporting us to the eighteenth century, when women had behaved with tact and gentility. We bounced and jostled down the canyon and finally turned left onto a narrow street.

"I'm pissed enough to get out and walk home," I said loudly. "I don't appreciate your macho-man tactics."

He didn't say anything. The street wound around under a blaze of cottonwoods, and the little frame houses got sparser, the yards wilder. Stuart slowed at a curve. I pushed the button and the music stopped. "Did you hear me?"

"It's okay," he said. "We're here."

He stopped in front of a yellow house with a big front porch and a wooden fence that had rosesbushes cascading over it. One, deep red, still bloomed. Spiky rosemary grew beneath the roses, its blue flowers a delicate contrast to the red rose. Stuart turned off the ignition. Suddenly, it was very quiet; then I heard wind chimes tinkling from the eaves of the porch, and music, but certainly not Mozart.

"Here," I said. "Where is here?"

For a moment, he stared straight ahead over the steering wheel, not looking at me. Actually, he hadn't looked at me since I'd arrived at his house, busying himself instead in a flurry of activity, the way I've seen defense attorneys do when they have no case at all, continuing to present irrelevant detail after irrelevant detail in hopes of confusing the jury.

"I didn't tell you 'cause I thought you might say no," he said. "This is Erica Hill's house and we're taking these ribs to Troy."

"Troy?" I hesitated, then said reluctantly, "I don't know if I should. I'm under the impression he's a suspect. Wouldn't—"

"Bull*shit*!" Stuart exclaimed, cutting me off. "Who told you he's a suspect?"

Frankie and I had only speculated. "No one, really," I said. "I mean . . . Well, they did question him with an attorney present."

"That was just Ed Masters being a dope. Troy skipped school the day Erica was killed, and Ed wants to be a hotshot. Troy's a *victim*, for Christ's sake, and he needs to be treated him like a human being."

"Okay, then, fine," I said.

* * *

Stuart opened the front door and shouted over the music. "Troy!"

"Ray, Ray, go away," someone, a female, shouted back.

I followed Stuart inside, wanting to look at everything, see Erica's house, but there was too much going on.

The music was nothing like Mozart. It went for the gut, the real seat of sorrow, and kept on punching. Hypnotic and insistent, it obliterated what must have been a pleasant room, a living room, maybe some walls torn down to make it bigger, all windows in front, art books on one wall, ferns thriving, a rocking chair, a cherry-wood desk. A woman was singing in a voice that had worked through pain and emerged into anger.

"Someday you will ache like I ache."

Sitting on a couch covered loosely with Guatemalan fabric was a young girl, head shaved except for a shock of green hanging over one eye. Big brown plaid shirt, black fishnet stockings with a rip in one leg, black combat boots. "Troy," she said.

"Is it *Ray*?" a voice called from the other room. "If he's drunk . . ."

"Don't worry," said the girl, sounding bored. "It's not Ray."

Troy came into the living room. He still had the puppyish lope I'd noticed when I'd seen him walking down the street with his mother. He was wearing baggy black shorts to the knee and an electric green tie-dyed T-shirt, but the élan, the flair, was gone. He tugged at one blond dreadlock anxiously. He stopped dead when he saw us, looking relieved.

"Stuart." He wore glasses with heavy black frames—nerd glasses, the kind that kids who weren't nerds wore to look cool. Behind the frames, his blue eyes were soft and blind-looking. "Pepper, it's Stuart, my lawyer."

The girl on the couch glanced at us and raised one arm, then dropped it as if it were too heavy to hold upright. "Hello, lawyer."

Troy smiled at us apologetically. "This is Pepper, Stuart. She's a friend of mine."

"They all work for the same government," Pepper said warningly.

"And this is a friend of mine," said Stuart. "Chloe. We brought you some dinner. Hope you like ribs. What's that god-awful music?"

"It's all right," said Troy. "It's just Pepper's music. Courtney Love. We could turn it off, except Pepper can hardly live without it. Let's go in the kitchen."

In the kitchen, Troy closed the door behind us. The room was small and somewhat untidy, with dishes piled in the sink. A wooden table stood along one wall, two rush-bottomed chairs pushed in beneath it. On the table, next to a stoneware vase full of dead roses, was a geometry book and an open notebook. The pages of the notebook were covered with drawings of swirly dragons with big smiling teeth, little dragons popping out of the bigger dragons' heads. The refrigerator was covered with more drawings in the same style.

"Troy," said Stuart, "I hope Pepper's not stoned on anything."

"No." Troy's voice was protective. "She's just being Pepper. She's depressed a lot."

"Girlfriend?" Stuart asked.

"Not a girlfriend," said Troy. "She's my sister."

"What?" said Stuart.

"My cosmic sister," Troy explained.

"Better than a girlfriend," I added.

"It is." Troy tried to smile at me, but his mouth trembled. I saw now that his eyes were not so much blind as numb with pain. Any qualms I might have had about being there vanished. The hell with Ed.

"And who's this drunken Ray?" asked Stuart. "Not the neighbor, I hope. The one who's looking in on you?"

"No, no," Troy protested. "That's Nelson. Nelson and Larry. Actually, they're not exactly neighbors. They live down the street, in that new-looking pink house. Nelson's a *counselor*. And Ray, he's just Pepper's . . . I don't know, not Pepper's anything." He looked disgusted. "He's her mom's boyfriend. He's a creep. That's one main reason Pepper spends so much time over here."

"Troy," Stuart said, "you got to be cool. No parties, no wild stuff. And sooner or later, you're going to have to call your aunt." He set the ribs down on the counter.

"No!" Troy's voice rose to a wail. "She lives way over in California. She won't want to come here."

"We'll discuss that later." Stuart snapped his fingers. "Left the slaw in the car. Potato salad, too." He looked at me reproachfully. "Be right back."

I sat down on one of the rush-bottomed chairs.

Troy looked at the ribs Stuart had put on the counter. "They look good," he said unconvincingly.

"What's wrong with your aunt?" I asked.

"She and my mom weren't speaking, not for seventeen years. She won't care if my mom's dead, and she hates me."

"How can you know that? You weren't born seventeen years ago. And Troy, sometimes people who care about each other a lot have fights. She deserves to know."

There was scratching at the screen door. Troy went over and opened it and a large shaggy black dog came in, propelling himself with wiggles. He wiggled over to me and put his paws on my lap.

"You must be Krishna." I scratched behind his ears as he drooled on my arm. "Hi there, Krishna."

"How'd you know?" Troy smiled for real this time. "How'd you know his name?" He sat down across from me at the table, peering at me intently through his glasses. I could see light down on his cheeks—so young.

"Your mother mentioned it," I said.

Troy's eyes lit up. He rubbed his nose with one hand. His fingers were inky, and on his wrist was a little dragon swirl. "I wanted to name him Axl—for Axl Rose," he said. "You know, Guns n' Roses? I was into them back then. But Mom said Krishna might be better, that an Axl can turn on you sometimes." He paused expectantly. "Get it?"

I smiled. "Yeah."

"She was always saying funny things like that." He bit his thumbnail. "I like the Beastie Boys now," he confided. "Sir Mix-A-Lot, Biohazard. Nirvana, too. Ween. *And* Hole. When I play them real loud, I can vanish. Nothing exists. That's what Pepper's doing now."

He looked thoughtful, then, eyes full of hope, he said, "You knew my *mom*?"

I had no idea what that hope was for. Everything around us—the flowers, the chairs and wooden table, the lace curtains at the windows—had all been chosen or found by Erica, and Troy would have to think about that every minute, for a long time.

"I knew her many years ago," I said, "when she lived in California, before you were born." My voice turned into a lull, as though I were telling a fairy tale—memories coming back, ones I didn't even know I had. "She lived upstairs in the house where I was staying. There were bamboo shades on the windows where she lived and she had an orange cat named T. S. Eliot. She was the most beautiful person in Venice, California. My brother James was her best friend."

"He was?" Troy leaned across the table and said earnestly, "Maybe I could meet him sometime."

"I wish you could. But James is dead."

Troy blinked. "Oh," he said sadly. "You must *miss* him."

"Yes, I do."

We sat in a kind of shared silence for a minute, sadness, like a big woolly blanket, covering everything around us, oddly comforting.

Then Stuart came back and broke the mood, holding up his quarts of slaw and potato salad. "Want this stuff to go in the fridge?"

"Okay," said Troy stoically.

From the floor beside me, Krishna let out a low growl. I got up, the dog following, and went to the window to see why. Outside was Stuart's truck; another car, a white Geo Metro, had just pulled up behind.

A big man got out of the Geo and walked through the gate.

Krishna whined and let out a short bark.

I said, "It looks like you have a visitor."

Krishna barked again.

The man was big and slow.

"Stuart," I said. "It's Ed Masters."

"You're shitting me." Stuart came over and looked out the window. "You aren't."

"They already searched the house," said Troy anxiously.

Stuart stared at him. "They did?"

"He took my best notebook, too."

"When?"

"I . . . I don't know. I . . ." Troy stuttered, terrified.

I wanted to put my arms around him, calm him, but Ed Masters was outside. "I shouldn't be here," I said.

"Right," Stuart said. "Stay in the kitchen, okay? You listen. If he's going to search again, I'll ask to see the search warrant. If you hear that, you go out the back door."

Stuart put his arm around Troy. "Probably just a couple of questions. You've got your lawyer present. No problem, okay? Let's go."

Shit, shit, shit, shit, I thought, alone in the kitchen. I'd actually believed a *defense* attorney. But how could Troy be a suspect? Pepper's music was way too loud for me to hear what they were saying in the living room. Then, suddenly, it went off and I heard Ed's voice, genial and ponderous. "Troy Hill, I'm sorry, son, but I'm going to have to take you into custody."

"The charges?" Stuart's voice boomed out.

"First-degree murder in the death of Erica Hill."

chapter eight

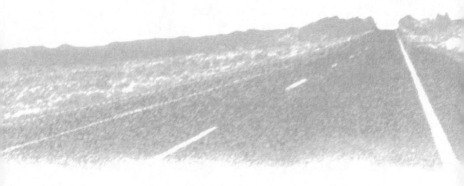

"NO!" SOMEONE SCREAMED. I WANTED TO scream, too.

"You stupid, stupid, *stupid*—"

Krishna barked and barked.

The voice kept on shouting. "Asshole! Dumb shit!" Pepper.

"Krishna!" Troy commanded in a broken voice.

"Pepper," Stuart said. "Calm down. You're not helping Troy."

"Son, do something about that dog," rumbled Ed, "and young lady, don't make me take you into custody, too."

"Good dog!" said Troy.

Pepper's voice stopped abruptly. Krishna whined. It was all I could do to stop myself from going out there and kicking Ed Masters in the balls.

Stuart said, "Officer, I'd like to take Troy down myself, as his attorney, so he can turn himself in, show cooperation."

I could have kicked Stuart, too. What kind of an attorney *was* he?

"That's your privilege, counselor." Ed's voice was polite, embarrassed even. I imagined his beefy face slowly turning red.

"Let me just get my wallet," said Stuart. "I left it in the kitchen."

". . . feed Krishna for you," Pepper was saying plaintively.

Stuart came through the door, his face tense. "This is a crock of shit," he whispered vehemently. "Wait till Ed's gone, then walk home. I'll be in touch."

"What . . ." I began, furious. "Stuart, you can't let this happen."

He gave me a blank look. "I'm not God," he said; then he was gone.

Would they be handcuffing Troy? No, Stuart was driving him. I heard footsteps, the front door closing.

I went to the window and looked out through the lace curtains. Ed was getting into his car, starting it up. Stuart walked slowly into view, Troy beside him, his head down. Stuart had his hand on Troy's shoulder and was talking, but I couldn't hear what he was saying. They got into Stuart's truck.

I thought of Troy, the nerd glasses, the dragon swirls inked on his wrists, what we'd shared in the kitchen. Juvenile detention, full of abused, angry kids, wise before their time—Troy didn't fit in there; he was still a child. And no one had tried to save him from it, myself included. *Asshole, dumb shit.* No one, that is, but Pepper.

Where was she?

If she's still here, I thought, maybe I should talk to her. I talked to victims, went to court with them, but what about the friends and relatives of the suspects? How often they blamed the friends and families of the victims, glaring at them across the courtroom, marching in early for the front-row seats. But they're heartbroken, too, I realized. Everyone a victim, everyone in massive denial. I *knew* Troy hadn't killed his mother. Or I was in massive denial, too?

Anyway, in this case, the friends and relatives of the suspect and the victim were one and the same. And what *about* relatives? That aunt needed to be notified. Erica's sister. They hadn't seen each other in *seventeen years*?

Troy was a juvenile. That meant Ed could determine probable cause and arrest him for six hours only, and then if the juvenile prosecutor also decided there was probable cause, they could hold Troy another twenty-four hours, at which point, the juvenile probation department had to step in. Victor, the prosecutor I'd talked to the other day, would be off this case then and Felix would take over, Felix Lambert, who was the juvenile prosecutor.

Juvenile. They would want him released to a guardian, and Troy didn't have anyone but his aunt, as far as I knew. Though he had to have a father. Where was he? *Who* was he? Erica's lovers had been a favorite topic of conversation between James and Erica—lovers who'd always seemed a little foolish—overzealous, too full of hope.

Like Andy, feigning toughness, so transparent. I hadn't told Ed they'd been lovers, and I probably should have. I could tell Victor—no, it would be in the hands of the juvenile prosecutor, Felix Lambert. He was the one I needed to tell. Better Andy than Troy, I thought heartlessly.

What had Ed found on that search that he thought was enough for probable cause? Big, plodding Ed—he wasn't a hotshot like Kyle had been. Maybe they would just let Troy go right away.

Meanwhile, where *was* Pepper? Then I saw her, walking through the front yard with Krishna on a leash, angrily dabbing at her face. And I saw something I hadn't noticed when she'd been sitting on the couch in her big plaid shirt. Pepper was pregnant. Maybe five months along.

No wonder she was depressed.

I sat down heavily on the rush-bottomed chair, exhausted. The ribs were on the counter, still in their wrappings. After a moment, I got up and put them in the refrigerator, next to the slaw and potato salad. I could take the food with me, but it would be too much to carry if I was walking, and what if they let Troy go soon? It would be nice if there was food in the refrigerator when he came back. There wasn't much else in it, except for a plastic container growing mold, various condiments on the door shelf, a carton of milk, and half a hot dog in a Circle K wrapper. Was there a car anywhere? Did Troy have a driver's license?

There had to be a car. If Troy was accused of killing Erica, then he had to have had a way to get out to the valley.

I opened the back door and looked out at a patch of straggly tomato plants and an assortment of herbs, carefully weeded—basil, rosemary, sage, parsley. The backyard extended up the mountain and turned into desert a little way up. Over on the left was a cracked cement driveway and, sure enough, a car. The same car Erica had

driven to the training class—the odd pumpkin-colored car of indeterminate make and vintage.

I closed the back door, locked it. Erica's sister was still in the
back of my mind; she was a legitimate victim, entitled to all the rights
that victims have. Plus, if she'd been in conflict with Erica, she might
take it even harder, things still unresolved, now never to be.

She needed to be notified right away; it was outrageous that she
hadn't been. If I'd been thinking more clearly, I would have gotten
her name and phone number already. Then I could have set up a way
to do a death notification, maybe through local law enforcement in
California. You didn't want to notify people by phone. And they had
victim advocates in California.

The neighbors, Nelson and Larry. In the new pink house. I could
go see them and find out about the sister—her name, phone number. Now I felt legitimate, a victim advocate working on getting
rights for a victim, which was what I was when I walked back into
the living room.

Emptied of Pepper and of Courtney Love's angst, the room
looked beautiful to me; a rich patina of age and use hung over it—
pleasant, comfortable, and full of things that seemed selected not for
effect but for meaning. I looked around, curious.

Among the ferns and art books were several framed sketches of
Erica in tights and a leotard, some good, but most amateurish. It
looked like she'd once done a stint as a model, posing for an art class;
it was the kind of job she might have gotten. On one wall, over a
small table full of votive candles, was a poster of the Virgin of Guadalupe.

Ringed by roses and atop a small angel, the Virgin, crowned and
serene, stood in an attitude of prayer. Rays of holy lights surrounded
her; a green cloth studded with stars covered her hair. Perfect,
blessed. And it wasn't hard to notice how much she resembled Erica.

I honestly wasn't prepared for the sudden anger that rushed
through me, so strong, I felt dizzy. Come off it, Erica. *Narcissistic.*
And you had a son; you were so proud of that, and now look. You
couldn't even take care enough to protect him. My hands were shak-

ing. Abruptly, I sat down in the rocking chair, holding its arms tightly, and rocked myself back to calm. The anger was inexplicable.

Troy was a good boy, and Erica had once been my brother James's best friend.

If there was anything, at all I could do for her now, I would.

There was a hall off the living room. I got up, still a little shaky, and walked down it.

Two bedrooms. I peeked in the first. What was I looking for? *Clues?* Or the source of my own anger? The first room was tiny. I noticed an unmade bed, a tangle of socks and T-shirts on the floor, a skateboard.

But the walls were amazing, more dragons and beasts carefully and lovingly painted on in bright colors, their eyes glaring at me, benign and baleful at the same time. On the ceiling were stars; when the room darkened, they would glow—one of those kits of the starry sky, pasted on the ceiling so Troy could learn his constellations while he lay safely in bed.

I suspected the stars were from an earlier time. When you're sixteen, you sometimes seem to whirl in constellations farther away than the ones on the ceiling. Paperbacks lay stacked in a corner, something by Clive Barker on top.

I tiptoed down the hall. Why was I tiptoeing in Erica's house, with no one there to hear me? The other room was bigger, full of clothes—clothes hanging on a metal rod, along one wall, probably more in the closet. Masses of clothes, Guatemalan and Indian, faded antique clothes from the thirties and forties, and loads of pillows on the wide bed. Jewelry was piled in a bright jumble on a battered pine dresser; shoes that had been kicked off now lay scattered on the floor. But the bed was made. A book rested on the bedside table, a bookmark sticking out of it. I could not resist looking now, any more than I had been able to at Stuart's.

The Letters of Flannery O'Connor: The Habit of Being. Heavy-duty stuff. And the page where the bookmark was, blasphemously marked with yellow Hi-Liter: "All human nature vigorously resists grace because grace changes us and the change is painful."

Maybe not so blasphemously. I looked around at the room, at the excess of clothes and jewelry and pillows, thought of Erica's flamboyance, her ever-changing jobs, her wit: Sometimes people's best-kept secrets are in plain sight, and we stare at them and do not recognize them for what they are.

Erica, what on earth was going on in your life? I had changed from the days at Venice Beach; Erica had to have changed, too. But the pictures in my heart never changed; I held them there, and they flipped past me one by one, the pastel buildings on Ocean Front in the soft air, the palm trees and green benches, the sun shining on the faded thirties houses, dogs chasing the seagulls out on the beach—my last good times with James, when he was himself.

And now he was dead. It was so cruel. Something you could never prepare for, never accept. It woke you in the night, years later, the pain as sharp as if it had just happened. Death had come prematurely to so many people I'd once known, and yet we thought we had embraced life so thoroughly, we scarcely believed in death.

Maybe what I had seen in Kyle was something utterly opposite this. Suspicious and self-sufficient, he was overwhelmingly prepared to defend himself, a kind of warrior, in control of death.

Where was he now?

Time to leave. I turned, and walked back through the hall. The whole house was empty, yet everyone had left so recently. Someone told me a story once about tornadoes, how if they hit a house just right, they create a vacuum that sucks the air from the lungs of the inhabitants, killing them, yet leaving everything intact: suspended in airless time.

I tiptoed out the front door.

The phone rang just then. Too late. I reached in, flipped the lock, then closed the door behind me.

chapter nine

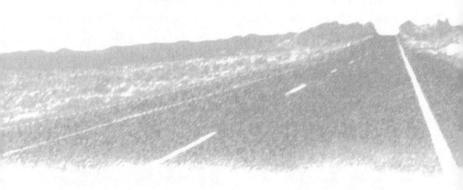

IT WAS STILL LIGHT AND THE EVENING WAS balmy as I walked back down the narrow road that curved and wound its way to Tombstone Canyon. Overhead, the cottonwoods rustled; under my feet, the leaves of the live oaks, which had shed in the spring, made a carpet of slippery burnt orange. The road felt like the quintessential country lane. I'd run a gamut of emotions back at Erica's, and now I was empty. A mood of deep and incongruous peace came over me.

I passed a couple of shabby little shacks, gray wood showing through faded paint, old toys in the dirt yards. As I rounded a curve, there was the little pink house, immaculate, its teal and white trim gleaming. You could almost smell the paint drying. An old gray Volkswagen and a brand-new red Cherokee were parked in the driveway. Among pots of pink geraniums on the front porch, two men, spiffy in cream-colored pants and dark polo shirts, sat in white wicker chairs, radiating domesticity.

I stopped. I didn't have a purse with me, no card. "Nelson?" I asked. "Nelson and Larry?"

"That's us," the younger one said. He was in his middle thirties, maybe, with tousled streaky blond hair and a face like a well-tanned Grecian god. "At least Larry's me." He smiled charmingly, sure of pleasing, and jerked his thumb at the other man. "And that's Nelson."

The other man, dark-haired, older, nodded—polite but serious among the pink geraniums. Deep lines ran from his nose to his mouth, setting off an extremely handsome mustache.

"I'm Chloe Newcombe, a victim advocate from the county attorney's." Come to ruin a pleasant evening, I thought. "Could I talk to you for a minute?"

They looked at each other; then they both stood up.

"We'd *appreciate* that," Nelson said. "We knew something was going on. Come up. Come up."

I climbed the porch steps. Nelson held out his hand. His brown eyes were warm, his grip strong, sincere. Of course. He was the counselor.

I shook Larry's hand, too. I didn't know what Larry was, but there was a seductive edge to him, a whiff of the hustler that you sensed immediately. His beautiful face invited your eyes to linger. Not just invited, dared. I looked away.

"We're *dying* to know what's going on." Larry's voice was animated with suppressed animal energy. "We saw that detective drive by, Masters, and then poor little Troy in a truck, looking so forlorn. Whose truck was that?"

"His lawyer's," I said.

Larry looked indignant. "What does he need a lawyer for? Why—"

"I'm a licensed counselor," Nelson said, interrupting him. "I told that detective I'd be responsible for Troy, at least until his aunt shows up. Troy told me he'd call her, but so far, he won't even tell me her name."

"It makes you wonder if there *is* any aunt," Larry added. "Erica never talked about a sister."

Nelson paused, looked at me attentively, and then said to Larry, "We've exhausted her."

"Coffee?" asked Larry, sounding contrite. "We have some fabulous coffee."

"Coffee would be nice," I said.

I followed them into an extremely beautiful room and sat down on a club chair slipcovered in white duck. I wrote down their phone number, said I'd keep them updated, then told them as much as I could as I sipped at incredibly powerful coffee. Troy was a juvenile and I didn't want to say he'd been charged, so I hedged and said I thought he was being questioned.

Nelson looked at me skeptically, stroking his moustache. "He's been questioned before, and with a lawyer present that time, too. What that means to me is that he's a suspect."

"It's outrageous," Larry said vehemently. "Little Troy. We have to do something. Whom can we call? I have an uncle in the senate."

"In Vermont, you goof," said Nelson. "That won't help." He looked at Larry fondly, as though he were a small child.

Larry tossed his head. A becoming lock of hair fell on his forehead. "But we need to do something. We owe it to Erica. She was our friend, and so good to us, so welcoming when we moved here. A Florence Nightingale for nervous souls. We *were* nervous; we didn't know . . ." His voice trailed off and he shrugged gracefully.

"For years, I'd been coming here from Tucson to visit," Nelson explained. "I've always liked the place, but for a while there was a strong homophobic element here. We were concerned about being . . . pariahs."

"But it hasn't been a problem," said Larry. "Not that there isn't a cowboy element, but we're homebodies. We don't go to the bars." He bit his lip, glanced at Nelson. "I mean not *often.*"

"There's so much that needs to be taken care of. The mortuary." Nelson shuddered. "They haven't released the—*Erica's* body yet. I don't know what's wrong with Troy; his aunt needs to be here. And you have no idea why Troy was charged?"

I shook my head.

A silence fell. Both of them looked confused and rather beautiful as they sat side by side on a big couch, also slipcovered in white duck and adorned with cushions made from old kilims. James would have loved this room, I thought. The floors had been sanded and hand-rubbed with wax until they glowed. The walls were luminous white, sponged with pale peach, and the windows were hung in a dim mist of sheer curtains.

The coffee was so strong that, in this ethereal world, I felt as though I might burst in a bubble of light.

Larry leaned back luxuriously on the couch, put his feet up on the distressed pine coffee table, and said thoughtfully, "Maybe that detective found out about the fight."

I set my cup down carefully on a glass and wrought-iron end table. "The fight?"

Nelson took a sip of coffee, coughed, then coughed again. Larry patted him solicitously on the back.

"Erica and Troy had a terrible fight about three weeks ago." Larry smoothed the lock of hair back from his forehead. "It was bizarre, because they never fought. We heard it all the way over here. Shouts, glass breaking. We were *paralyzed*. Then someone called the cops, but it was over before they got there."

"Really?" I said, not wanting to sound too curious. "What was it about?"

"We don't know." Larry looked sad. "Nelson went to see if he could do anything, but . . ." He shrugged, playing with the top button of his wine-colored polo short. "I mean, he *tried*."

The distance between the two men seemed to widen, almost imperceptibly. Tension filled the room. Larry went on, as if apologizing, "I guess Erica really didn't want to talk to anyone about it."

He glanced at Nelson accusingly.

Nelson's shoulders dropped like a man who has conceded defeat. "I was wrong," he said simply. "I went for my ego—the counselor— but I should have sent Larry instead. Isn't that right, Larry?"

His voice conveyed something more than the question, almost a challenge. He said to me, "Larry and Erica had a true rapport." He put two fingers together, held them up. "Twin souls."

Twin souls. A true rapport. Erica and James had had it, too. But James had been more innocent, less aware of his power than Larry.

Larry leaned back and closed his eyes, his lashes shadowing his cheeks. His skin was perfectly tanned, his nose and cheeks a miracle of geometric planes. The curtains lifted in a breeze. Nelson looked at him for a split second, a look almost terrifying in its sheer love.

Or was I hallucinating on caffeine.

Nelson said very quietly, "Troy had nothing to do with Erica's murder. I'm as sure of it as I am of anything."

*　*　*

I left soon after. A fight, a terrible fight, I thought as I started home, jittery, speeding on caffeine. And something was going on between Nelson and Larry. Twin souls. Surely Erica and Larry hadn't been lovers? And why not? Larry's sexuality didn't seem focused, more like pervasive, that mixture of innocence and manipulation I'd seen in certain children who have been molested. Damaged.

And Nelson, a counselor, trying to fix him?

But I couldn't connect that with Erica and Troy. "I have to get home now," she'd said, her face lighting up. "I promised Troy I'd get right home. He's got some project. . . ." *Why* had they fought?

But teenagers did fight with their parents; they fought about almost everything. It was normal. Though according to Larry, Troy and Erica never fought. But you couldn't really know what went on in families, behind the facade.

Troubled again, I walked down the quintessential country lane, and my incongruous peace showed its other face; the menace in the slippery live-oak leaves under my feet, the facades of fresh paint over wood long rotting, a child accused of a terrible crime as the air cooled and evening turned to dark.

chapter ten

WHEN I GOT HOME, IT WAS DARK INSIDE the house. I turned on the lights, but there was no destruction in evidence and Big Foot was nowhere to be seen. I went out on the porch. "Kitty, kitty, kitty," I called loudly, already panicking. I couldn't lose him now, not with everything else.

But he came out from under the porch steps, a tailless lizard writhing in his mouth. I was beginning to feel a little desperate about my house—the refrigerator was still chirping and I hadn't mopped a floor in days and days, or was it weeks?

I checked my machine, but no one had wanted to call me, including Stuart. I was tired of trailing after him anyway, the lord and master. I was hungry, but it was okay, as I had a freezer full of Budget Gourmet Light and Healthy, or at least one, if I still even had a freezer, and maybe some asparagus. Then the phone rang and it was Stuart.

"What are you doing there?" he demanded.

"You *told* me to go home. How's Troy? You've got to get him out. Right away."

"I'm trying."

"And you said he wasn't a suspect. You lied to me."

"I swear I didn't. I was as surprised as you were. Come on down and have some ribs. I saved out some slaw and potato salad, too. You can eat while I make phone calls. If you're good, I'll take you to the Dairy Queen later, and if you're bad, even later than that."

"See you, then." I hung up, not bothering to respond to the last remark. Clearly, the emergency situation had robbed him of his senses. Ribs sounded better than diet frozen food. Who was I kidding? I could hardly wait to get down there and find out everything.

Did Stuart know about Andy? That would be useful information, if you were Troy's defense attorney.

As a victim advocate, I didn't strictly work for the prosecution, but I was supposed to make known any exculpatory information I learned in the course of my job. Exculpatory meant more than just relevant—it had to be information that tended to exonerate the person charged. It was the only exception to confidentiality. It would be revealed to the defense eventually by way of discovery, but it wouldn't sit well with the prosecutor if I revealed it to the defense first.

But Jude had asked me to tell someone about Andy and Erica, so there was no confidentiality involved anyway. I would feel like a snitch turning Andy in. But he hadn't been at work; he knew the bookmobile schedule, probably knew the Olanders weren't at home. Maybe Ed already knew Andy and Erica had been lovers; maybe Andy had a good alibi and I was agonizing over all this for nothing.

I thought about the other library people who had worked with Erica. Sally—so scared as she sat at the computer, with her pale albino hair, her childish clothes. Was she just a nervous type, or did she have a real reason to be so frightened? And Neva, the boss, calling Sally off just when she might have said more. Neva and Erica hadn't gotten along. Well, so what? Lots of people don't get along with their bosses. You can't choose them like you can your friends. Damn. How had Ed handled Sally anyway?

Or had he handled all the questioning except Troy's in a perfunctory way, not caring about the answers, because he was already on the track, attached to a theory.

I went over to Stuart's and found him in the dining room, on the phone. I walked back to the kitchen. The sink was full of dishes, barbecue sauce splashed all over the counters. The rubber soles of my Aerosoles were like suction cups on the sticky floor, and the trash can overflowed with take-out containers, empty cans of diet soda, cigarette butts. I could hear Stuart talking in the other room as I filled a plate from the dish drainer with slaw and potato salad and ribs.

"No, I'm not talking like a defense attorney. It's bullshit no matter how you look at it, and a guardian will be there, at the house—I can guarantee it—when he's released." His voice was forceful and full of conviction. "Or shortly thereafter."

He hung up as I came in the dining room. "Felix, the juvenile prosecutor," he said wearily.

I shoved a cupful of old coffee and soggy cigarette butts to one side and put my plate on the table. "Troy's getting out, then?"

"No." Stuart put his face in his hands and took a couple of deep breaths. The overhead light in the dining room was harsh; I noticed he needed a shave and that a button was missing on his denim work shirt. "He's probably not getting out. Not right away anyhow."

"But you said *when*—"

"No point in saying *if*."

"And this guardian stuff," I said. "Troy hasn't even called his aunt."

"I'm going to. I laid down the law on the way to the detention center. Troy hates her, but that's irrelevant now." He lit a cigarette, looking harassed. He smoked too much, ate junk food, couldn't even sew a button on his work shirt. Not long for this world, the way he was living.

"And what about Troy's father?" I went on, showing no mercy. "He has to have one. There isn't visitation or anything?"

"Troy doesn't even know who he is. A one-night stand maybe?" He looked at me slyly. "It's not so unusual. There're women out there just looking for sperm donors."

"Hah!" I said, looking at the place where the button used to be, thinking of the wreck of his kitchen, "And there're men out there just looking for mothers."

He didn't even flinch.

"*Why* was Troy even arrested?" I persisted.

"Circumstantial stuff of the flimsiest kind. Troy skipped school that day, for one. Ed found a gun in the house, a twenty-two no less, not even the right caliber. And Troy and Erica had a big, noisy fight about three weeks ago. The neighbors called the cops."

"I know."

Stuart looked at me with interest, through a cloud of smoke. "What do you mean, 'I know'?"

"I stopped in at Nelson and Larry's. They told me."

"Did they tell you what it was about? The night they questioned Troy, he told Ed he didn't remember."

"They didn't know," I said. "Ed knew about the fight when he questioned Troy? Why didn't he charge him then?"

"Because," said Stuart. He leaned back in his chair, put his feet up on the table. "It wasn't enough."

"Wasn't enough? There's more? Come on," I said impatiently. "I can ask Felix."

"Ed made a initial search that night, then went back to the house a second time and searched again. He found one of Troy's notebooks." He ran his finger around the collar of his shirt.

"Full of dragons," I said.

"Full of dragons, and a list. The list was titled 'How to Murder Someone and Get Away with It.' "

There was a silence. For the first time, I felt just a smidgen of doubt; then I said in a rush, "He's a teenager. You know what they're like. My brothers used to do all kinds of things—hang my dolls from the stairwell and—oh, boys that age, they have black hearts." My stomach gave a little lurch. "I mean," I said, "it didn't describe—"

"No. Let me see, one choice entry was 'Throw an electric heater in the tub when they're taking a bath. Take the body out to the desert so the cops will think they were struck by lightning.' Nothing about killing a mother, or a bookmobile driver, either. I told you it was flimsy." He paused. "Now you owe me. How come you never mentioned that you knew Erica?"

I blinked. "What are you talking about?"

He squinted at me behind a cloud of tobacco smoke. "Come on, Chloe—you told Troy. He was all excited about it."

"It was a long time ago. I ran into her once here. That's it."

"Ran into her recently?"

"I guess. A few weeks ago."

"Recently. You were friends from before—it must have given you an in with her. What did you talk about?"

Somewhere in my head, an alarm bell rang. I stared down at the ribs, exposed in the harsh overhead light—dry, overcooked. Why the third degree? He is a *defense* attorney, stupid, I told myself; a weasel. "We hardly talked at all," I said defensively. "She was on her way somewhere."

"So what'd you think from your . . . brief encounter?"

"I thought what I thought from when I knew her before—she was interesting, very alive, intelligent."

"Single. Sexy. Dressed to get noticed."

"How do *you* know?"

"I met her once when Troy got busted for marijuana possession. I was his lawyer."

"Umm."

"I heard she couldn't maintain a relationship for long," he went on. "Came on strong and fast then just when things are going great she says bye-bye. Probably drove men nuts."

I looked at him suspiciously. "You learned all that just from meeting her *once*?"

"You can tell." His voice was glib. "You know what the guys used to call a woman like that back in high school?"

I jabbed at the potato salad with my fork. Anger welled up inside me. "Two words," I said. "The first one starts with *P*. Or a *C*. I don't want to hear it. It's typical male thinking, so self-centered. Maybe she dressed that way because it's fun." *All human nature vigorously resists grace because grace changes us and the change is painful.*

I knew Erica was more than the picture Stuart had painted but that didn't mean I knew who she was. Not anymore, if I ever had.

"Everything a woman does isn't geared to how men react to it," I added.

"Okay," Stuart said, "you're right. How insensitive of me. Just trying to stir up a little reasonable doubt but I won't pursue that line of thinking. I'll let Troy rot in jail."

"Go to hell."

He took off his glasses, rubbed his eyes. There were pouches under them, lines on his face that hadn't been there earlier. "Damn, I've got a trial coming up next week, too. I planned to spend this weekend preparing." He picked up the phone. "I'm going to call the sister. Mariah's her name, by the way. Mariah Haskell."

"Stuart," I said pedantically, "there're definite ways to deliver a death notification; people can be damaged if it's done wrong. And telephoning isn't a good way."

"Well, it's in the hands of the philistines now. I'm calling. I think I'll do it from the couch. Eat."

He got up and went into the other room. I picked up a rib, bit into it. It was dry and cold, but I was eating from hunger, not for taste.

In the living room, Stuart was saying loudly, "Hello, Mariah, this is Stuart Ross. I'm a deputy public defender in Cochise County, Arizona. When you get this message, you can call me anytime, day or night, at . . ."

Answering machine. I stopped listening. Once the relatives arrived and applied pressure to get Troy out, everyone would move more vigorously, start exploring other avenues, like Erica's relationship with Andy and anything else that might be relevant. I hoped.

The table was littered with documents, disclosure files, and some kind of treatise, entitled "Prosecutorial Misconduct: A Domain Without Borders." I read it without taking it in as I finished three ribs and ate the potato salad from Safeway; it lacked zing and zip, but I ate a big portion and then a little vinegary slaw. After that, I took my plate out to the kitchen, rinsed it off, put it back in the dish drainer, and went into the living room.

Stuart was lying full out on one of the couches, head back, snoring faintly. He hadn't even taken off his cowboy boots. A trial coming up next week. It was lonely work, going out with defense attorneys. I walked home.

*　*　*

Neva Shumaker, the county librarian, had permed her salt-and-pepper hair and dyed it blond. She wore long, dangling earrings and she held an order pad in one hand. At least it looked like Neva, but I sensed it wasn't.

"I know it was you who did it," she said. "Now please place your order. I don't have much time."

"But I don't know what's on the menu," I said, "What's good?"

"Better ask the chef," she said, pointing.

I looked where she pointed and saw him in a little window behind the bar: Kyle, wearing a big white chef's hat. He had a large knife in one hand, and with the other he was holding up a side of beef, except when I looked closer, I saw it was a heart.

"I'll take the ribs," I said. "I feel safe with ribs."

"I wouldn't trust the ribs," said the waitress. "Not when Kyle's doing the cooking."

Then, with horror, I remembered that *he'd* ordered the ribs, too, the man Kyle had killed. If you couldn't trust ribs, what could you trust?

I woke up, my heart pounding. What did Stuart know? Whom and what could you trust? No one and nothing. It seemed like a valuable perception, a satori, maybe. Keep your wits about you and your emotions under control at all times. I got up, drank a full glass of water, and took two Advil just in case.

And as I stood barefoot in my kitchen, I suddenly thought of the man who knew Erica from out in the valley. Lucas. Dot, Erica might have known from the library, but this man Lucas—who was he? The more I thought about it, the stranger it seemed that Erica would have known someone, anyone, in the valley.

"How to Murder Someone and Get Away with It." It was kind of creepy.

chapter eleven

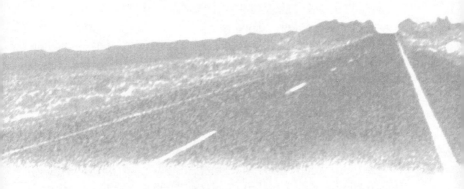

HEADS BOWED, TWO MEN IN SHACKLES, wearing orange jumpsuits, white socks, and tan sandals, got out of a prison van and hobbled toward the back door of the courthouse. I watched them through the windows in the reception area of the county attorney's offices. For a second, I imagined Troy, his blond head bowed, too, hobbling in behind them, leg irons on, feet chained together.

I marched through the door to the inner offices, then down the hall to the office of Felix Lambert, the juvenile prosecutor.

The door was open. Felix, Friday casual in a navy-and-white-striped polo shirt and Dockers, was tilted back in his chair, feet on the desk, reading something long and legal and tugging at one corner of his elaborate walrus mustache.

I tapped at the door frame until he looked up.

"Hey, Chloe."

"Do you have a minute?"

"Sure. Come on in." He set down what he was reading, but I could tell by the vacant look in his eyes that he was still with it.

I went in and sat down. His hair crept past the collar of his polo shirt and the room smelled of the patchouli he used as aftershave. He was more of a renegade than Victor. I wondered about his past and how he felt about the numerous marijuana possession cases that came his way.

"Troy Hill?" I said.

Felix was paying attention now. He tilted his chair forward. "Charged him last night. He's over in juvie."

"So what's going to happen?"

"To be honest, the case against Troy is weak. I'm still ruminating."

"Since he's been charged, I guess I should tell you this, since it might be exculpatory. I don't think Ed Masters knows. One of the women at the library where Erica worked told me Andy Marookian and Erica were lovers—they broke up just a few weeks ago. Andy"—I paused for effect, traitor that I was—"Andy's the regular bookmobile driver."

He didn't jump up and down for joy, but then, he was a lawyer. He stroked his mustache for a moment. "Interesting," he said after a moment. "Maybe Ed should pursue that a little more, huh?"

I shrugged. "Whatever."

I went back to my office on rubbery legs. All this agitating about Troy. Betraying other people in the hopes of getting him released. Even Felix thought the case was weak—after all, there wasn't any physical evidence. But what if I was wrong about everything? About Troy, about Erica's relationship with him. The fight between them was disturbing, the list scary.

But my conversation with Troy in Erica's kitchen kept coming back to me. No. No way he did it. No way.

I called Frankie.

"I've got to be out in the valley today," I told her, lying. "I thought I might do a follow-up with Dot. Want to give me her number?"

"Five five five–one four five seven," said Frankie. "You going to tell her Erica's son's been charged?"

"He didn't do it, Frankie. I'm sure. And the juvenile prosecutor hasn't made a decision yet."

"Well, Ed was here earlier, walking around with his lip stuck out at least three feet, whining and going on about lawyers destroying the country."

"Oh, good," I said. "That means he's worried the charges won't stick. I'll just tell Dot there's a possible suspect and leave it at that."

I hung up and called her.

"Well now, I think I'd like that," she said when I offered to visit. "People out here are enough to drive you crazy with their worrying and all. And my boy Ernest is the worst. I'd like to talk to someone got some sense."

"Worrying?" I said. "Anything in particular?"

"Hogwash is all. Just a bunch of hogwash."

Half an hour later, I was driving through the Junction under an overcast sky, thinking about all the people out here who must be worrying about hogwash. Feeling sad, too—I'd spent time here a couple of summers ago. I passed the sign advertising the Harvest Festival, passed the wood and adobe houses and the double-wide trailers, the Hitching Post bar and the Junction Church of the Latter-day Saints, the Horseshoe Café, the Valley Cooperative Feed Store, and the Valley Baptist Church—sign out front saying RUMMAGE SALE. The Wagon Wheel bar.

I'd gone to the Wagon Wheel once with an old friend, gotten drunk and danced with a couple of cowboys to George Strait and Randy Travis on the jukebox. Drunk but still innocent back then; walking out to the parking lot, looking up at the stars reeling in the summer night. Now it was fall, strings of red chilies for sale at Valley Mercantile, and the leaves of the cottonwoods, the chinaberries, and the oaks smoldered gold under the pale gray sky.

The Junction seemed closed against me, like an old friend who didn't recognize me anymore. Those summer times were gone, and I thought of Kyle, so much a part of them, gone, too. There had been hot winds, and torrential rains that summer. Beautiful balmy evenings, too, and on one of those evenings, Kyle had made a decision, fired a gun, and changed his life forever.

And certainly made an impact on mine.

* * *

Fifteen miles down from the Junction, following the directions Dot had given me, I slowed, turned right onto a dirt road. A blue van was driving toward me, driving fast enough to raise the dust; then suddenly, gravel shot up from its tires as the driver braked. The van swerved, stopped abruptly, resting in a diagonal across the road, blocking my way.

There was a house far down the road and another one off in the distance, but basically there was nothing else. It was deserted here, as deserted as it must have been at Olander Meadow when the bookmobile had pulled in. Then I saw the sign on the truck: STONE'S APPLIANCE REPAIR. Stone. A relative?

I backed up, pulled over next to a clump of rabbitbrush, which was going to seed in a cloud of white fluff. A man climbed out of the van in dusty overalls, a faded plaid shirt, his movements urgent. White fluff swirled around him. I wound down my window as he approached, and white fluff blew into the car.

"You the lady from the county attorney's?" His face was ruddy, middle-aged, lines like apostrophes between his watery blue eyes. Under his feed-store cap, a tuft of graying hair stuck out.

I nodded.

"I'm Ernest, Dot's boy." White fluff clung to his eyebrows, as though he were turning into Father Time before my eyes. "I got to git going, but I wanted to tell you about this rumor going round everywhere, all over the damn Junction. Somebody's got to talk some sense into her."

"What rumor?" I asked.

He brushed at his eyebrows, voice full of indignation. "That Ma saw the one what shot that librarian lady, saw him real good. So she could identify him."

I stared at him in disbelief. "I don't think so."

"Look." He removed a bit of fluff from his lower lip. "My ma needs *protection*." His face got redder. "That's what we pay taxes for, ain't it? I been trying to get her to come stay with me, but she won't budge. I'd appreciate it, you'd talk to her. And now I got to git. My kid's got a ball game."

He started to walk away. Down the road, a jackrabbit loped along, stopped, big ears quivering.

"Wait," I said. "What does your mom say about this?"

"They're all saying Ed Masters told her to shut up about it."

"They have a possible suspect," I said. "I can't say who, but Ed would have had Dot over to Dudley to identify him if that was true."

"Damn it, it better be the one, 'cause if it ain't, it don't matter if it's true or not whether she saw him. Not if the killer hears about it."

Little goose bumps rose on my arms.

He reached into his overall pocket and walked back toward my car. "Here, let me give you my business card."

I leaned out the window and took it, a grimy rectangle.

"You let me know what's going on," he said over his shoulder as he got in his van and drove off, raising dust behind him.

Rumors, I thought as I watched him go, they're like the telephone game that kids play. You start with a sentence and whisper it down a line of people and see how it ends up. It ends up hogwash, Dot would probably say. But it didn't matter, like Ernest said, not if the killer heard about it.

chapter twelve

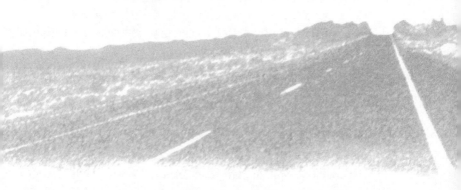

IN THE DISTANCE, DOT'S HOUSE WAS A pale green cinder-block rectangle with a screened-in porch, and next to it the pecan orchard, site of Mr. Stone's demise. A heart attack, leaving Dot out here all alone. I bumped down into a wash; my tires spun, then caught as I bumped back up. When it rained, the wash would fill up and the road would be impassable. The orchard wouldn't provide the house much shelter; the sun would burn down like fire on its roof, the wind rattle everything loose, kick up the dust, push the unstable right over the edge.

And if that weren't enough, whoever had emptied a gun into Erica Hill might want to do the same to her. Why would she *want* to stay here?

I parked in front of the house, next to a white van—JESUS IS THE LIVING WORD painted on the side and, under that, VALLEY BAPTIST CHURCH. A little brown mutt came around by the side of the porch, barking frantically.

I half opened my door and he backed away, still barking, into the fenced-in yard full of marigolds and two chrome and green plastic strip chairs side by side. The door of the house opened.

Two women came out, followed by Dot, who was dressed in men's khaki pants and a gray sweatshirt, a pair of binoculars around her neck, a shotgun under her arm.

"Fudd," she shouted. "You shut up! Chloe. Don't you worry—he won't bite." Fudd got on his belly and whined, grinning up at Dot. "You musta passed my boy Ernest," she said. "He just left."

"He stopped and introduced himself," I said. "Gave me his card."

"You hang on to it, then. He's a good boy," she said in a distracted voice. "Mr. Fix-It Man."

The two women, middle-aged, and pretty in their flowery dresses, smiled at me.

"This is Beulah and Molly," said Dot "They came from the church to comfort me. And this is Chloe, from the county attorney's."

"We're pleased to meet you, Chloe," Molly said graciously, a blond, rosy woman in a blue dress with a starched white collar.

"Dot was just reminding us how Erica Hill came to our church— why, not even that long ago, maybe two months," Beulah said. She was blond, too, almost platinum, her rouged and powdered face like crushed petals.

"Erica went to your church?" I was astounded. Underlining sentences in books by Catholic intellectuals was one thing, Baptist churches another entirely. I looked at the women as they flittered in the yard like two butterflies. "Are you sure?"

"Well, of course we are," said Molly. "She came twice, Dot said, but I only noticed her once."

Beulah said, "If we'd realized, we . . . we could have *prayed* for her."

"We will now," Molly said. "We certainly will."

Dot looked at the two women skeptically and shifted the gun, slinging it as casually as a purse.

Molly looked wistful. "We'd better get back to the sale. You know, the pastor's so softhearted, if we don't watch him, he'll be giving everything away. Dot, you go on over to Ernest's now, *please.*"

Dot harrumphed.

Molly kissed her and Beulah gave her a hug; then they drifted to the white van.

Dot, like a plain gray rock, looked after them as they drove off. "Well," she said dryly, "I'll be safe in the arms of our Savior for a while."

"Erica went to the Baptist church?" I asked.

"A couple of Sundays is all. I'm sorry to say that no one was real friendly to her, even the pastor, though he was courteous, of course. So that second Sunday, I went over and spoke to her. Curious, I guess. I invited her back to the house and we talked. That's how come I knew her."

She looked up at the overcast sky, which softened the light and made the red marigolds in her yard glow like embers. "I sure hope it's not going to rain. There's pecans sacked out there in the orchard. If I could persuade you to help me out here, you might win yourself a sack."

"We'll start at the end and haul 'em as we go," said Dot as we walked between the trees.

The wind had suddenly gone and everything was still under the gray sky, the turning leaves silent. Looking through the rows of trees, I could see the Chiricahua Mountains in the distance and, miles away, another house, floating on the desert. The smell of living plants on the verge of decay pricked at my nose.

"We planted this orchard a long time ago," Dot said. "Me and Daddy and the kids. Each kid had a special tree that was theirs. Now I got more pecans than I can use."

My feet crunched on old nuts. Fudd trotted beside us, sniffing at things. "So you have other children?" I asked her.

"Three altogether," she said "Ernest is the middle one. Wasn't much in school, takes after his dad. But he's a real good mechanic. Then there's my baby, Ruthie. She works with the U.S. Forest Service, over in California. Fights fires and all. Got her master's degree in forestry."

"You must be proud of her," I said.

Dot nodded absentmindedly, as if something else was on her mind. We reached the end of the orchard, where the mesquite, tumbleweed, and creosote began. Fudd loped out and began to circle in the mesquite. A burlap sack lay by the last tree in the middle row; under the tree was an old metal chair, its white paint cracked and peeling.

"Those are the kids' trees there at each end," Dot said, pointing. "Ruthie's is at one corner and Ernest's at the other. Right here is Henry's."

"Henry?"

"My oldest. Star quarterback in high school. All *A*'s and *B*'s, and good-looking, too. Don't know where that came from—the good-looking part."

Dot set her shotgun against the tree and sat down on the metal chair, ignoring the burlap sack, as if she'd forgotten why we'd come out to the orchard. "Have you heard about what they're saying in town?" she asked. "About me seeing the killer real good?"

"Yes."

"It's just nonsense." Her face was stubborn, even in the soft light, eyes impregnable behind her glasses. "Everyone's saying how dangerous it is to be out here alone. But I'm sitting here, and I can see for miles every way." She touched the binoculars hanging around her neck. "Who's going to sneak up on me here? Besides, I got my shotgun. Fudd's a good barker, and I keep him in at night." She looked at me, her face bleak. "They're trying to make me go stay with Ernest."

I shifted uncomfortably. "Maybe it wouldn't be such a bad idea," I said. "For a little while anyway."

She shook her head. "It's funny," she said. "Daddy died out here, and I found him, and it hurt, but it wasn't like finding Erica." She sighed. "I keep wondering about her. Wondered about her from the minute I saw her, sitting there in the pew all neat and dressed appropriate but not really fitting in. There's something on her mind, I thought. I wonder what it is."

Everything was so quiet, the air cushioning us at the edge of the desert. I held my breath.

"Tell me about Lucas," I said.

Dot leaned down and picked up a pecan, threw it into the desert. "Lucas. She picked our church 'cause he told her about being saved, a few years after his roping accident."

"You mean she went to church to see him?"

"No." She snorted. "He wasn't coming anymore when she showed up. Hadn't been for years. He got saved, but it didn't last."

I waited, saying nothing.

"Lucas Delton Lucas," she went on. "His daddy named him after his own last name." Her face softened. "Mame Olander told me he's been over to that meadow the last two days, leaving flowers right where she was killed. They used to be good friends—that's what Erica told me—but she hadn't seen him for a long time."

I picked up a rotting pecan, running my thumbnail on one cracked edge. "Then you got to know her pretty well?"

"I wouldn't say that. She came to my house and we kind of chit-chatted, but in the end, I talked too much, and now I'm ashamed."

"Ashamed?"

"Well, she asked me all about the church, said she had trouble believing and how did I come to believe?" Dot took off her glasses and pinched the bridge of her nose. "I had to be honest. 'Erica,' I said, 'it's for the companionship. That's why I go. They'll tell you faith is just work, plain and simple, but to me, it's a gift, and no one's given it to me.' And you know, she didn't come back after that."

Her feet planted firm on the earth, Dot leaned back blindly, her face naked, reached out and patted the trunk of the tree. A leaf floated down and caught in her white hair. She didn't seem to notice. She put her glasses back on.

"So all that is going through my head. I just had to speak my mind, but maybe she could have found something there if it wasn't for me being a meddling old woman. I been coming out here a lot since she got killed, I like to sit by this tree—Henry's tree—and think about it. I sit here and I ask Henry, Now, what do you think? It's the closest I can get to faith."

The pecan cracked, fell through my fingers. The bits of nut meat were worm-riddled, pungent with mold.

"Henry got killed in Vietnam," said Dot. "His buddy came out to talk to me, oh, maybe a couple of months after. He told me all about Henry, some funny little stories and then how he died, my pretty boy—it was a mine exploded right under him, so it was quick, and I hope it was quick for Erica, too. But neither of them ready to go."

I looked past Dot to the desert as tears stung at my eyelids, blurring my view of the mountains. But it wasn't for me to cry as Dot sat there, stony-faced.

"I'm not leaving my home and Henry, not for anyone," she said. "Death don't scare me, not one bit." She patted the shotgun. "Maybe that coward will come sneaking up on me after all, but if I catch him, I'll shoot him as many times as it takes."

She glanced at me. "The courts," she said. "There's always something wrong; somebody picks something up with the wrong hand or something. Even if they convict, we got two boys from around here on death row, been there ten years or more, and I don't know when they'll get around to doing it. I swear, if I wasn't so old and arthritic, I'd hunt him down. Kill him and then sleep all the night through."

chapter thirteen

AS I DROVE AWAY, MORE CLOUDS OF RABBIT-
brush were going to seed on the edges of the wash, gathering in drifts like false snow. A hawk swooped. The woman I was leaving behind was half creaky old lady and half one-woman vigilante with shotgun loaded and ready. Ready not only to avenge Erica but, in some obscure way, Henry, too.

You couldn't accuse Dot of being Christian; she was Old Testament all the way. "I'd hunt him down. Kill him and then sleep all the night through." And maybe going to get herself killed for it.

And what about Erica, who'd already gotten herself killed? What had she been looking for, at the Baptist church out in the valley? To get saved like Lucas Delton Lucas? She hadn't seen him for a long while when she died, but he went and put flowers on the only grave she had at the moment.

I reached the highway, turned left instead of right, headed for Olander Meadow. Clusters of sunflowers lined the road, bursts of brown and bright yellow under the milky sky. If you were planning to kill the bookmobile driver, how would you go about it?

"How to Murder Someone and Get Away with It"—Troy's list. I put it out of my mind.

First, you would almost certainly have to drive to get here. But would you drive clear up the dirt road? No. So where would you stop? Then I saw it again—the abandoned house Frankie and I had passed just before the turn. I pulled over and got out of the car. The house was at the end of a short circular dirt driveway, obscured among big oaks and bushes. I walked to where I could see it properly. It was frame, the boards silvery gray. One side was stoved in, a cluster of white prickle poppies growing up through the sagging porch.

But somehow, you could still see the builder's intention; the porch extended from the house like welcoming arms. You could imagine the residents sitting out there, before television kept people inside, long before the new blacktop road, the trees still young. Now it was dying, melancholy and peaceful in the autumnal light.

You'd park in the driveway, of course. The trees and bushes would block any view of a parked car from the road. Then you'd walk through the field of dry grasses behind the house, not on the dirt road, so you wouldn't leave footprints. You'd walk diagonally through the field up to Olander Meadow. The bookmobile schedule was posted in all the newspapers; all you had to do was to go to the stop and wait. You could easily hide behind the stand of tamarisk at the edge of the meadow.

I shivered. Okay. The bookmobile shows up and you do what you came to do. But just as you're leaving, Dot Stone pulls up in her gray station wagon, and there you are, stuck in the middle of a field of yuccas. She gets out and goes over to the body. Instinctively, she looks around. She said just a glimpse in the rearview mirror, but maybe she saw you sooner, before she got back into her car. Standing there in the yuccas, with their stems the color of old bones. Does she see you real good?

Did she?

If she did, then why didn't you kill her? Maybe you weren't sure she had. Maybe you froze and, in that little bit of time, she got back to her car and pulled out, in a big hurry.

Anyway, after you saw Dot, you'd want to get out of there fast. You'd go back the same way, check for cars coming on the road. You could see forever and ever. The highway continues on clear to the I-10; you wouldn't have to drive through the Junction, pass anyone who might see you and remember. If you were really thinking and not too panicked by Dot, you'd stop and brush away any tire trucks and footprints you'd left in the dirt driveway.

You, whoever you are.

Spooked, I could almost feel someone watching, palpable on my shoulder blades. I turned—to nothing. Uneasily, I walked back to my car, rubbing my foot over the faint prints I'd left in the dirt as I went.

Then I drove the rest of the way to the dirt road, turned, and drove to the meadow, stopping by the tamarisks. The meadow stretched out, golden grass, white poppies, a few pink thistles, and all the desolate white skeletons of the yuccas. Empty now, all the people gone; abandoned, like a fairground after the show is over.

Where the bookmobile had been parked were flowers, two bouquets of pale, dried-up roses on the top. Erica hadn't seen Lucas for quite a while, but now he brought roses to where she'd been killed.

Something serious had been going on in Erica's life two months ago. Not only had she started going to church but a few weeks later, she'd gone to the Victim Witness training class. "There was something on her mind," Dot had said. "I wonder what it was."

And Erica had said to me, ". . . let's get together sometime and talk." But I hadn't called her. Had there been something specific she'd wanted to talk about?

If I'd called her, would I be standing now by the tamarisks at the edge of Olander Meadow, on a cloudy day with the birds singing? They were singing now. Had they stopped suddenly, in warning back then, when the murderer showed up? Had Erica noticed and stupidly, because she panicked, run for the bookmobile?

The birds had stopped singing.

A man in a cowboy hat stepped out from behind the tamarisk. He was not too tall. Had a flat sunburned face, forehead hidden by the fawn hat.

My hands and feet turned to ice. I might have run, but I couldn't move, like someone in a head-on collision who automatically brakes and the wheels lock, so the driver can't even steer to get away.

"Mind if I ask what the hell you're doing here?" he said.

"Nothing, really," I said. "Just looking."

Folds of fat ringed his neck, submerged his eyes. He was wearing one of those Aztec-print cowboy shirts, his belly hanging out over low-slung jeans. "Hope you're not one of them damn reporters. This is Olander property." His voice was threatening.

"I'm not a reporter," I said hurriedly. "I work for the county attorney."

He scratched his nose and looked apologetic. "Sorry, then. I'm Buddy Olander. Couple them reporters came down here from Channel Four news and just about pestered everyone to death with questions. I seen your car, so I walked over. When we all got back, after the murder, Ed Masters and a couple deputies had just about wore out this poor old field, walked all over it, must have been a hundred times."

"It must have been awful for you. I'm Chloe Newcombe, from the Victim Witness Program." I extended my hand. His grip was flaccid, uninvolved. "The victim's sister will be coming to town, so I thought I'd better look things over. Sometimes people who've lost someone need to know every little detail."

He shrugged indifferently, took off the hat, then put it on again. "They got a suspect yet?"

"Maybe," I said. "They'll let us know, when it's for sure."

"Well, I got my own theory about it. There's a load of manure over behind them trees. Pretty fresh. Ed's not the type to notice manure less he steps in it, and even then, not till he takes his boots off." He smiled at me unpleasantly, the sun glinting off one chipped tooth.

"So here's what I think," he went on. "They got those forensic guys you see on TV can trace just about everything. 'Cause of that DNA stuff. Hell, maybe they can round up all the local horses, get some horse DNA, see if it matches that shit. Then you got your horse." He started to laugh.

From somewhere came the sound of a vehicle, coming closer. Buddy Olander looked past me, over my shoulder.

"Shit," he said. "We ought to build a damn parking lot here and charge admission."

I turned and saw a white pickup pulling in. The driver parked next to my Omni and got out.

"Hey there, Lucas," Buddy said. "We got the county attorney's rep right here. Best you turn around and go on home, wouldn't you say?"

I stared at Lucas. Tall and thin, but broad-shouldered, wearing a beige cowboy hat, faded jeans, white shirt. He was holding a bunch of marigolds, squashed in his fist. "This lady here?" he said. "What for? I'm pleased to meet someone from the county attorney's. Hold on. Let me lay down these flowers."

He walked slowly, with a slight limp, to the meadow and laid the marigolds gently on top of the mound of flowers. For a moment, he stood absolutely still, looking down.

Buddy spat in disgust. "I got to get on home." He began to walk away. "Luke there is slow," he said to me over his shoulder, leering. "But you watch it. He always gets there anyhow."

Lucas looked after him without rancor, then walked stiffly backed over to me, his hand outstretched. "Lucas Delton Lucas here. Pleased to meet you."

I shook his hand, the skin calloused and hard. But his smile made his blue eyes tender, utterly without guile, like the smile of an idiot or a saint. It was unnerving. I introduced myself, name and title.

Lucas looked over at the tamarisks. "I'd sure like to talk to you, ma'am, but that Buddy is over there, hiding and watching. That's the way he is. No life atall of his own."

I looked toward the tamarisks, too. They were full of shadows.

"I live just over close to the Junction," Lucas said. "You must be going back that way anyhow. I could offer you a cup of coffee or a soda pop, you stop and visit with me. Tell me what's going on. Got to make one little stop on the way, but you could follow me."

I hesitated.

"Don't worry." He smiled his tender smile again. "You're safe as safe with me."

chapter fourteen

I FOLLOWED LUCAS'S WHITE PICKUP TO THE outskirts of the junction, thinking of his tender smile. When had I last seen a man smile like that, in this paranoid day and age? Had he and Erica been lovers? He would certainly be a more dangerous choice than Andy, if you wanted to own your own heart.

He turned left onto a paved road and stopped half a mile down, in front of a little wood house, painted white, spick-and-span. I stayed in my car and watched as he went to the bed of his pickup, wondered about his stiff walk, slight limp. He pulled back a tarp and took out a TV set. The door of the house opened and a tiny white-haired woman came out, walking slowly, using a cane.

"Mama," Lucas said. He called over to my car. "Chloe, why don't you get out, meet my mama."

I did.

"Mama Lucas, this is Chloe," said Lucas.

She bowed and smiled at me, leaning over her cane, the smile unfocused, her eyes as blue as Lucas's.

"Chloe here works for the county attorney." His voice was so polite as to be from another century. "You two chat about that and I'll run this TV in and hook it up for you."

"Where'd you get that TV?" She looked at him suspiciously.

"Now never mind. It ain't hot, I swear it." Lucas winked at me, then went in the door with the TV, leaving me alone with Mama Lucas.

She twisted up her face and squinted as if the light was too bright. "That damn Cyra still the county attorney over there, Mary Ann? Dumbest boy you ever met; then he went and got elected."

"No," I said, "it's Melvin Huber. But my name's Chloe, Mrs. Lucas."

She nodded, lifted her cane, and poked at peppergrass growing in the dirt. There was a long silence. Then she said, "I just call 'em all Mary Ann. I'm too old to remember all those different names. Mary Ann was Lucas's *wife*."

Lucas came out of the house just then. "She was, Mama, twenty years ago."

His mother shrugged.

Lucas picked her up and gave her a big hug. "You're my girl, Mama. I love you forever."

Over his shoulder, Mama Lucas grinned like a little girl.

"You keep your doors and windows locked, now, you hear? And don't go opening the door less you know who it is. I'll be back later, sit with you."

I wondered if Mama Lucas owned a shotgun.

"All this fuss," she said, but without rancor. "Everybody hiding in their houses. Why don't they just arrest her husband? Get it over with."

" 'Cause she didn't have one," Lucas said.

Mama Lucas screwed up her face and looked wise. "Well, somebody else's husband, then."

Following Lucas, I drove back through the Junction; past the Horseshoe Café and the Valley Cooperative Feed Store, the farmers and cowboys loitering; past the pickups and old seventies cars parked along the street; past the sign advertising the Harvest Festival. A little farm town on the verge of autumn, nostalgic and, until now, peaceful. I wondered, Does every pickup and every car have a gun handy on the front seat? Are people hiding in their houses, like Mama Lucas said, sitting behind locked doors at night, armed and ready?

Lucas turned down a dirt road and stopped in front of a battered double-wide trailer. A bed of marigolds and petunias and fading tomatoes in oil drums were in the front yard. Back behind were a couple of sheds and wooden fencing, the top rails gnawed at the way horses will. A big black-and-white dog with one blind eye ambled over to Lucas when he got out of the pickup and butted its head against his leg.

I got out of my car. The air was dense and close and somehow unreal, as though I were in a dream. Lucas's white shirt looked washed a million times, his jeans faded to the color of dust. Everything about him was earth-colored; he was like a figment of the landscape.

"Lucas," I said as I followed him to the front door, "I've been worrying about Dot Stone."

He paused, hand on the door. In his blue eyes was a look, as though he saw something coming from way far away but it wasn't close enough yet for him to see what it was. "Don't," he said.

Inside was a couch covered with a faded blue chenille bedspread and a big leather chair with the stuffing leaking out. It was plain but neat as neat—the room of a man who needs no one.

"You sit. I got coffee or a soda pop, that diet stuff all the ladies like. Course, I do got beer."

"A diet soda would be fine, thank you," I said.

I sat on the leather chair, fretting. Out the window, the Chiricahua Mountains floated in the distance. Lucas came back, calm and slow, a beer in one hand, diet soda in the other.

"Monsoon season, I like to sit right where you're sitting and watch the storms coming in," he said "Watch the lightning." His voice caressed the words. "Feel safe."

Feel safe.

He smiled. "Some dream, huh? Just right for an old broken-down cowboy, living on odd jobs and disability."

Bitter words, but you couldn't tell it from his face; his face was miles away, thinking peaceful thoughts. He shrugged. "The truth is, that there is all I got left to brag on."

He gestured. On the wall was a large square of plywood, sanded and varnished, with big belt buckles mounted on it. Curious, I stood up to look.

"Belt buckles?" I said.

"Roping trophies. Team roping, me and Clyde Daugherty—we was partners before I had my accident."

Framed photographs hung on the wall next to the trophies, group shots of cowboys grinning and holding a banner saying RODEO COW-BOY ASSOCIATION and one with just two men. "That's you," I said, and leaned to look closer.

Lucas, fresh-faced and eager to take on the world, stood against a dusty backdrop of fences. His arm was around another man; a smart-alecky-looking cowboy with a crooked grin.

"Me and Clyde," said Lucas. "That Clyde was mean as they come. Always had to keep an eye on him."

Clyde grinned back at me, mean as they come; insouciant, brash, not caring. "What happened to him?"

For a moment, Lucas was silent, staring out the window. brooding. An odd feeling came over me, as though I'd asked him something he didn't want to answer, something terrible. Then he sat down on the couch and looked over at me. "What do you mean?"

I shrugged, looked at Clyde again, brash, cocky. "I just wondered what happened to him after you weren't his partner is all."

Lucas leaned back, relaxed a little. "Aw, he tried working with other guys, but nothing ever clicked. So he drank a little more, got meaner." He sighed. "But the two of us had some good times together till that horse bucked me, rolled on me, wrecked my leg, 'bout to broke my back, and just like that my roping days was over." He added sardonically, "Clay O'Brien Cooper and Jake Barnes must be real relieved about that."

"Who?"

"World champs. You don't know nothing about rodeo, I can tell, just like Erica."

Knowing nothing about rodeo, days ago Erica had lain in her own still-warm blood on the grassy meadow, the copper taste of death in her mouth. What did Lucas Delton Lucas think about that? What did he think about anything? Clyde, he thought something about Clyde, something, it seemed to me suddenly, dark and sad. What? Nostalgia for his lost youth? But other than that, under his sweet country manners, disengagement swirled around him like a mist.

Then he surprised me. "Now you can tell me straight out, 'cause it ain't going beyond this room—what's this I hear about Erica's boy being charged?"

I stared at him. "Where'd you hear that?"

"I got a friend who's a deputy—never mind which one—but it's gotta be bullshit. Erica and I stopped seeing each other two years ago, so it's been a while since I seen Troy, but your basic kid don't change. They got any *evidence*?"

"Between you and me?" I said. "Very little."

"Course there's very *little*. Just Ed Masters's dirty little mind. And if what else I hear is true, that Dot saw who did it, why didn't Ed drag Dot over to Dudley to ID him? He didn't, did he?"

"Not to my knowledge." I took a deep breath. Under all that peaceful slowness, Lucas wasn't stupid. "Dot denies it, anyway."

He chugged his can of beer and set it on the floor. "Damn Dot— excuse me—but she's been hanging out there in the middle of nowhere with a bunch of ghosts too long."

"Lucas," I asked, "how did you know Erica?"

"Erica? Met her at that hippie food store in Old Dudley. Grew a bunch of organic tomatoes and I was selling them over there. She was working the register. Prettiest thing, and real feisty."

He leaned down and picked up his beer again, looking past me out the window, the back one, not the one where you could watch the lightning and feel safe. "Yeah." He looked at me then, his blue eyes so guileless, so kind. "You remind me of her."

I felt my face getting pink, zapped suddenly by Lucas the lady-killer. I scrunched up my toes, as if that would stop it.

"I can still hear her voice," he went on meditatively. "Bossy, you know, like a schoolteacher. She was so smart and so dumb all at once." He rubbed his chin regretfully.

"Dot told me Erica was going to the Baptist church for a while," I said. "Because you told her about being saved."

"Now, I didn't know that." He looked mildly surprised. "She went to church?"

I nodded.

Lucas rubbed his chin. "I was saved all right, for a little bit. After the accident, I felt like a big gray cloud had fell on my head. I did some mean things then, things I'll never understand. Anyway, I went to church and got saved. Erica used to ask me so many questions, about who lived in every house in the valley, and when we got to the pastor's house, I told her about it."

"Were you seeing her for a long time?"

"About a year. A few times, I went to her place. But I don't breathe freely in Old Dudley. So she used to come out here. Brought Troy with her sometimes. I taught him stuff. Roping tricks. How to shoot."

Taught him how to shoot. The clouds must have parted—a shaft of sunlight came suddenly through the window behind Lucas, silhouetting him in its beam. I shivered.

He rested his hands on his knees, leaned toward me. "He was never much good. Shot like a girl, afraid of the gun. Nice kid, though. Sharp in his way. I kind of missed him when it ended."

"Two years ago," I said. "You and Erica had a fight?"

"Not exactly. A little girl from the Junction started coming round to see me. Going through a divorce, wanted a shoulder to cry on. One day, this little girl—we'll call her Patsy, but that's not her name—shows up and Erica's here. Patsy starts crying, calling her names, and Erica looks over at me and says, 'Bye, Luke.' And left. I never saw her again."

"Oh." There was a silence. I looked at the mountains and felt sad. "You mean she was jealous?"

"Who, Erica? I wouldn't know. But I never owned her and she never owned me." His voice had turned smooth, seamless. "Didn't mean a thing, none of it. And Patsy married again and lives up in Flagstaff."

"But you knew Erica well. Lucas, something was going on with Erica. I think it started a couple of month ago. That's when she went to church. It could have something to do with her being murdered.

Can you think of anything . . . anyone . . . from when you knew her, anything that could have started going bad?"

He was looking at me directly and I bent toward him, and thought I saw, in his blue eyes, something like a tiny door opening. "There *is* something," I said.

He blinked, looked away. "Anything she mighta told me, I got no license to repeat. It was couple years ago anyway. Who knows what she was up too after that."

"If there is something, why not tell me?" I stared at him, but he seemed far away, back behind that mist of disengagement. "She's *dead*, Lucas."

"Sorry," he said politely. "I won't."

It was no use; his face had closed off. It wasn't a mist; it was a wall, three feet of solid glass. I imagined a million women beating on it, trying to get through to his heart.

Angry, I jabbed at him. "After Patsy, did you call Erica, talk to her about it?"

"I ain't got a phone. She knew she was always welcome here."

"Maybe she didn't, not really."

Lucas looked at me questioningly. "So I got to go now and put those flowers where she was killed every day, just in case?"

"I don't know," I said. Trying one more time to reach him, I added, "Lucas, I knew her, too. Long ago, back in California. We were supposed to get together, talk, but I never called her. She might have confided in me, told me things. That *haunts* me."

"And maybe she wouldn't have told you a thing." Lucas tilted his head, looked at me. "Sounds like maybe you need to do a little flower picking yourself."

chapter fifteen

"BUT I NEVER OWNED HER AND SHE NEVER owned me." Two people, friends for more than a year, and then suddenly it was over. Were there no regrets? Or was it a question of pride winning out over feelings? Lucas was right, though—it was two years ago, after all, and surely even the dead have a right to privacy.

It was strange to drive back into Old Dudley, with its coffee shops, art galleries, and tourists, so close to the valley and yet, at the same time, a million miles away. I parked near the post office and checked my mail—a water bill and a flyer from Wal-Mart. Drifts of kids, late teens and early twenties, hung out near the iron railings in front—displaced kids from the cities and the suburbs.

Old Dudley drew them like a magnet—wanderers in grunge clothes, with tattoos, nose rings, educated, middle-class voices. Maybe the children of the hippies who had hung out on Venice Beach so many years ago, living out their parents' discarded dreams. Though maybe not as hopefully.

Yet once, Erica had arrived here, like these kids, and she'd made it out to the valley. Had she been fascinated by it the way I was? I mulled this over as I walked down Main Street to the newspaper office and bought two back issues and that day's *Dudley Review*. The *Review* didn't cover much valley news; it had no more interest in the valley than the kids by the post office. But this was a fairly sensational murder, and besides, Erica had been a Dudley resident.

Wednesday's headline blared out at me: HOMICIDE IN THE VALLEY, and then, in smaller print, *Dudley Bookmobile Driver Murdered.*

I got in my car and quickly scanned the articles. "Cochise County Sheriff's Department detective Ed Masters stumped by brutal murder," it said. Stumped. Ed would love that. I read on. No mention of Troy, in any of the three articles; no mention of Dot Stone by name, just "bookmobile patron." In the follow-ups, some quotes from Neva Shumaker, county librarian, about Erica being an excellent employee and a warm and friendly human being. Nothing I didn't know in any of the articles, except maybe the comment about Erica's excellence as an employee.

At least, if Erica had been killed by someone in Old Dudley, there was nothing in the newspapers to encourage the killer to drive out to the valley and murder Dot Stone. I started the car, drove back to work to check my messages, the last day of the week, just in case there was some last-minute emergency.

Despite the bright yellow of her T-shirt, Gigi looked tired, manning her desk, while a skeleton staff waited for five o'clock. "There're some people waiting for you," she said. "Outside your office. It's locked, so they couldn't use the waiting room. I told them I didn't know if you'd be back, but . . ." She shrugged her shoulders.

I grabbed a sheaf of messages and walked outside to the front of my office. A lanky, pale man stood on the patch of grass by the steps, arms out, grabbing at leaves that fell from the tree by my window.

"Got one!" he shouted. "Look, Jude! Look, Neva! I got a *leaf!*"

He looked familiar; then I remembered. Myron. The man sweeping at the county library. Jude's brother, from interlibrary loan, who was now sitting on my steps, along with Neva Shumaker, county librarian.

Jude's shoulders were hunched over, and she wore a grayish garment of no particular style or cut. Neva, in a denim dress buttoned to the neck, sat prim and straight-backed beside her, arms around her knees. Somehow, they seemed united as they sat there, cut from the same cloth; grown-up, conscientious, their faces patient, as if they were used to waiting, had spent their lives waiting for something that had never turned up.

"Look!" shouted Myron. "It's a real *pretty* one!"

Jude and Neva ignored him, their faces solemn; then they saw me. Neva half-rose.

"Hi there!" Myron said to me. "Want to see a pretty leaf?"

His aging face was joyous, as if care had never reached him, as if he were just a newborn on a cloudy day in the fall. My heart was touched. I looked at the leaf he held out, bronze, veined with red. "That *is* pretty," I said.

"Miss Newcombe, we're very worried," Neva said. "It's Sally. Sally Smith, our reference librarian?"

As if I needed reminding. Forty going on fourteen, blond as an albino. The nervous one—nervous? More like scared out of her wits. "He's going to kill me, too," she'd said.

"Yes," I said. "What about her?"

"She's *missing*." Neva's voice was ominous.

"Missing?" I stared at her.

"She didn't show up for work yesterday." Nervously, Neva touched the top button of her dress. "It's not like her. She didn't call in sick or anything. I called her, but no one answered."

Myron held the leaf to his mouth, as if to taste its colors. He looked sad. "She dead, too," he said resignedly.

"Myron," said Jude in a long-suffering voice. "You come sit down now."

"I was worried, so I called Detective Masters," Neva went on. "He went to her house, but no one was there. Her car was gone. I got her license plate number for him from our travel forms, and he said he'd have the deputies keep a lookout for her car. Then he asked me questions, like whether Sally and Erica were *close*." She shuddered.

"They didn't *act* like it," Jude said. "But Sally told me once she knew Erica before Erica got hired at the library." She smoothed her gray garment.

"Oh?" Neva looked at her. "I didn't know that."

Jude turned her head away, her face a blank. Once again, I had a sense of undercurrents. What was it between these two?

"Jude?" said Neva sharply, as though she were speaking to a child. "If I'd known that, I would have told Detective Masters."

"Well, it wasn't something you'd notice." Jude's voice was defensive. "Like I said, they didn't act like friends."

Neva sighed.

"Sally was very upset when I talked to her," I said. "She didn't strike me as a stable person at all. She *is* seeing a counselor."

"Right." Jude sniffed. "She's always going on about him, 'My counselor' this, 'My counselor' that. It is not healthy, if you ask me."

Neva said, "Detective Masters asked me about relatives. She has a sister, Annie, but I don't know her married name." She started to wring her hands but then thought better of it. "Detective Masters said I need to report this to the Dudley police, since it's their jurisdiction. And then the Dudley police told me you can't file a missing persons report for forty-eight hours. It's so ridiculous. Of course she's missing. She's worked at the library for twelve years, and she's never once stayed home from work without getting in touch with me."

"Reliable," said Jude.

"Bam," said Myron loudly.

"Give me your phone number at home," I said. "I'll see what I can find out and then I'll let you know. That's the best I can do."

Myron squirmed on the steps, dropped his leaf. "Bam," he said again. "Bam bam and she dead, too."

When I got home, there was a message on my machine from Stuart. "The sister's coming Saturday. She's hot on victim's rights and wants to see an advocate. How about it? Call me." I called but got his machine. Shit.

I called Frankie in the hopes of reaching Ed, to see if anyone had spotted Sally's car, but I only got a recorded voice, telling me to call Dispatch if it was an emergency.

It was almost four, a calm Friday afternoon, Big Foot snoozing on the front porch. Leaves were beginning to drift into the flower beds in my front yard; purple asters had sprung up uninvited. "Bam bam and she dead, too," Myron's words. But I didn't want to get hung up thinking about Sally; she was clearly nuts long before any of this had happened.

I did a wash, and mopped the floors at last. The house felt empty, but it was me who was empty—as bad as Stuart. Just keep running, keep busy, and you won't have time to think too much.

What's the rush?

I went outside and called across the fence, and pretty soon, my neighbor Lourdes's face and shoulders appeared over the top. She looked as casual as she ever looked, wearing a fuchsia sweatshirt and big pearl earrings. Her dark, glossy hair was freshly done, little tendrils framing her face.

"Chloe, I'm doing my wash. We can talk while I hang it." She disappeared behind a large pink towel. I watched as she clipped on a clothespin, stretched the towel, clipped on another one. The two pins were exactly equidistant from the ends of the towel.

"I wanted your recipe for chicken mole," I said. "The one you're always bragging about."

Lourdes flung a flowered sheet over the line. "Chloe, you never asked me for a recipe before. She looked at me knowingly over a stretch of tulip bunches. "Is he handsome?"

"Never mind," I said. "Lourdes, you went to high school here. Did you ever know Jude—Jude . . . I'm not sure of her last name. Plain? Serious? Maybe older than you."

"Jude? Must be Jude Moffit." She looked piqued. "She's a *lot* older than me. I didn't really know her, but I knew her brother, Myron. Everybody liked Myron. And now . . . Oh, it's terrible."

"What?"

"He was in a car wreck, about seven years ago. He got brain-damaged." She pulled the sheet smooth. "He's like . . . like an *idiot* now. People say it would have been better if he'd just died." She sighed. "Let me get you that recipe."

Waiting for Lourdes to come back, I thought about Myron catching the leaf. He seemed happier than a lot of people I knew.

"Myron was engaged to be married, too," Lourdes said when she returned with the recipe. "Before it happened. But I mean, would you . . ."

"I guess not."

"Now you make a nice pot of beans with that and some rice, maybe a little salad."

I took the recipe inside and read it through. I had not one single ingredient on hand, and there was no way I wanted to drive to Safeway. Anyway, what was I thinking? I didn't have time to have a man to dinner. I made some Smack Ramen with lots of somewhat-soft butter; I could have dinner late, Budget Gourmet Light and Healthy, and maybe the asparagus was still okay.

By eight o'clock, Stuart had not called back. I opened the refrigerator and took the asparagus out of the vegetable keeper, which hadn't been keeping. I'd bought it out of season because it was my favorite vegetable, and the expensive tips were now infected with some sort of slimy mucus. My life was going to hell. I held it, tips away from me, debating, and then someone knocked on the door. I threw the asparagus in the trash and went to answer it.

Andy stood outside, face pale, eyes bloodshot.

"Andy." The man I'd betrayed just this morning. "How *are* you?" Guiltily, I wondered if I had to let him in.

chapter sixteen

ANDY DIDN'T LOOK LIKE MUCH OF A THREAT.
He wore a white T-shirt and jeans—the dash and flare of bandanna, shades, and vest now gone. Even his pompadour looked deflated. No .357 Magnum tucked in his waistband, either.

"I know I'm way out of line here." He gulped, Adam's apple bobbing, and patted the pocket of his T-shirt, where a pack of Camels protruded. "But I'm feeling kind of . . . desperate. I thought about going to your office, but it's the weekend tomorrow. So I asked around, and someone at the Co-op told me where you lived. Could I talk to you for a few minutes?"

"Sure. Come on in," I said. "Is it about Sally? Have they found her?"

"Sally?" he said blankly. "Oh, Sally. I don't know. She's so crazy anyway. Maybe she checked into a nice mental institution."

He pulled out a Camel and lit up. His hands were shaking so much, it took a couple of tries. When he spoke again, his voice was agonized; chords on his neck stood out visibly. "It's about something else. I . . . I think I might be a *suspect.*"

He flicked his cigarette, spilling ash on the kitchen floor.

I felt terrible. Poor guy. He looked so forlorn, and I'd snitched on him, plain and simple, as Dot would say.

I grabbed an ashtray off the top of the refrigerator and handed it to him. "Here. Let's go sit out on the porch."

Outside, it was still warmish; the cloud cover had kept the temperature from dropping its usual twenty degrees. From down the hill, you could hear the bar bands working themselves up. Andy propped his feet on the porch railing and lit another Camel.

"That detective, Masters, came to my house this afternoon," he said. "He asked me again where I was, when it . . . happened. I told him I was home all day reading *Deadwood.*" His voice thickened and he stopped. "Of course, nobody *saw* me."

He inhaled, sucking in the nicotine greedily, the tip of his cigarette burning brightly for maybe an inch.

"It's one of the best books I've ever read, and now when I see it, all I can think of is Erica." His voice was bitter. "Anyway, then, right out of the blue, Detective Masters asked me why I hadn't mentioned that Erica and I had been lovers."

He glanced at me. "We were. For maybe six weeks. I helped her get the library job, and then right after that, it was over."

"Oh," I said.

"I don't know how he found out. Unless Neva . . ." He shrugged. "She can be such a bitch. Anyway, he asked me how I felt about Erica. And I told him that when we broke up, I was really angry for a couple of weeks. Why the hell did I tell him *that*?"

"Well, at least it was more credible than saying you didn't care."

He looked out morosely into the shadows of my garden. "Anyway, I got *over* it. After all, I should have known. She was a big flirt, Erica, in a sneaky kind of way." The bitterness was back in his voice. "Even Myron had a crush on her. Poor Myron. He used to come sweep the Tech Services offices three or four times a day."

He sighed resignedly. "I guess I should have told Detective Masters about the relationship right away."

"Probably," I said. "But that doesn't automatically make you a suspect, Andy."

He nodded, letting out a long, shaky breath, which turned into a cough. "There's some other stuff I didn't tell him, either. When I talked to him, it hadn't even occurred to me yet."

"Oh?"

"After Detective Masters left this afternoon, I was scared, and I was pissed, too. The cops in this county really suck. It reminded me of this big discussion some of us in Tech Services had. Erica was there. Neva was out of town and we were goofing off. It was about this cop, the one who killed the man out in the desert and got off scot-free?"

I took a deep breath. Past the porch was my garden and beyond and below that was the street. I could get in my car anytime I wanted and drive down the street, out of town, and into the desert. I could go to the very spot, look down and imagine the blood, seeped into the ground and nourishing the peppergrass, the prickle poppies, the mesquite.

"I know the cop you mean," I said. "Kyle Barnett."

"Yeah. Barnett." He threw off the name casually. "Anyway, we were all saying it was typical of justice in this county. The cops can do anything they want and get away with it. But Erica defended him. She said she knew Barnett from a long time ago and she thought he was basically a good person, and that even if he had killed the man, he'd been cleared of everything."

"Yes, he was," I said. Leaves drifted down from the ash tree in my yard. Erica had known *Kyle*? I picked at a splinter on the wood of my chair arm. "I don't understand what you're getting at, Andy."

"Wait." He refueled with nicotine and went on. "I was surprised at the time that she would know a cop, so I'd always remembered it. Then all of a sudden this afternoon when I was thinking, I remembered something else. Something she said, the night we broke up."

"What was that?"

"She told me things were surfacing, things that had happened to her a long time ago. I didn't notice that night, but now I realize those were the exact words she used when she was talking about the cop, Barnett. 'A long time ago.' Maybe whatever was surfacing was connected to when she knew him—a cop. If there was a cop, there was a criminal. What's a criminal? *Someone who kills people.*"

He flicked his cigarette into the garden, as if putting it out in the ashtray wasn't dramatic enough. It sounded vague, a little far-fetched, but Erica had broken it off with him a few weeks after she'd gone to the church, around the time she'd gone to the Victim Witness training class.

"You didn't ask her what she was talking about?" I said.

"I didn't want to hear it." His voice was forlorn. "I knew things were screwed up between us. I could tell by her tone of voice that the end was probably going to be that night. I thought she was going to tell me some sad story and make me feel sorry so I couldn't get mad. I *wanted* to be mad."

There was a long silence.

After awhile he said, "You work with cops, don't you? You could talk to Officer Barnett, ask him about it."

"He doesn't live here anymore. Someone would have to locate him. Or maybe look through the old police reports. 'A long time ago' isn't exactly specific. But I'll see what I can do."

Andy said sadly, "The worst of it is, if I'd really listened to her, maybe it would have brought us closer together. Maybe everything would have been different and none of this would have happened."

Pain. Pride. Low self-esteem. That which we fear most, we bring upon ourselves. Sally's words: "He's going to kill me, too." And now Kyle was somehow involved. Two separate worlds I carried around with me, on the verge of colliding. I wanted to go to bed and sleep a Rip van Winkle sleep till they both went away. Maybe this would be my lucky night and I wouldn't dream at all.

But I did dream. In the dream, Lucas was sitting in the big leather chair in his trailer; I was on his lap. Big gray clouds were building up outside, over the Chiracahuas, but I felt warm and comfortable and safe. "You're my girl now, Patsy," Luke was saying, "I'll love you forever."

"My name's not Patsy," I said. "My name's . . . my name's . . ." But for the life of me, I couldn't remember what my name was. I thought I should get up, find my purse; my name would be on my driver's license, but I couldn't move.

"Look out, Patsy," Luke said. "The lightning's coming; it's knocking at the door."

Then the door opened, and Erica floated in. She was dressed all in crinkled rose silk, the way she'd looked at the class, but her hair was bright, bright red; it trailed over her shoulders and down her arms. "Get out of my life," she said. The words were so clear and distinct, it was as though they came from somewhere else. Somewhere closer.

"Erica, I'm only trying to help," I said. If I could get up, I could find my purse, because I remembered now that it wasn't my card I needed to find; it was the flowers. Somewhere in my purse was a bunch of flowers. I could show them to her. Then she'd know. But I still couldn't move.

"Sally Smith," I said suddenly. "Erica, where is Sally Smith?"

Erica began to scream, little intermittent screams.

"Stop! Stop that!" I said, and sat up in bed. The phone on the bedside table was ringing. I picked up the receiver.

"Hello?"

No one said anything. The clock on the bedside table gave a patient click and turned over from 1:03 to 1:04.

"Hello?" I said again.

"Oh, sorry. Hello there, Chloe. Stuart here. It was ringing so long, I forgot who I was calling. Plus, I started reading this brief."

I slumped back against the pillows. "Anything to keep the mind engaged."

"The aunt's flying here tomorrow, late afternoon or evening, and she wants to stay at the house. She doesn't want to talk to me; she wants to see a victim advocate. That's you. Mariah's her name. Mariah Haskell."

"Mariah," I said.

"The key to the house is under a rock by the front door. I thought maybe you and a volunteer could go tidy up, so she can see that Troy is a clean, responsible young man. And you could leave your card for her to call you. Doesn't Victim Witness do things like that?"

"Usually not in the service of the defense. But wait a minute— her nephew's in jail and she doesn't want to talk to his *attorney*?"

"It's a long story," said Stuart. "I mean, it must be. Oh, and listen—get those damn ribs and stuff out of Troy's refrigerator. Bring them over here tomorrow night and we can eat them."

"Fine," I said, and hung up.

The room was dark and haunted with the residue of my dream. Why did I ask Erica where Sally was, I wondered, as if the rest of my dream made sense. I closed my eyes. Behind the lids, I could see Erica as she'd been in the dream, hair red as blood; could almost sense her presence, spying on me. No. What was I thinking? Erica was the *victim*. Where *was* Sally? Was she a victim now, too?

interlude

SHE CHECKED THE FRONT DOOR AND THE back door. They were always locked, but she needed to be sure. She checked that all the windows were bolted and the curtains drawn all the way, so there weren't any cracks. The gun was always getting in the way—so big and unwieldy, and she had to keep it pointed at the ground and away from her body, in case it went off.

"Sugar," she said. "Bedtime."

The cat saw her coming and dodged playfully under the dining room table. "Sugar, please?" Tears came to her eyes. It was hard, frustrating to grab Sugar and hold on to the gun at the same time. Finally, she had to put the gun down and get on her hands and knees.

In bed, she put the gun on the bedside table and stroked Sugar until they both quieted down. She clicked the remote and the TV came on. Conan O'Brien was interviewing an Italian-looking man, the Italian man doing most of the talking. He moved his lips fast and fidgeted in the chair, but she couldn't hear what he was saying because the sound was so low. He was too plain to be a movie star, so he must be a comedian or something, except Conan wasn't laughing.

She was afraid to turn up the sound, in case someone was trying to break in and she wouldn't hear it. The only possible *way to get in would be through a window, so she needed to be able to hear the sound of the glass breaking.*

She was exhausted; every inch of her body cried out for sleep, but she was afraid to sleep. One part of her was normal, doing what you did when you went to bed; that part set the remote for sleep and lay back on the pillow. After all, she thought, even if I'm asleep, I'll still be alert enough to hear glass breaking. I'd wake up instantly, and the gun's right here.

Did I check the doors?

She got up again, carrying the gun, so tired, she had to force herself to move. She checked the doors again, checked the windows, made sure the curtains were drawn so there were no cracks. She went back to bed and lay down. She closed her eyes and drifted.

Didn't sleep, but thought of her father—dead now for years, but she could see him clearly—he was building the addition onto the house in Mesa, and she and her little sister, Annie, were helping him. It was a beautiful winter day, one of those days that, for no reason, you carry with you always, though you don't realize that until later. She and Annie took turns handing their father the nails, so he could pound them in. He did it so perfectly, just two or three hits with the hammer, and they went in straight and clean.

She and Annie were both wearing red sandals, and socks with Mickey Mouses on them. After awhile, her father would let them each pound in a nail, and when her turn came, she kept seeing Mickey Mouses grinning at her, even when she wasn't looking at them. It made her giggle, so she couldn't pound right.

"You have to concentrate," said her father. "You have to be the hammer. Remember that; it's true of everything in life. Concentration."

What a funny thing to remember, she thought, and opened her eyes.

It was morning. Even though the curtains were drawn, sun shone through the fiberglass material. She had made it through the night and she was still alive. Thankfulness flowed through her body; for a moment, she was totally relaxed.

She got up and went to the window, pulled back the curtains. The leaves of the desert willow outside hung heavy on their branches, Mikey's tricycle gleamed as if it had been freshly painted; in the flower beds, the gold chrysanthemums were flattened, the dirt beneath dark, almost black.

It had rained last night, not just a sprinkle but a good heavy rain. It had rained, and she hadn't heard it pattering on the roof, hadn't heard the eaves dripping or awakened to the sound of the torrents that came down the rainspouts from the gutters—at least as loud as the tinkle of breaking glass.

She put her hand to her mouth, bit down hard on the flesh of the upper joint of her index finger. He could have broken the glass, raised the window, come in, entered the bedroom; even unarmed, he would have seen the gun on the nightstand, picked it up, and shot her, and she wouldn't even have known till the gun went off.

Tears of exhaustion filled her eyes. I lost it, she thought. I lost my concentration. I can't let it happen again. I mustn't go to sleep again!

chapter seventeen

DURING THE NIGHT, SOMETHING CHANGED.
I felt it the minute I woke up. I sniffed; it was the smell of damp. It had been warm enough the night before to leave the window open a crack. I got up and looked out; it had rained, nothing much, just a sprinkle—fall rain. The washed leaves had turned a deeper shade of yellow. Something was bothering me. Well, a lot was.

Like where Sally might be. Had Ed found her? I got up and went to the kitchen, grabbed the phone book. I looked for her name; there were Smiths aplenty, but no S. Smith. I called information—she was unlisted.

I fed Big Foot and took a shower. In the bathroom mirror, my face looked peaked; it hadn't been a restful night. I thought about having cereal, but the milk in the singing refrigerator was warm and smelled funny, so I ate a handful of Cheerios straight from the box. Then I called Bobbie, my favorite volunteer in Dudley. Bobbie, Kyle's sister.

We usually got together, the two of us, a couple of times a month, often at some restaurant in New Dudley, where they cooked things right instead of fancy-dancy. We talked about lots of things, but never about Kyle.

She answered the phone in a shot, as if she'd been standing right there, waiting for excitement. I asked if she'd like to help clean Erica's house for Mariah's visit.

"That bookmobile murder," she said. "Nasty. Sure, I'll help. They charged anyone yet?"

"Not yet." My voice was glib.

"I'll meet you in the parking lot down from your place in hippie-dippy land."

I put together a victim packet, along with my card, to leave for Mariah, then drove down to the parking lot. The clouds had parted and sun was coming through now.

Five minutes later, Bobbie pulled in next to me, her white Honda, scarred from previous hits, just missing my back fender. She leaped out, little and wiry, wearing jeans and a ruffled gingham midriff blouse, about as Anglo-Saxon all-American as you could get. I thought, as I always did when I saw her, how much she looked like her brother.

Driving down Tombstone Canyon, I told her most of the story so she would get involved and draw her own conclusions—about Troy first, then Andy's visit and what Andy had told me about Erica knowing Kyle. "So what do you think?" I asked.

She didn't answer, her silence like an accusation. I realized then that eventually I would have found some way to reach Kyle, no matter what. It felt like my whole life up to that point had been in limbo, waiting to talk to Kyle. In silence, we turned on to Erica's street. Overhead, the trees formed a yellow canopy. Everything smelled delicious.

Bobbie whooshed out a sigh. "Nice to have a little rain. I heard it really stormed in Tucson. Supposed to be a bunch of little storms coming through."

It was up to her. I couldn't push her any more than I had. Kyle and Bobbie were so alike; under Bobbie's energy and cheer was the same fierce silence.

"So you want to talk to my brother," she said finally.

"I just want to call him up," I said, "and see if he remembers."

"You can't call him," Bobbie said. "There's no phone."

We passed the dusty pink cottage with the teal trim and the pink geraniums. Nelson and Larry's house. Friends of Erica. Nelson the counselor and Larry the . . .

"Oh, well then," I said. "Just forget about it. Maybe I can find the police report. Here we are." I stopped in front of Erica's.

Bobbie put one hand on the door handle and turned to me. "It would be pretty hard to find the police report," she said. "Let me think about it."

Music blared out from the house. We didn't need to look for the key under the rock, because the front door was half-open. Bobbie looked at me as we went up the porch steps.

"I thought no one was here," she said.

For a second, I imagined Troy had been released after all, some last-minute stroke of genius from his overworked attorney, but the music was familiar: The angry woman who had worked through pain.

"I think I know who it is," I said.

We walked inside. Pepper was lying on the couch on top of the Guatemalan bedspread, Krishna on the floor beside her.

"Hi, Pepper!" I said brightly. "Bobbie, this is Pepper. She's Troy's friend."

Pepper looked at us balefully. Her shock of hair was now a strange shade of yellow, not what you'd call blond. She was barefoot and bare-legged, wearing a full, short flowered dress that stopped several inches above her bony knees.

"Mind if I turn this off," said Bobbie, "before I commit suicide? My nieces like Hole, too. It must be some kind of mass hysteria."

I went and sat on one end of the couch while Bobbie found the stereo and turned it off. The room seemed different somehow; then I realized the door to the hall that led to the bedrooms had been open when I'd been here last. Now it was closed.

"We're here to tidy up the house a little bit," I said to Pepper. "Troy's aunt is coming today."

Pepper swung her legs over to the floor and rested her hands on her stomach. "Who? *Mariah?*" Her voice was full of scorn. This close, I could see the black mascara ringing her eyes. She looked like a little girl who'd gotten into her mother's makeup. Who *was* her mother anyway?

"Oh, honey," said Bobbie, not unkindly. "How far along are you?"

"Five shitty months." Pepper rubbed at her eyes, smudging mascara. "And Mariah's not welcome here. Troy doesn't want to see her, and he's getting out soon. I set things straight with his attorney." Her voice turned haughty on the word *attorney,* a fancier, more knowing word than *lawyer,* as if she consorted with them all the time.

"Did you now." Bobbie's mouth twitched.

"I sure as fucking hell did," said Pepper. "I explained all about Tino and the list."

"Who's Tino?" I asked her.

"The guy who got me pregnant. He's a *vato loco.*" For a second, she brightened. "He's really handsome. When Erica and I talked about if I should get an abortion, she said, "well, the baby will be good-looking anyway." Erica was dead set against abortions—she got one once and it got screwed up, and she thought she could never have children after that. Then she got lucky and had Troy."

She looked gloomy. "I hate that *vato.* Troy hates him, too. That's why we made the list—Troy said it would be good therapy. It's all the bad things I was going to do to him."

"Like throw a heater into the bathtub while he was taking a bath," I said suddenly, "then take his body out to the desert so it would look like he was struck by lightning?"

Bobbie blinked.

"That was Troy's best," said Pepper happily. "Mine was 'Tie him to a horse and run him through cholla cactus eight feet high,' but Troy said it wouldn't be fair to the horse." Her eyes widened. "How'd you know about that?"

"Never mind," I said.

"Anyway, Mariah can't stay here," said Pepper. "She's a first-class bitch. She hasn't been Troy's aunt and Erica's sister since I don't know long. She told Erica they weren't fucking sisters anymore."

"Pepper," said Bobbie firmly, "families have fights, but family is family. From what I hear, Troy needs some family right now."

Pepper said between her teeth, "She doesn't care. Now that Erica's dead, no one cares about Troy in the whole world but me and

Krishna." She rubbed Krishna's back with her foot. "Krishna's been so bummed out."

He did seem depressed. Pepper bent over and stroked his head. Then she sat back, her face suddenly vulnerable. A little tear, blackened with mascara, rolled down her face to her mouth, and she caught it with her tongue.

"I'm going to get started," Bobbie said.

"I already cleaned," Pepper said. "Can't you tell? Except the bedrooms. The hall door was closed, so I thought it would be rude."

"Didn't you close it?" I asked.

"No, I didn't close it." Pepper stood up heavily. "I never had tits before," she groaned. "Now they're fucking weighing me down."

"It was open when—" I began.

But Pepper interrupted, staring past me, eyes on the front door. "Jesus fucking Christ."

I turned my head. A woman in large black sunglasses stood in the doorway, impossibly slender, impossibly clean, from her impossibly perfect hair in shades of pale golds down to her pale linen espadrilles. And on her shoulder was a video camera, running.

No one really looked like that. It had to be a reporter. Shit. About to be immortalized, and possibly on the Channel 4 news, where people who did not know us would see us more vividly than they saw their intimates—my tired face, Bobbie's midriff blouse, showing maybe a little too much extra stomach, Pepper's condition.

The woman spoke. "This is the interior of Erica's house," she said, "as you walk in the door."

I went toward her, putting my hand up to cover the camera, just like all guilty people do when they are cornered by *Inside Edition, 60 Minutes, American Journal.* That was how you knew they were guilty. "Turn that camera off," I said.

Pepper slipped past me, past the woman, Krishna behind her, and faded out the door. Bobbie went into the kitchen.

"You have no right," I said, all alone now.

"I have every right," she said. "You're the ones without the rights. This is my sister's house."

"Mariah," I said.

chapter eighteen

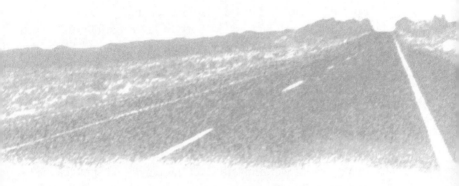

A VICTIM, HURT, IRRATIONAL, I REMINDED
myself. "My name's Chloe Newcombe and I'm a victim advocate," I
said gently, "I'm here to help you, but I don't want to be videotaped.
It's too . . . constraining."

"Oh." Reluctantly, Mariah lowered the camera and rubbed her
shoulder. "All right. I guess."

Where had Bobbie gone to?

Mariah sat down abruptly on a rocking chair and moved her big
sunglasses to the top of her head. She had the body of an eighteen-
year-old, but her face was closer to forty. The light from the window
exaggerated the lines around her mouth and her eyes, despite her
careful makeup.

"Why would you want to videotape this anyway?" asked Bobbie,
suddenly returning. Her voice was hostile. Bobbie was great with dirt-
poor women battered by drunken husbands, but she had the suspi-
cion of the small-town native toward more urban people.

"Bobbie," I said warningly. "This is Erica's *sister.*"

Mariah ran her fingers through her long hair, each strand a different color, and somewhere among them was maybe her real color,
too. "It's important to document *everything.* My sister's murder. Not
many people have a chance like this."

Bobbie stood in the kitchen doorway in her faded jeans and midriff top, irritation plain on her bare, freckled hillbilly face. She didn't

say them, but somehow the words were palpable in the air, heavy with sarcasm. *Aren't you lucky.*

"Bobbie," I said, "could we talk for a minute?"

In the kitchen, Bobbie said, "Sorry. I know I'm blowing it with her. If it's okay with you, I think I'll take a hike. I need it." She patted her midriff. "Here." She handed me a CCI form folded.

I put it in the pocket of my black one-pocket T-shirt.

Bobbie left by the kitchen door.

In the living room, Mariah sat rocking, her body tense and fighting the motion. Her eyes were blank, as if she'd forgotten who I was.

I sat on the couch.

Outside, there were footsteps on the porch and someone called out, "Honey, I'm here."

Mariah stopped the motion of the rocker with her feet.

"I hurried as fast as I could, sweetie." A tall man in a bleached jeans outfit that set off a tan too deep to be healthy walked in the door. "I got you ibuprofen, Tylenol, and Excedrin." Seeing me, he stopped abruptly.

"This is Clo, the victim rights person." Mariah said my name so it rhymed with Flo. "This is my husband, Wally Haskell."

Mariah's husband thrust out his hand with alacrity. His face was boyishly handsome in a well-preserved sort way.

"It's Chlo-*e*," I said, taking his hand.

He smiled. "Chloe. It's a pleasure." He got the name just right. "This town has sure changed. Mariah and I were here seventeen years ago. I thought it was going to be like the Old West, cowboys and stuff, but it was just boarded-up shacks and a bunch of hippies." He brushed awkwardly at his hair, a youthful cut, strands just separate enough to show off a deeply receding hairline.

"I was going to buy an authentic cowboy outfit," he went on doggedly, as if driven by polite social urges beyond his control, "and I ended up having to drive clear to Sierra Vista to get one. There were hardly any stores open here then—Erica's house went for seven thousand. We helped her with the loan."

"Wally, please." Mariah sighed and leaned back in the rocker, sweeping her hair up and back with her fingers.

"Sweetie, your *headache*." He dumped the sack onto the coffee table and fumbled through the bottles. "Water," he said.

I took him to the kitchen.

"There are some things you'll need to know," I told him, since he seemed to be obstensibly the one in charge. "There're two neighbors who've been looking after Troy; I'll leave you a packet of information and I'll write their names and number on it. You'll need to make arrangements after Erica's body is released—for the burial. There's a list of mortuaries in the packet and various phone numbers that might be useful."

He nodded, worry lines etching his face. "This is hell on Mariah," he said. "Her mother's been dying for ages now. They thought it was Parkinson's, but now they say it's some rare disease affecting the ganglia. She's not coherent anymore. And Erica had pretty much re-signed from the family. Mariah's had to do everything."

Under his good-hearted-helper demeanor was panic, barely restrained. Blindly, he began opening and closing cabinets.

"Plus, there's the business," he went on, picking up a Baggie of brown rice. "I'm out of town a lot, going to conferences, so she takes care of all the day-to-day stuff. We run a dating service, Happy Hearts, out in the San Fernando Valley. We use video a lot, and Mariah does all the taping." His voice rose. "She can hardly manage as it is, and now *this*."

He stared down at the rice.

I took it from him, handed him a glass from the dish drainer.

Mariah's voice came plaintively from the living room. "Wally?"

"Just a sec, sweetie." He moved closer to me and said in a low voice, "When we were here seventeen years ago, Erica and Mariah fought all the time; they've been . . . estranged ever since. We've never even *met* Troy."

His eyes bored into mine pleadingly; I could see the bubbles of his tinted contact lenses floating on their surface. He was holding the empty glass so tightly, his knuckles were white.

"Here." I took the glass from him. "Let me fill this for you."

"The lawyer," he said, "the one who called Mariah? He made it sound like Troy is innocent."

I turned on the water; it coughed and spat from sitting unused in the pipes. "I understand the evidence against him is pretty weak. He may be released very soon."

"Well, that's good." His voice was dubious. "It would be a terrible thing . . . We'll do everything we can for him, if he really is—

"*Wally?*"

"Coming, sweetie."

I gave him the glass of water.

"It's so hard for her, coming back here." His face trembled with emotion. "Erica was tough on her. *Cruel.*"

Cruel. Erica had been tough on Andy, too. Maybe tough on Lucas. "Wally," I said, "don't forget to take care of *yourself,* okay?"

He nodded at me politely, my words not really sinking in, and headed back to the living room. I found a plastic bag under the sink and got the ribs and salad from the refrigerator. I could take it into the living room and carry it off when I left. I didn't think they'd notice.

Wally and Mariah were murmuring together in low voices, but when I went back into the living room, they stopped. Mariah was in the rocker, Wally beside her, sitting awkwardly on the floor.

"We were talking about Troy," Wally said. "You said the case against him was weak?"

I set the ribs bag down by the door, then sat on the couch. "Yes. You need to think about what will happen if the charges are dropped. He's still a minor. He'll need a guardian."

Mariah looked aghast. "We're supposed to take him in? Someone who might have *killed* Erica?"

"The case against him is extremely weak," I said.

"Sweetie," said Wally, "let's cross that bridge when we come to it. Right now, you need to rest."

"How can I rest," said Mariah indignantly, "when I have to keep thinking about *Erica.* She didn't even love me. She had nothing but disdain for everything I've ever done."

Her eyes were very bright. She crossed her legs, one linenespadrilled foot kicking in compulsive little jerks. "And *she* never did *any*thing."

"Sweetie, hush, it's *okay*," said Wally.

"If she wants to talk, let her," I said to him.

"When we were growing up," Mariah went on, "for a while she wanted to be a nun—can you believe that? Then she majored in Eastern religions in college, but she never finished. When I was taking all those business classes, she just drifted around Venice Beach." Her hands clutched at the rocker arms, perfect manicured pale nails digging in. "Not a care in the world. Being *spiritual*."

"You're the real spiritual one," said Wally stoutly.

Mariah ignored him. Her voice rose. "It was just like her, to get herself murdered. Murdered, and now *I'm* expected to take care of her child."

There was an awful silence.

Suddenly, Mariah closed her eyes. "I don't mean that," she said. She looked a little less tense now, but very tired. "Erica was my big sister. I loved her. For a long time after we had the fight, every time the phone rang, I would think for a second, It's *Erica;* she wants to make up. But it never was."

Wally reached over, patted her hand.

"Then," said Mariah, "she finally did call. Just a few weeks ago. No one was home. She left a message on the machine for me to call her, but I . . . I never did. It had been too long." She opened her eyes. "She could have called back," she added plaintively.

For the past few weeks, Erica had been reaching out and everyone, *everyone,* had failed her. Myself included. But Erica had failed people, too. A free spirit who left the hard stuff to her little sister.

Mariah's face was blank; she reached down and took Wally's hand. "Maybe I *would* like to rest, take a nap." Her voice had turned childlike.

"That's a great idea," Wally said. "And I want to ask Chloe here a couple of things."

Mariah stood up shakily. "Remember?" she said. "The spare room where we slept?"

The spare room, which would be Troy's now. I wondered if she realized.

"Need a hand, sweetie?" Wally asked.

"I'm okay."

We watched as she walked through the living room, past the ferns and the desk, past the shrine to the Virgin of Guadalupe, who looked like Mariah's beautiful sister. We watched her open the door to the hall. Who had closed it. The wind?

Now that Mariah was gone, Wally's shoulders slumped. For a moment, he stared at nothing, deflated from his ride on Mariah's roller coaster.

"Wally . . ." I began.

"Wally?" Mariah was back, leaning against the door. "Clo?" Her voice trembled. "Something's . . . Someone's . . ."

"What?" said Wally. "What's wrong?"

"I . . . I was going to go the *bathroom,*" Mariah said. "And Erica's room is straight ahead. I couldn't help . . ." She put her arms around her body, hugging herself. "It's . . . it's . . . Oh, *Wally,* Clo—come *see.*"

We got up quickly, followed her down the hall, and stopped at the door to Erica's room.

"All human nature vigorously resists grace because grace changes us and the change is painful."

Only two days before, I'd stood in Erica's room and read those lines from a book by Flannery O'Connor, thinking of James and Venice Beach and Kyle, the warrior of death. The room had been full of clothes, but it was a civilized room, with the neatly made bed, the pillows, the book lying on the bedside table.

Now the metal clothing rod I'd noticed on my first visit was empty except for a dress that hung in shreds from a wooden hanger. Her clothes, or what was left of them—bits of colored cloth—covered the bed, the bedside table, the floor, hung from a lamp shade: torn or cut with a jagged knife, ripped to pieces, reduced to ragged, brilliant confetti. All traces of civilization had been obliterated, replaced by an aura that still hung in the air, the aftereffect of what felt like uncontrollable and primitive rage.

chapter nineteen

"SON OF A BITCH," SAID WALLY, ALL TRACES
of the good helper gone from his voice.

For a second, everything seemed unreal. Wally's face and Mariah's
floated at me like white balloons, painfully close yet miles way.

"I thought . . ." Mariah began. "I . . . I thought she was killed
someplace else. No one said it was *here.*" Her thin shoulders quiv-
ered. "Why didn't anyone *tell* me?" She began to shake.

"Mariah, these are just *clothes.*" My voice sounded harsh, shock-
ingly loud. I took a deep breath, struggling for control. "She *wasn't*
killed here."

But in its way, it was as shocking as if she had been. At Olander
Meadow, someone had emptied the gun, but it had been from a distance; here, they must have grabbed at the clothes, ripped them to
shreds with a sharp instrument in a frenzy of destruction—clothes
that had touched, clung to Erica's body, clothes that, in a sense, had
described and defined her. The gun had killed her, but this seemed
more brutal, terrible in its intimacy.

Mariah began to shake violently. Wally put his arm around her.
"We don't have to stand around," he said, *"looking."*

We all turned, went back down the hall, bumping one another in
our haste, like frightened children. In the living room, Wally picked
up the video camera; Mariah sat shakily on the very edge of the
couch.

"I don't think we can stay here," Wally said. "I think we should check into the Copper Queen." He leaned down and took Mariah's hand. "Now, sweetie. Right away."

I nodded, standing in the middle of the living room, still in shock, uncertain what to do next. It wasn't a pleasant, comfortable room anymore, despite the ferns, the books, the Guatemalan spread on the couch, the shrine to the Virgin—a room I had seen as the center of the house. Because the whole house had changed, its focus shifted to Erica's bedroom, that was its center now, its heart—a heart of rage.

What if Troy had been there when the intruder came in? Would he be dead, too?

I went for the phone. "I'll call the police," I said.

Officer Bill Soto, of the Dudley police, dark and sincere and handsome, hair graying around the ears in a most distinguished way, whistled through his teeth. *"Jeez."*

He turned from the door of the room. "Criminal damage," he said. "Maybe breaking and entering. Guess that's about the most you could charge the perp with. It's a shame."

I followed him back down the hall.

"Any damage anyplace else?" He stopped at Troy's room; the door was closed.

"Not in the living room or the kitchen. I didn't . . ." *Couldn't* bring myself to look in Troy's room.

He opened the door. The unmade bed, the tangle of socks and T-shirts on the floor, and the skateboard were untouched; the dragons and beasts painted on the wall still glared out, both benign and baleful. I breathed a sigh of relief.

"I didn't see any signs of a break-in," I said. "I mean, the kitchen door was locked. I checked. Unless they found the key, which wouldn't be hard—it's usually under a rock." Should I mention Pepper had been here when I'd arrived? No, somehow, I didn't want to involve Pepper. Anyway, she hadn't known about what had happened or she'd have told me and Bobbie. Surely she would have.

Soto gave a short laugh and strode across Troy's room to the window. "See this? He gestured. "It's locked, right? You can see it looks like it's caught, here under this thingamaboby." He put both hands under the bottom of the window where it didn't quite meet the sill, gave a push. The thingamaboby gave way and the window sprang open. "When you close it again, it still looks like it works, but it don't." He looked at me triumphantly.

"In the window, out the door," he said. "These Old Dudley houses, they're just junk. You go to bed at night, everything locked up, and you think you're safe. They oughta tear them all down, start from scratch. Half the time, these hippies types don't even bother to paint 'em. What's wrong with some nice aluminum siding? Save you big money in the long run."

He closed the window again. He wasn't even wearing gloves, maybe smudging existing fingerprints, destroying evidence.

"You've got to get Ed Masters over here," I said, "even if it's not his *jurisdiction*. I'm willing to bet the same person who did this was the one who killed her."

I was also willing to bet Soto thought the same, but I could see his cop eyes sneering at me, *Civilian.* "You don't know that," he said with dignity. "Could be kids, knew the house was sitting empty."

"Cranked up on methamphetamines," I said.

"That's right," said Soto, "it's a real bad drug."

"Hello," called a voice. "Helooooo?"

A man appeared at the doorway to the hall, backlit by the light from the living room.

"Chloe?" he said, coming toward me. I recognized him then— Larry, in khakis and a cobalt blue cotton shirt. Handsome Larry, lover of Nelson, the counselor. And Erica's twin soul. "I saw the cop car outside," he said. "What's—"

He stopped, staring past me into Erica's room. *"No."*

"Sir," said Soto. "Sir, would you step back, please."

But Larry brushed past him, reached the room. He stood frozen. "Rape," he said in a choked voice. "It's *rape*. I mean, what *else* would you call it?" He leaned down and picked something up.

"Sir," said Soto. "That's evidence."

Larry ignored him. "Look!" He held aloft a bit of white cloth edged with embroidery. "Her Mexican wedding dress. She never wore it; it was too . . . fragile." He pressed it to his cheek, his voice dazed. "I . . . I used to tease her, tell her, No one cares about that sixties hippie stuff anymore; it's the glamour sixties that's in now.' " Grief contorted his beautiful face, making it vulnerable, real. "I said, 'you should maybe search around and find some old' "—his voice broke— " 'Puccis.' "

"Sir, you're obstructing justice here." Soto's voice was losing patience.

"And *Nelson*, Nelson hated . . ." Larry dropped the cloth and put his head in his hands. "Oh, he just hated this whole thing."

Soto took a step toward him.

"Can't you see he's in shock?" I said to Soto. "He and Erica were good friends." I walked over to Larry, put my hand flat on his back, and propelled him down the hall.

"Everything comes back," Larry said as he strode up and down in Erica's yard, ducking the rosebushes cascading over the wooden fence. He stopped and looked over at me, his cobalt shirt brilliant against the green backdrop. "That's what she said when I teased her about hippie dresses." He flung his head back, running his hands through his sun-streaked hair. "Too much."

"Larry," I called to him from the porch steps. "Sit down, for heaven's sake."

"I can't," he said, striding faster. "And now the poor little match girl's missing. Did you know that? That horrible Neva woman called, looking for Nelson." He wrung his hands. "But Nelson's had all he can take. He took off, on a retreat."

"The poor little match girl?"

"Oh, Sally, Sally something."

"Sally Smith," I said. "Why did Neva call *Nelson*?"

"Neva thought he might know where she was—he's Sally's counselor." He strode over to the porch, sat down beside me on the steps, and put his head in his hands. "I'm not supposed to know the names of Nelson's clients, but I came home early one Tuesday night, a couple of months ago, when Nelson had group at the house, and there was Erica coming out the door with this little mouse, and she introduced us."

I looked at him surprise. "*Erica* was in Nelson's group?"

He made a disdainful face. "It was a new group. He starts one up every few months, but mostly the same people come back over and over. Erica only went to that one, thank God."

"What do you mean, 'thank God'?"

He shrugged. "Counseling's fine for some, but for *Erica*? I said to her, 'You want him to fill your head up with those *words—dysfunctional, abusive, codependent*?'" He paused. " *'Victim?'* We didn't use those words, Erica and I. We were strong."

Strong, I thought, and that little memory that had been haunting me came back, sitting on Venice Beach with James and Erica. They'd talked and laughed. How powerful James became when he talked to Erica, powerful and knowing—he was different with her, more beautiful, and crueler. I'd sat on Venice Beach, drawing little x's in the sand, shut out from my favorite brother, kind James, gentle James.

She stole him away that summer, and how I had hated her for it.

Suddenly, my head seemed to spin. I could hardly get my next words out. "Larry," I said, "Erica *was* a victim, wasn't she—some time, someplace?"

"We both *knew,*" said Larry. His face was anguished. The hustler I'd sensed the first time we met was gone, wiped out by his pain. Some other time, he would be a nice person to be around, witty, caring.

I stared at him, his every move so graceful, so attractive, as if he had been trained somewhere to be that way. Sometime, someplace, I thought, he had been a victim, too. I wanted to reach out to him, let him talk.

"She stood out," he said. "It was just who she was; it wasn't on purpose. They want to own you, and if they can't they'll get even." He turned his head away from my stare, arching his neck proudly. "We knew," he said, "but we never talked about it."

chapter twenty

SOMEBODY HAD TO TELL TROY. AND STUART
seemed like the best person. I caught him as he was coming out of
his front door. I was happy to see him—he seemed so solid, so sane—
well, sort of.

He looked stunned when I told him what had happened; then
he looked thoughtful. "I could get Troy off on just what you've told
me. Not that I expect it to get that far. It's a preemptive fact if I
ever saw one."

"Is it now? What's a preemptive fact?"

"If Ed ever gets around to finding a reasonable suspect and I get
him as a client, my first line of defense would be to tell the jury that
if they can't prove my client trashed Erica's room in an insane frenzy,
then the real suspect's still out there somewhere. It's enough for reasonable doubt in and of itself. Hope they're taking photographs with
the lens cap off. Hope—"

"Stuart." I stared at him indignantly. "Could you just *stop*!"

"Stop what?"

"Being a damn *lawyer.*"

He looked harassed. "Fine for you to say. *You* don't have to pick
up Troy at juvie detention and tell him what happened."

"He's being released?"

"Charges dismissed, without prejudice."

"That means they can recharge him?"

"Only if they come up with new evidence. The poor kid never should have been a suspect in the first place." He sighed. "There's no way he can go home. He can stay with me. I'll call the relatives at the Copper Queen when I think Troy's ready to handle it. As soon as I pick him up, we're driving to Sierra Vista to get him some new running shoes—his only pair look like Krishna lunched on them. Then we're coming back and, about sixish or so, we'll go across the line and have some Mexican food. You're invited."

I felt breathless. "What about the ribs? I've got them in my car."

"Got to run," he said. "Put 'em in my frig. The door's not locked." He started to walk to his truck. "Oh, and Chloe?" he said.

"What?"

He looked inept, helpless. "There's a futon, in the room I use as my office, where Troy can sleep. Maybe you could throw a couple of sheets on it?"

He jumped into his truck, revved the engine, and drove off.

I got the ribs from my car and walked into Stuart's house. I'd only been inside twice, once before going to see Troy, once after, but somehow it felt as familiar to me as if it were my own home. The ugly beige couches, where you could sink down and put your feet up. Argue. Say what you felt like saying. A sanctuary. It even smelled like Stuart.

What was I thinking? It smelled horrible, like a cheap cigarette burning. The ashtrays on the big coffee table were full of stubbed-out butts, burned down to the quick. It was no place for a *child*. I set the plastic bag down and opened one of the two windows; nothing caught under a thingamabob here. The other window seemed to be painted shut.

I picked up the bag again and went through the dining room, finding more full ashtrays, and half-full coffee cups, where drowned cigarette butts floated in a milky scum. The dining room table was piled with files. In the kitchen, the sink was still full of dirty dishes and the floor still sticky under my feet. I shoved the bag in the re-frigerator between a two-liter bottle of Coke and two jars of extra-hot salsa.

Then I went around opening more windows, moving briskly,

keeping busy so I didn't have to think. I opened the front door, the back door, then went down a little hall. The house had two bedrooms; in one, the turquoise scatter rug was bunched on the floor, the king-size bed a tangle of zebra-print sheets and blue electric blanket. Full ashtrays rested on top of newspapers stacked on the end table.

It came to me how, back in New York, with a long-ago lover, we always stayed in bed on Sunday mornings, read the *New York Times,* ate English muffins with bacon, scattering crumbs all over the sheets.

Maybe Stuart could cut down on the smoking, just a little.

But oddly, there were no clothes on the floor. The closet door stood open, revealing rows of dress shoes and fancy cowboy boots, neatly pressed dress shirts, jackets, ties, two suits. Even Stuart's jeans and Dockers were hung on hangers.

For a second, I thought of Erica's clothes, torn to shreds, Larry with the bit of Mexican wedding dress pressed to his cheek. "And *Nelson*, Nelson hated . . ." Larry had said, holding the cloth; then he'd dropped it, put his head in his hands. "Oh, he just hated this whole thing." Was that what Larry had started to say? I didn't think so. What, then?

"Who the hell knows," I said out loud in frustration to the clothes in Stuart's closet.

Then I went down the hall to the other bedroom, which was furnished with a high bookcase full of law books, a desk, an office chair, and a couple of filing cabinets. The futon was against one wall. Sheets—where were they?

I found them in the hall closet and banged my shins several times trying to get the futon to be a bed. When I finished, I sat down. The muscles bunched at my shoulder blades, and anxiety touched a little spot under my rib cage with a burning finger, but my mind was blank. Not even enough energy for a little despair.

Fresh out of emotions, I stared for a while through the window at the pyracantha bush growing just outside, bright with red berries. Then I looked around the room.

No wonder Stuart worked on the dining room table. The desk was invisible under the paperwork in here. Framed on one wall was a law degree from the University of Arizona. On the floor by my feet was a wicker basket full of trash. No, not trash, but a mass of snapshots, stashed there in lieu of a photo album. I leaned down and picked one up. Stuart with a bunch of guys in Dockers, palm trees and a swimming pool behind them. Probably some legal conference.

I dropped the snapshot back into the basket, picked up another. Out of focus, Stuart getting into his truck, waving at someone. Aha. *His ex-wife.* There had to be photographs of her, probably at the bottom. Who could resist? I bent, shoved my hand deeper, pulled another out. A woman—it might be her—thin, maybe blond, maybe light brown hair, but wearing a sweatband, so you couldn't tell, domestic out on a patio.

A slim little cheerleader nose, perky, holding up a can of beer. It looked like morning light, but she wouldn't care. It might not be his wife anyway, maybe just a friend, someone who didn't own him and he didn't own her.

Had Stuart said what his wife's name was? I didn't think so.

I dug down farther and pulled up another photograph, this one formal: Stuart, his hair short, face younger and thinner, wearing a dark suit and standing beside the same woman, who now wore a white dress. A wedding dress. So it *was* his wife. They were holding hands and smiling at the camera. She was prettier in this one, Stuart handsome, innocently youthful. Before the drinking caught up to them. Before she smashed his computer with a ball-peen hammer.

Shamelessly, I took a whole handful of photographs, put them on the futon beside me, so I could sort more efficiently through Stuart's life. After all, it's a scary world out there, and the only weapon we have is information. Here was a drunk one with another couple, at a bar or restaurant, bottles of wine on the table, all of them red-eyed and overly joyous. And another patio picture with an Irish setter. Did she get the dog?

Now here was someone else, a dark-haired woman, standing by a river. Standing in sunshine, backed by shadows of trees and glinting water, in a flowing skirt and high-heeled boots. I stared at the photograph and my mind went blank. I turned my head, looked out the window at the pyracantha bush, bloodred berries clustered thickly on its branches, burnished by the sun, sharp and insistent as neon.

I looked again at the woman in the snapshot. Her smile was cool and confident, her hair remarkably thick and luxuriant. "She stood out. It was just who she was; it wasn't on purpose," Larry had said. Absurdly, lines from Edgar Allan Poe flashed through my mind:

> *Strange her pallor, strange her dress,*
> *Strange indeed her length of tress.*

Erica.

There was no getting away from her.

I searched thoroughly, but there were no more snapshots of Erica in the basket. But why were there *any*? Stuart had told me he met her once, when Troy got busted. Met her *once*.

I went around Stuart's smelly house, banging windows closed, slamming doors. Then I got in my car, slammed that door, too, and drove fast up the hill. Not fast enough. Tourists, generic in shorts and T-shirts, littered the back streets, taking pictures of the charming houses with their corroded, inadequate plumbing, electrical wiring smoldering in the attics, windows that didn't lock, while, thanks to these same tourists, everyone's taxes doubled and tripled yearly.

Impatiently, I honked at a family of four walking right in the middle of the street. Startled, they scattered like dumb animals put out in an unfamiliar pasture; the smallest child tripped, her mouth open in an **O**. Her mother caught her. The child began to wail.

Heartlessly, I sped on up the hill. So maybe the photograph had been in the disclosure file when he defended Troy, portrait of defendant's mother—*sure*. Stuart had known Erica better than he'd indicated. It was nice she could take time out from her busy schedule as single mom, library worker, and religious maniac to get to know every man in town.

So what? Suddenly, I was ashamed. I slowed to fifteen miles an hour and took a deep breath. I wouldn't have known any of this if I hadn't shamelessly sorted through Stuart's personal belongings, like a possessive, voyeuristic lover. Erica was dead, brutally murdered. And there was Troy, an innocent, who didn't deserve any of this. What? Then Erica *did*?

I pulled in my carport, got out of the car, and went inside. I sat down on the couch in the living room, trying to sort through my feelings. Big Foot plip-plopped slowly past me, visibly shedding fur. He went out the open French doors, then stood on the porch in quiet despair. He would never have a real life—proper owner grooming and attention, canned cat food every day—the kind of life a cat of his bulk deserved.

I giggled, the giggle turned into a laugh, and the laugh went on and on, a cataclysmic laugh, invading my body and shaking me like a car-test dummy in a staged fatal collision. Then something dissolved inside me and the laughter turned to tears. When they finally subsided, I felt much better. I sniffed and wiped my eyes on the sleeve of my T-shirt.

So I'd been jealous of Erica, way back when I was young and foolish, jealous to the point of hating her, primitive emotions, but I'd never acted on them, except possibly through omissions. At least I could make it up to her now by doing all I could for Troy—still alive, vulnerable, and, judging from the destruction in Erica's bedroom, maybe even in danger.

I needed to shower, change, get ready to go out to a Mexican restaurant with Troy and Stuart, possibly one of Erica's exes. I went into the bathroom, pulled my T-shirt over my head. Paper crackled in the pocket. I pulled it out.

The client contact information form that Bobbie had handed me that morning, which now seemed so long ago.

Had she actually filled out a CCI? She'd never been that good with the paperwork. I unfolded it and saw at once that she hadn't. On the blank bottom of the back were directions; she must have scribbled them hastily in the kitchen while I dealt with Mariah. The name of a town, Alpine, in the White Mountains and a tiny map. On the map, she'd written, "Milepost 23, left on dirt road, right three miles." And she'd drawn a little star and marked it "Kyle's place."

Bobbie had given me permission.

James's good friend Erica, linked with the most unlikely people— Sally Smith, for instance. Her life had reached out to the valley, to Lucas and the Baptist church, and now possibly included Stuart. And Kyle—a long time ago, if what Andy had told me was true, even Kyle had known her. I felt trapped in a sticky mesh, like an insect in a spiderweb, while the truth, like a giant spider, lay in wait for me.

chapter twenty-one

WHEN I TURNED MY HEAD AND LOOKED
through the back window of the cab of Stuart's truck, I could see
Troy sitting in the truck bed, sniffing the air like a puppy just released
from the pound. His feet were enormous and resplendent in the new
black-and-white running shoes. We jostled down Tombstone Canyon
and turned left on the street before Erica's.

"Troy wants to talk to Pepper," Stuart said. "Ask her to dinner
and see if she knows anything about the break-in."

"Did Troy have any ideas?"

"The only person he could think of was Ray."

"Ray."

Stuart shrugged. "That's Pepper's mom's boyfriend. He and Erica
were barely on speaking terms. And Troy and Pepper hate him."

Pepper's street was shabbier than Erica's, sad; jammed with un-
renovated shacks, many with FOR SALE signs hung on twisted metal
fences. Even the trees seemed bereft, leaves drying up before they
yellowed. A mature voice in my head said, You can wallow in suspi-
cion or you can just ask him about Erica. "That's a thought, then,
isn't it?" I said. "Ray."

"Just one of the many," said Stuart, "that go through my mind."

Troy tapped on the back window and pointed.

Stuart pulled over and parked on the edge of the narrow road,
behind an old white van, a big pink pig holding a can of beer painted

on it, amateurish and sloppy. The house was a typical miner's shack—chipping white paint over faded gray boards, the original integrity ruined by a mélange of add-ons in tin and plywood. An orange cat slept on an old beige couch that sat on the sagging front porch; in the front yard, near a large but barren ocotillo plant, a rusty rake lay beside a pile of trash, as if years ago someone had started to clean up and then had run out of energy.

Troy jumped out and came up to Stuart's window. "That's Ray's van." He stamped on the ground as if testing his shoes, then walked toward the house, stopping by a pomegranate bush. He let out a long, low whistle.

Pepper materialized, wearing a long black sheath dress that hid nothing. They stood by the bush, whispering, Pepper's face contorted, indignant.

Suddenly, the cat leaped from the couch and scuttled under the porch. A man in dirty jeans and a black T-shirt came out the door with a can of beer in his hand. He had long light brown hair that hung in sticky strands past his shoulders.

"Son of a bitch," he said to Troy. "It's the jailbird. How'd you like them orange jumpsuits? I hear they got red ones now, too, for the real bad guys." He chuckled. "They give you a red one, Troy?"

"Hi, Ray," said Troy. His voice was polite, but small.

Ray stared at him, rubbing his stomach, which hung over his jeans, not fully covered by the T-shirt. He looked like he'd been athletic once, maybe even a stud, but now everything had blurred. "Pepper, you get inside."

"We wanted to know if she'd like to come have dinner with us," Troy said, still polite.

"She already ate. Time to go, Troy. *Hasta la vista.*"

Head down, Pepper trudged past Ray, up the porch steps, and inside. Ray went in, too, and closed the door.

Troy came back to the truck, walking disconsolately, a smudge of dirt on his new shoes. "She didn't know anything," he said sadly.

* * *

We drove across the line into Mexico to a restaurant on a side street where dark and vibrant children played in the dusk. The restaurant was small, plants spilling out from the window ledge. *Norteño* music blared from a radio in the kitchen. We sat on vinyl and chrome chairs at a table covered with an oilcloth that was strewn with cherries. We ordered *carne asada* and Cokes, two diet, one classic, from a tiny waitress, pretty as a doll.

"Who's the father of Pepper's kid anyway?" Stuart asked.

"Tino." Troy played with his fork, turning it around and stabbing cherries. Behind his nerd glasses there were smudges under his eyes. "Tino Alvarez."

"He just abandoned her?"

Troy shrugged. "He's a *vato loco*—you know, a crazy dude? All the girls like him. I thought he was pretty cool myself, once." His eyes got a faraway, dreamy look. "You kind of want to be friends with those *vatos*; they know all this stuff about life and nothing bothers them— school, grades, not even girls." He looked wistful.

"And sooner or later, they show up in court," said Stuart morosely, "and I get to defend them."

We all sat and digested the thought that Troy wasn't even a *vato loco* and Stuart had had to defend him, too.

"I met someone the other day who knows you," I said to Troy. "Lucas."

"Lucas?" His eyes lit up. "He was my favorite of all my mom's boyfriends. Stuart, he was the *coolest* guy; he was a roping champion. He was teaching me how to rope!"

Stuart looked at him with interest. "When was that?"

"A couple of years ago, when I was just a kid. And one day, his old roping partner showed up! This guy Clyde."

"Clyde." I knew the name, tried to remember . . . then I did. The young cowboy, cocky, brash, in the photograph on the wall of Lucas's trailer; Lucas had had his arm around him. Saw Lucas, brooding by the window, when I asked about him. "Clyde *Daugherty,*" I said. "You met him?"

"Yeah." Troy wrinkled his nose. "I was all excited at first, 'cause

Lucas had told me lots of stories about him and Clyde, how crazy Clyde was. He showed me pictures, too, but when I met him, he looked different. Gray-looking and *old.*"

Clyde had looked so young in the photograph, not afraid of anything, certainly not about to grow old. And Lucas had seemed sad about something—what *had* happened to Clyde. Troy tugged at a dreadlock and looked thoughtful, contemplating crazy guys getting gray and old.

"Anyway," he went on, "they were going to show me all the tricks, but Mom wasn't feeling good. And before I got a chance to go back again, he and Mom broke up. She was *always* doing that, breaking up."

He took off his nerd glasses, licked the lenses, and rubbed them with his shirt. Suddenly, his lower lip trembled. He said to Stuart, his blue eyes suddenly vulnerable, "Why couldn't she like someone for *a long time?*"

The question seemed to reverberate in the air, bouncing off the stucco walls.

Why indeed? Was it not wanting to lose her independence? Wanting only the unattainable? Hooked on the thrill of endorphins racing through the blood? The *norteño* music pulsed from the kitchen, insistent with heartbreak and longing. Outside the window, a motorcycle revved up and I heard a child's laugh, joyful.

Troy was still looking at Stuart.

Stuart touched his gold earring, smoothed back his thinning blond hair. "I have no idea, Troy." He looked tired. "I'm just a lawyer."

"And I was really, really hoping my mother and Lucas might get back together," Troy said. "She went and saw him, less than two weeks ago."

"She did?" I stared at Troy. Lucas had said he'd never seen Erica again—after the fight about Patsy, *he never saw her again.* That was two years ago. "How do you know?"

"She came home late one night and she just said, 'Oh, Lucas says hi.' I wanted her to tell me more, but that was all she would say."

He looked up as the waitress arrived with plates of *carne asada* and flour tortillas. She was so pretty, her dark, shining hair a beauty school's dream. She smiled at Troy when she put his plate down. *"Un pequeño mas por el muchacho."*

"Mucho gracias, señorita," said Troy with great cool, blushing.

So Lucas was a liar, too. Like Stuart. For a while, we all fell to eating, wrapping the smoky steak strips in tortillas and dipping them into salsa and guacamole. Why had Erica gone to see him? Stuart glanced at me as if he knew what I was thinking.

"Lucas," he said to Troy, wiping up the juice on his plate with another tortilla. "You liked him a lot, huh? Is that maybe why you and your mom had that fight? You wanted her to go back with him?"

"No." Troy took a breath. He grabbed for his Coke and sucked ice at the bottom with his straw. "It wasn't about Lucas at all. It was before she went to see him. It . . . It was . . ." He looked like he was about to cry, here in the brightly lit restaurant with the waitress who'd given him a little more. "It . . . It was about my *father.*" He gulped.

There was a little pause. Troy stared down at the oilcloth miserably.

"Tell you what," said Stuart, "there's a little park down the way. We can buy some gelati and go sit on a bench and you can tell us about it."

Young trees lined the square and there was grass, scruffy but green, underfoot. It was not quite night, the sky a deep purple, and above us hung a fingernail moon, like a prop from the *Arabian nights.* We sat on a wrought-iron bench across from a pink bandstand, Troy in the middle, eating gelati. Mine was almond, creamy and sweet, and it sent icy little stabs of pain to the roots of my front teeth with every bite.

"My mom had been acting funny for awhile." Troy finished his coconut gelato with a series of neat little nibbles. "She would hardly even talk to me at dinner, like she was thinking about something else all the time."

He licked his gelato stick clean and began to notch grooves in the stick with his thumbnail. "I was feeling . . . you know, lonely." He sighed. "Maybe that's why I was thinking so much about my dad."

"You told me he was dead," Stuart tossed his gelato stick and lit up a cigarette.

"Yeah. In an automobile accident. Mom told me that years ago, when I was just a little kid. Whenever I tried to find out more, she'd get really upset, so I stopped asking, but I kept thinking and thinking about him. Finally, I decided I had a right to know stuff, like . . . like where he was buried. I could go to the cemetery. *She* wouldn't have to go. I had what I was going to say to her all planned out, so she couldn't clam up this time. It was right before dinner; she was cooking a big pot of spaghetti sauce."

Troy snapped the gelato stick in half and began to shred the ends. "I made the salad, even though I hate chopping all that stuff, and I set the table. Then . . ." His voice broke. "Then I asked her where he was buried."

Across the square, young men strutted. Someone was playing a guitar. I could feel the tension coming from Troy in little waves, and I clenched my jaw. I wanted him to stop talking. It would be easier. Then we could all go home.

He went on resolutely. "She was standing at the stove, and she turned around with the pot in her hands, and dropped it on the floor. All this spaghetti sauce spilled out all over. She said, 'Never ask me about your father again, do you understand? Never.' And then she walked over to the table—I thought she might even hit me, but she never did that—and she picked up the salad bowl and threw it so it hit the window and broke, and the whole time she kept on yelling, "Never, never, never."

There was a long silence. Finally, Stuart asked, "Then what happened?"

Troy whooshed out a breath. "She went into her bedroom and slammed the door. I stayed in the kitchen and cleaned up all the sauce and the broken glass. I guess one of the neighbors called the cops, 'cause after a while they showed up."

A trio of mariachis began to strum vigorously across the square.

At the bench over from us, a tall, dark woman in a red dress stood up, threw her head back, and laughed.

"The kitchen was already clean by then, and Nelson came over and talked to them." Troy dropped the shreds of gelato stick on the ground. "They finally went away."

Beyond the square, beyond the trees, down the street past the shops by the border, you could just see under the lights a small section of the newly erected twelve-foot-high, four-mile-long metal wall. Put up to keep dope dealers from crossing freely over the border. Put up to keep the dope dealers and the aunts and uncles, mothers and fathers, brothers and sisters, nieces, nephews, the old friends, and all the people who came across to dance in the dance halls from freely crossing the border.

But still they crossed.

"Heavy-duty," Stuart said. "That's pretty heavy-duty stuff."

A chilly wind came up across the square, scattering the leaves of the young trees. How fiercely, how violently Erica had protected her secret. Bobbie and I had never ever talked about Kyle. Stuart, Troy, and I sat on the cold metal bench, together but separated by our insecurities, our lies, and our secrets. I thought of the barriers people erect between each other, subtle and intangible, but more insurmountable by far than any twelve-foot-high, four-mile-long metal wall. I shivered.

Stuart ground out a cigarette with the heel of his boot, looked at his watch. "Time to get going."

chapter twenty-two

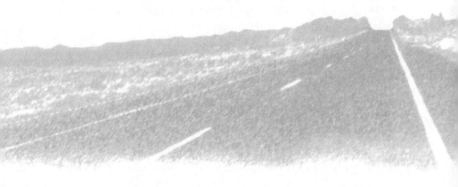

CLOUDS SCUTTLED ACROSS THE FINGERNAIL moon as we drove back to Dudley. It wasn't late, maybe nine o'clock on a Saturday night. The lights were bright down on the Gulch, rockabilly music twanging, parking lots jammed with pickups, vans, and cars. Saturday night—you could feel it in the air, expectant, fizzy, like a sip of champagne; too soon for the drunks, the shouting, the gunshots, and the whine of the cop cars.

Stuart cleared his throat. "I don't know," he said. "How long can you carry a grudge?"

"What?"

"I'm thinking about Erica and Troy's father."

We both glanced behind, through the back window, where Troy sat, oblivious, a blank look on his face.

"It seems to me she could have handled it better than throwing a pot of spaghetti on the floor." He'd lowered his voice, but the hostility still came through. "If the guy's dead—why not paint a nice picture for Troy, so he has something to live up to?"

"When you've reached the point of throwing spaghetti on the floor, you're not exactly in charge anymore," I pointed out.

Stuart shook his head. "I don't buy that. Everyone has to take responsibility for their own actions. I'm a recovering alcoholic; if anyone understands that, I do."

"But can't you also understand what it's like not to be in charge?"

"Sure, I understand." Stuart shifted gears as we drove up past the Copper Queen. "Self-pity, self-indulgence. I plead guilty to all those. *Guilt's* the key word here. Whatever Troy's father was like, Erica could have put it aside for Troy."

"Come on," I said. "Maybe he was really awful."

"And Erica was just an innocent victim?"

"Something like that."

"No one's truly innocent," he said firmly. "It's recognizing that that leads to responsibility."

"That's fine, but you're blaming. Guilt's different from blame. Guilt, we take on ourselves; blame, we assign to others." My voice was self-righteous.

"Okay, okay," Stuart said.

"You mean you're actually conceding a point to *me*?

"Did I say that?" His voice was irritable. "Am I taking you home or what?"

"Stuart, I need to talk to you about something."

"I *knew* it."

"Knew what?"

"You're pissed."

"All I said was that I needed to talk to you."

"Let me drop Troy off at my house first." He bent over the steering wheel, shifting gears again, doggedly beleaguered.

Honestly, I thought, so *immature*. My hands were cold.

Stuart dropped Troy off, then drove up to the parking lot below my house and stopped next to an ancient Volkswagen van. "I don't know if I want to try the truck on this hill again. We can talk here."

He lit a cigarette. There was a silence. I watched the shadows of the ailanthus trees flickering under the streetlight, read the bumper sticker on the van: DUDLEY, ARIZONA—THE TOWN TOO DUMB TO DIE. It was hard to know how to begin. The silence grew.

After awhile, Stuart said gloomily, "Here you are, pissed off, and you're not even telling me what I did."

"Who said I was pissed off?"

"Forget it."

I felt as though I were back in high school, having a teenage fight. I leaned back in the seat and put my feet up on the dusty dashboard of the truck, breathing in nicotine-tainted air, maybe the equivalent of a drag or two. "I guess I was wondering why you didn't mention you had some sort of thing with Erica."

Stuart gave an exasperated snort and banged his hand on the steering wheel. "Jesus Christ. Who told you that? This town is nothing but a fucking *rumor* mill."

I said nothing. There was another long silence. Up the hill, a dog barked.

"I met her when I first moved here," Stuart said finally. "It was no big *deal.*"

"I thought it was when you were defending Troy."

"That was months later. I defended Troy because she asked for me. Some nerve, when you think about it."

"Oh?"

"It's a long story. No. A short story. Very short. When I first got here, I went to everything. I mean, I didn't know anybody. I went to this art opening; there was a woman lying on a table and she was completely covered with yogurt."

"Erica?"

"No. Erica was wearing this slinky black dress and she had little gold stars pasted all over her face. She was behind the table where the wine was, and she offered me some. I told her I didn't drink, and one thing led to another and we got into this AA discussion, so I asked her to dinner. That was okay. So I asked her to go out to the San Pedro River with me a couple of days later, and that was better."

He opened the door of the truck and stuck his legs out. "I mean," he said, "she was very *friendly.* I thought we had a lot of fun."

"But she didn't?"

"I don't know. I tried to make further plans that day and she said to call her. And then when I called her, it was always the machine or Troy on the phone, saying she wasn't there. I left messages, but she never called back. After awhile, I quit trying, end of story."

Stuart flicked his cigarette, the still-burning end dancing and skittering across the parking lot. "All she had to do was tell me she wasn't interested, instead of leaving me twisting in the wind."

Resolutely, he squared his shoulders. "Anyway, I wasn't going to sit around asking myself what I'd done wrong. I figured it was *her* loss, not mine."

"Very healthy," I said.

"That's *right*. Some guys wouldn't take it that way. Some guys wouldn't help her out later, defend her son and all. I did it for Troy, of course, not her. And even then, she was acting like, Thank you so much, Mr. Ross, like she hardly knew me. Some guys would get *mad*." His voice was strained, touched with a residue of anger. "I've thought all along that it was some guy that she treated like shit who killed her. I said as much to Ed Masters, but he never listens."

"Now there's a librarian missing," I said. "Sally Smith. Not exactly the kind of person who treats guys like shit. No one knows where she is. She might even be *dead*. Where would she fit in?"

"For Christ's sake," said Stuart, a little irritably. "If we had apple pie, we could have apple pie à la mode if we had some ice cream. There's no evidence she fits in anyplace. Maybe she just left town. Some people get pretty nervous when someone they know is murdered. It's not like they found this Sally person's body."

Not yet. My stomach felt hollow.

Stuart lit a cigarette, then looked at it with disgust. "Anyway, I'm a lawyer, not an investigator. As long as Troy's in the clear, I'm off this case. It's got nothing to do with me."

"That's right," I said. "Who cares who killed her, anyway?"

"That's right," said Stuart. "Who cares?"

"And you're so defensive," I said.

"Only when attacked."

"Guess I'll go home," I said.

"Hasta la vista."

I got out of the truck.

Are Stuart and I still speaking? I wondered as I walked in my kitchen door. The client contact information form Bobbie had handed me was lying on the counter, with the map to get to Kyle's. It wasn't my fault if Stuart couldn't behave in a mature fashion. I'd had a right to ask him about Erica, and I wasn't going to sit around now wondering what I'd done wrong. So there.

I picked up the CCI form. I hadn't done any paperwork for a long time. No CCI for my call-out with Frankie to the crime scene, my call on Dot, no CCI for my visit to Nelson and Larry, or my session with Wally and Mariah. As my boss had told me repeatedly, it didn't matter what we did, because if we didn't fill out the paperwork, we might as well not have done it.

This was in keeping with my personal opinion that all-government-funded agencies exist only to generate reports.

The problem was, if I filled it all out, my hours would be so huge, I could sue the county right then and there. If they didn't fire me first—for going far beyond my duty and using my position as victim advocate to conduct my own personal investigation.

Instead, I should start a new life, go to Safeway, fill up the refrigerator with fruit and vegetables, little packages of skinless, boneless chicken breasts and tofu cakes. *Were* Stuart and I still speaking?

More importantly, had he told me the whole story? I wanted to believe him, wanted to believe someone. I went and sat on my porch, my feet up on the railing, and thought about this.

Let's say we *were* still speaking. I could buy the ingredients for chicken mole and have Stuart to dinner. There would be flowers on the table and candles in colorful Mexican candleholders, the ones I'd stored in the back of the cabinet after Big Foot knocked them over and broke a little bird off one of them. Mozart would play in the background. A perfect life lies in wait for all of us, if we would only realize it.

After awhile, it got chilly, so I went inside and sat on the couch, picked up the remote, and surfed for a while. A perfect Saturday night, me on the couch, channel surfing. I stopped at MTV.

They were playing a video of R. E. M. singing about how everybody hurts sometime. The video was in black and white and full of lonely people hurting all the time. Their eyes, full of pain and uncertainly, stared out at me.

So what? I was tough. Tired, too. I fell asleep.

* * *

I woke, lying on the couch, sometime long after midnight. No longer Saturday night, but Sunday morning. Young women wearing next to nothing were gyrating on the TV screen. I felt sad, peevish. *Put on some clothes; get a job.* I clicked them off. I wasn't feeling happy, but I wasn't tired anymore. I'd been bumping my head against various walls, and not only that—everything I learned just seemed to add on another suspect.

Let's face it, none of us go that innocently about our lives. We live with anger and pain every day, live in secrecy; it's just part of living. I wanted knowledge; I wanted some certainty.

I got up, took a long shower, and dressed carefully, not in black, my usual color, but in pale blue jeans and blue plaid shirt, like some imaginary all-American person. I filled a serving bowl with cat food, set it on the floor, along with the biggest pot I owned, filled full of water. I grabbed the CCI off the counter and got in my car.

By 3:00 A.M., I was driving through the valley, headed for Willcox, then I-10 to Clifton-Morenci and, after that, the White Mountains. The lights of the electrical plant twinkled in the distance like a fairy castle and small animals froze in my headlights, but I missed them all. No one would be out at this time of night except the animals and maybe some drug runners, a drunk or two, and possibly one murderer.

I didn't really think so. Anyway, I saw no one. All the time, I was thinking of seeing Kyle in a nebulous way, but I was full of exhilaration and a sense of acute freedom. Spooky under the fingernail moon, the skeletons of yucca, like souls of the unresolved dead, seemed alive parading through the fields, headed for some Yucca Jamboree.

chapter twenty-three

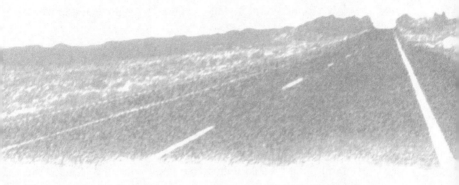

MILEPOST 23 WAS ONLY A FEW MILES OUT OF the town of Alpine, in the White Mountains, home of survivalists, gun nuts, and retired cops. I turned onto the dirt road marked on Bobbie's map and wound down my window; the chilly air smelled of pine and dew. Wooden cabins were scattered among the pines and the brilliant deciduous trees, the sunlight so sharp, it hurt my eyes.

I fumbled in my purse, pulled out sunglasses, put them on. My hands were shaking. *Get a grip.*

A little blond girl on a big black horse looked at me as I drove by, turning her head to watch as I pulled away from her. My foot trembled on the accelerator as I shifted down to second. On my left was a stand of mailboxes, and one of them said BARNETT in small red letters. I turned down the narrow road beside them, rutted and bumpy under a carpet of fallen leaves. A bright red cardinal sailed from one tree to another. Blue jays scolded and somewhere a dog barked warningly.

The road wound around for a while, then stopped at a sign that read KEEP OUT PRIVATE. Beyond that was a driveway, covered in pine needles. Down a hundred yards or so was a little cabin, with a white compact parked beside it. The same one he always drove, just as Ed drove a white Geo, anonymous. He didn't even buy a pickup for his new life? I thought.

I took a deep breath, drove down the driveway, and pulled up behind the white car, then stopped and just sat there. Now I could hear cicadas singing, more jays. Maybe the jays scared the cicadas, because they stopped after a while. I sat in the silence and looked at Kyle's cabin, rustic, rough dark wood.

On the front porch was a wooden kitchen chair, straight-backed, so you couldn't get too comfortable, lose your edge. A houseplant was next to it, some sort of creeping charlie, which is hard to kill, but someone had been making a good effort. The door was open, but the screen door made a dark barrier to the inside.

As soon as I was certain I could handle it, I would get out and walk up the steps, past the wooden chair, the houseplant, and knock on the screen door. I could almost see his stern, unwelcoming face appearing at the screen. I rehearsed what I would say, get it out at once, so he wouldn't think I was intruding for no good reason.

"Hi, Chloe."

I yelped, jumped in my seat, and banged my thumb knuckle on the steering wheel.

Kyle stood outside my window. His hair was cut as short as a new recruit's and he wore jeans and an old white T-shirt that said SHER-IFF'S POSSE on it. In spite of the logo, he had the wiry, alert look of someone who spent his spare time planning how to hold up a liquor store.

"Kyle, you *shithead!*" I said accusingly. "You snuck up on me." I sucked my knuckle.

"Anyone could of." He was almost smiling.

"Why would they want to?"

"No point in waiting till it's too late to find out. Who's sneaking up on who anyway?"

I took off my sunglasses, blinking in the glare. "I drove up the driveway, in plain sight. I've been on the road for hours." Now I wondered why I'd been so nervous; it was just Kyle. "Aren't you even going to offer me a cup of coffee?"

"You want curb service?" He stuck his hands in his jeans pockets and cocked his head.

I got out of the car. I guess I must have closed the door, but I couldn't remember doing it, because in a split second we were holding each other tightly. His T-shirt smelled of sweat, pine resin, faint detergent residue. I kissed his neck; it tasted of the ocean. We were the perfect size for each other, all parts fitting, welded together into one person, only we weren't. One of us was lean and dangerous as a wildcat; the other was me.

I stepped away.

Kyle looked dazed, his gray eyes unfocused. I'd done that to him; could taste it, sharp and sweet as a fresh raspberry on my tongue: power.

"What's so funny?" he said.

"Nothing."

"I'm still married to Laurie, you know." He tugged at his T-shirt neck, like a man whose tie is too tight. "We're trying to work things out."

"I can tell," I said sarcastically. "You're blaming this on *me*? Anyway, I've been seeing a *defense* attorney."

He looked at me in disgust, as if he'd just found a rodent in his can of beer. "The reason I'm still going to offer you some coffee," he said, "the *only* reason, is that you came so far."

He turned and walked inside. I followed.

"Sorry about the mess," he said.

It wasn't much inside—small living room, wood-paneled walls, kitchen in back, separated by a counter. It smelled like beer. Some amateur with dulled tools must have made the rough pine furniture. The cushions were covered in a matted brown velvet. On the floor was a brown-and-green braided rug. There were two doors, one closed, which had to be a bathroom, the other open. Beyond, I could see a bed with a rumpled sleeping bag on top, saw it with a kind of shock. Then Kyle walked across to the room and closed the door.

Avoiding my eyes, he began to pick up beer cans from the floor and the coffee table. Several of them were crumpled up, men showing each other how strong they were.

"You had a party or something?" I asked.

"Couple guys stopped by last night is all." He walked behind me, giving me a wide swath, picked up more cans.

I turned toward him, the air between us charged. *"Cops."*

"Sure. So what?" Kyle moved away to safety behind the counter, beer cans clanking. "Cops know about it when another cop moves into their area. As a matter of fact, this place belongs to a sheriff's deputy."

"The brotherhood." I couldn't resist needling him a little. *A wimp*—that was how Bobbie had once described Kyle's wife, Laurie. But I could imagine life with Kyle, trying to sleep while he and the boys sat in the living room swapping stories and crumpling beer cans. You could never belong, never. All we really had between us was chemistry. Who could explain it?

I walked over to the counter and sat down on a wooden stool. Kyle was at the stove, fiddling around, separated from me by the counter. We were a little mad at each other. I could tell he was by the way he set a mug of coffee on the counter, still avoiding my eyes.

"Milk, sugar?"

"Both."

He set a half-gallon carton of milk in front of me, along with some packets of sugar he must have lifted from a restaurant. His movements were stiff, restrained.

"So what are you doing with yourself nowadays?" I asked, trying to neutralize the tension.

"I'm thinking about getting a job as a deputy over in Pinetop." He poured himself coffee and sat down. "I can't spend the rest of my life not working. I got child support."

"I thought you were through as a cop," I said, surprised. "I thought that was why you quit."

He looked at me then, over the top of his coffee cup, his calm gray eyes steady. "You thought what was why I quit?"

I stared back. "Well, of course. I mean . . ." Suddenly, I couldn't look at him. Because you couldn't stand the thought that you'd killed someone, someone unarmed, killed them in cold blood, was what I meant, what I'd been assuming all along, but I couldn't say it. Couldn't say it, because now I knew, sitting across from Kyle, knew from the calm in his eyes, that it wasn't true. It was a revelation. He'd done what he had to do, and that was that.

Suddenly, I felt very alone: a wimp, burdened with a set of moral scruples unknown to someone like Kyle. Not that he didn't have his own—they were just different, and what he'd done fit right into them.

I stared down at my cup. "Kyle, you never told me anything. We never talked about . . . you know." I reached for the milk, added some to my coffee; it coagulated in little clumps. My stomach turned. I looked at him then, angrily. "I have a *right* to know things."

"Women," said Kyle. "I can never figure out what they're talking about."

"What a tired old platitude, and your milk's sour," I said in disgust.

I got up and went around the counter and poured the coffee into the sink, rinsed out the cup. One of us had to be brave. Then I put my arms around Kyle from behind, rested my head on his stiff, puritanical shoulder, breathed in the sweat, pine, detergent residue.

The comforting thing about loving a cop is knowing he's prepared to defend you on a moment's notice; the challenge is breaking through all those defenses. I felt him tense, then relax.

"We may never see each other again after today," I promised, whispering in his ear. *"Please."*

"The only thing I ever regret about not working in a big city," said Kyle musingly, "is the chance to use some good equipment. The equipment in Cochise County was never worth a shit. All the new fancy things they have now, and we got the shit. I remember the time I wired someone up, had big hopes, state-of-the-art Nagra reel-to-reel—and all I got was a bunch of static. Pissed me off so much, I took the damn tape and, instead of just throwing it away, I burned it."

Why was he telling me this in such a roundabout way when the someone was me? And I knew he'd gotten more than a bunch of static. Of course, he was telling it like that in case I had a wire on right then. He had to have known I didn't. A cop, through and through. But I believed that he'd burned it—the tape that had haunted me for so long was gone forever. I backed off and got the coffeepot from the stove. I poured a fresh cup and went back to my side of the counter.

Kyle was grinning at me, not a big grin, but it reached his eyes. "Happy now?"

"Happy as I'll ever be about it, I guess." Part of me was relieved, but there was another part that would still have to live with it forever. Maybe the frequency would diminish, but I'd never get rid of the guilt; now and then, I would take it out and examine it; still whole and perfect and all mine.

As if reading my thoughts, he said, "Put it out of your mind. It's not your deal. Some things are personal, one-to-one, and they can't be solved in a court of law." He looked weary. "So. You got what you came for?"

"No," I said. "There's something else. A case you might have had a long time ago, involving a woman named Erica Hill. Maybe you won't even remember."

For a moment, he didn't say anything. Then he leaned back, put his arms behind his head. "I remember," he said. "It was right after I quit the Dudley police and moved over to the county Sheriff's Department. I remember those days better. I was just a deputy, not war-hardened yet. Kind of tore me apart, 'cause we never even came up with a suspect."

"Oh?"

"Happened out by Cochise Stronghold, just before the point that would make it Forest Service's jurisdiction. She was camping out there by herself, and around one, two o'clock in the morning, some guy in a cowboy hat with a bandanna over his face held a gun to her head. Not looking for her money."

I closed my eyes. "Raped her?" I asked.

Kyle nodded. "Whatever you can think of, he done."

I kept my eyes closed, thinking of Kyle and me, the little measuring dance we went through to stave each other off, a ritual that kept our pride intact. Rituals Erica must have played out many times. Saw her, proud, flamboyant, laughing with James on Venice Beach while little sister sat and stewed. Just one memory she must have had out of the countless memories that make up a human being, and none of them mattering out by Cochise Stronghold, wiped out as she lay faceless, terrorized in the dark—obliterated, zero, zilch, nada. How utterly lonely she must have been.

chapter twenty-four

"CHLOE?" SAID KYLE. "YOU STILL WITH ME?"

I opened my eyes. For a moment, everything seemed blurred. I held the edge of the counter to steady myself, remembered I hadn't had much sleep. "I knew her."

"Knew?"

"She was murdered. A few days ago, out at Olander Meadow. There's no suspect, but someone caught just a glimpse of the shooter. He was wearing a cowboy hat, too."

"Yeah," said Kyle. "Him and every other guy in the valley." He looked at me skeptically. "You're not thinking it was the same guy? Because if you are, I'll tell you right now to forget it."

"There's . . ." I began, reaching for my cup, my hand knocking against it, tipping it over. A pool of coffee spread over the counter. "Shit."

"Let's go outside," Kyle said. "Get you some fresh air."

We sat on the porch steps. The sun beat down directly now, but clouds were coming in from the west, occasionally blocking it, making the air turn chilly. I told Kyle everything I knew. Then we sat for a while in silence as a breeze came up and swirled the leaves in the yard, but it didn't ruffle a hair of Kyle's fascist haircut.

"Well," said Kyle finally, "it's not much, but in the absence of a suspect, if I were Ed, I *might* run with it. Except for one thing—we never had a suspect in the first place. She couldn't describe him past the bandanna and the cowboy hat. There was a full moon, but he covered himself pretty good."

"There's nothing else at all she remembered?" I asked, disappointed.

"His voice, maybe. He called her some names. But she wasn't even that hot to prosecute. A couple of months later, she called me up, said she hoped we weren't pursuing it, 'cause she'd forgotten everything anyway."

"No way she'd forget," I said. "No *way.*"

"Not much of a case, reluctant witness." He shrugged, got up off the steps. "Forget it, Chloe." He pulled one leg up to his chest. Then he pulled the other. He groaned. "Arthritis in the kneecap. One I injured playing football. I swear I'm getting old."

"Maybe later she heard a voice that reminded her?" I suggested. "It wouldn't even have had to be his voice. Or if not that, then something else, maybe something as small as a slant of light."

Kyle looked dubious.

"Post-traumatic stress disorder," I said. "Things come back after years and years. Maybe she started having flashbacks and remembered something else she never told you because she'd repressed it. Emotional memory is really specific, compared to intellectual. Maybe she suddenly figured out who raped her.

He shook his head. "So what? You know how hard it is is to make a sexual-assault case? And I figured it wasn't someone she knew. I hate it when they know the guy. Damn defense attorneys always make a big deal out of that."

He glanced at me.

I stared off into the pines.

"They're all weasels," he said.

He walked over to the steps, picked up the houseplant, pulled it out of the pot, and threw it into the woods. "Been wanting to do that for awhile." He grinned.

"If we could figure out who raped her, there'd be a suspect in the homicide," I said. "Something to go on, to match up with the evidence."

Kyle looked serious. "Chloe, we can sit here and shoot the shit about it, get all worked up, but she's not going to tell us. She's dead."

"Statute of limitations," I said doggedly, "When do they run out on a sexual-assault case?"

"*What* case? By now, the evidence from the rape kit's deteriorated—if it hasn't been thrown out. If you're that bugged about it, go tell law enforcement; that's what they're there for."

"She had an old boyfriend," I said, "who lives in the valley. I think he knows something, but he won't tell me. Lucas."

"Lucas?" said Kyle. "The roper?"

I nodded.

A grin spread over Kyle's face. "Lucas," he said fondly. "A good man."

"Clyde," I said suddenly, "Clyde Daugherty. His roping partner. Do you know him, too?"

Kyle nodded, not grinning anymore.

"What *happened* to him?"

"What do you mean, 'What *happened* to him'? Nothing good, probably. Last I heard, he was drinking hard and getting into fights." He looked at me suspiciously. "Chloe, stop playing cop; you already got a job."

"There've been times I've played cop when you didn't mind so much," I said hotly.

Kyle turned his head away. "Shit."

"Besides, *Ed's* the investigator."

He kicked at a pinecone. "I'll say this for Ed—he was the best DARE officer I ever saw. Treated the kids like he was their father. Well, he's got eight of his own."

"Um," I said.

"Sure, he's slow, but I'll stand behind him. People think he's stupid, but that can work for you sometime. Have him look up the police report." He shrugged. "Who knows? Maybe he'll find something I overlooked."

"You never told me the year."

"Let me think. Cody was born around that time, and by then, me and Laurie weren't hardly speaking. Early March. Yeah. Cody's seventeen now, so that's it. Seventeen years ago, round about."

Seventeen years ago. It hit me then. Troy was seventeen. Born in November, a Scorpio, Erica has said that. My God. I couldn't think of the implications of this now, with Kyle here. My God, I thought again. March. Erica was raped in March.

"Funny," Kyle mused, "me and Laurie hardly speaking for seventeen years."

I struggled to focus. "But you're speaking now?"

Kyle's face closed down. Up the road, a pickup was coming slowly our way. "Shit. That's my ride. I told the guys I'd help out with the Sheriff's Posse Barbecue. Come inside; I got to put on a shirt."

I followed him into the bedroom, watched as he opened the closet, took out a red flannel shirt, put it on. He looked over at me. "I got to do this barbecue deal. The sheriff'll be there. I need a job."

"I understand."

"You can leave, or you can stay and wait for me," he said. "I don't know when I'll be back. Those guys'll want to do some carousing later."

"Work," I said. "I have to be back at work."

He looked at me closely. "You're tired. At least get a few hours sleep before you get back on the road. Rain's in the forecast, and the roads might be slippery."

I *was* tired. He walked across the room and I collapsed against him. The flannel of the shirt was soft, old and worn. I put my arms under the shirt so I could feel the muscles of his back, and I rested my head on his shoulder. I felt him responding to me, not fighting it, not trying to hold back the way he had when I'd arrived.

"Hi," said Kyle. "Chloe . . ."

Then though the bedroom window, I saw the pickup truck, a man getting out. He wore a baseball cap and had a big buck teeth and a huge belt buckle. "Hey, Kyle," he shouted. "You hot to trot?"

It pissed me off. Kyle wasn't holding back, because he knew he'd be leaving. It seemed to me like a cheap thrill.

"In a minute," Kyle shouted.

"Look," he said in a low voice, "you don't think it goes through my mind what I did? You think it was nothing to me? But I didn't have a choice; it was a family matter. What, you think he should be running around wrecking more people's lives?"

"No," I said, "it's just . . ."

"It's just nothing. You want it both ways. Him dead and nobody done it."

"Kyle!" the man outside shouted. "Move it!"

Kyle backed away from me. "Got to go. See you."

"Someday," I said.

I let him go then collapsed onto the bed, beaten out by the boys. I had to think about Troy now, my revelation, but I didn't want to. I wrapped the sleeping bag around me; it smelled like Kyle's T-shirt, all pine resin and sweat and faint detergent odor.

I woke up hours later, opened my eyes, and stared at the dust balls in the corner of Kyle's bedroom. Out the window, the sky was gray. I wasn't tired anymore, but my body felt heavy with loss. I looked at my watch—four o'clock. I had to get going soon; it was a four-hour drive back to Dudley. And I was hungry.

I got up, smoothed the sleeping bag over the bed, making it neater than it had been when I lay down on it. So he'd notice when he came home and think of me. I thought of Kyle now so as not to think of Troy. I went over to the pine dresser, looked in the spotty mirror at the dark-haired woman in the plaid shirt, who didn't exactly look like me. On the top of the dresser lay a Swiss army knife, a small pinecone, nail clippers, a quarter and three pennies.

Three pennies. Just what you need to throw the I Ching. Back when I threw the I Ching a lot, my house was full of little sets of three pennies, but there wouldn't be an I Ching in Kyle's house. Tentatively, I opened the top dresser drawer. It was full of men's briefs, BVDs, all folded in perfect little squares. I touched one of the little squares, imagining him folding it. But I didn't open the next drawer down; because he was a cop, somehow I thought he might know if I had.

I went into the kitchen. Outside, the clouds parted and late-afternoon sun streamed in through the windows. The coffee cups still sat on the counter. I picked them up, put them in the sink. There was a box of Grape-Nuts in the cupboard, but I remembered the milk was sour. I ate them straight, washed down with Gatorade.

Reluctant to leave, I wiped the counters with a sponge that looked like someone had been chewing on it, then stared out the back window at the oaks and pines going on and on behind the cabin, thinking of Kyle, the impossibility of it all, the wreck of his marriage.

But now I had to think of Troy and his desire to meet his father. And of Erica, who had once wanted to be a nun, a bride of Christ. The shrine to the Virgin of Guadalupe. And she'd called Kyle a couple of months later, saying she'd forgotten all about it. And she didn't believe in abortions; she'd told Pepper that—told her she thought she could never have a child but that then she got lucky. Raped and pregnant, Troy's father a rapist.

Got lucky.

Erica did what she wanted, always had, she was braver than most of us, but what a path she'd chosen, such a high lonesome road.

I drove down from the beautiful White Mountains, drove blindly through the ponderosa and the brilliant oaks, the juniper, the pi-ñon, thinking about Erica. Vain, flamboyant, narcissistic even, but independent, too, courageous, maybe even—that overworked word—spiritual. I wouldn't have done what she did, but I had to admire her for it.

By the time I reached Safford, it was dark. I drove through the ticky-tacky outskirts of gun shops and auto-repair places, drove past the Mormon, Baptist, the Assembly of God churches. God's will, that was how they thought in all those churches. Maybe she'd thought that, too, when she discovered she was pregnant.

"They'll tell you faith is just work, plain and simple, but to me, it's a gift," Dot had said. Light streamed from the windows of the houses of Safford, where people argued, talked, loved and hated, connected to one another. But I was outside, driving in the dark, literally and figuratively, wishing things could have been different between me and Kyle. So I could lie sleepless and unhappy in an ordinary world and listen to the boys guffawing in the living room?

Let go, I thought; you wouldn't even want it.

By the time I hit I-10, the night was pitch-black; clouds hid the moon and the stars. I exited just past Willcox, got onto a long, straight two-lane blacktop and opened my window. The dark wind rushed in, smelling of rain as my headlights made a tunnel of light through the darkness.

There's nothing so lonely as a country road at night. For company, I turned on my tape player—Emmy Lou Harris singing "This Sweet Old World," her voice haunting, achingly sad. Lights twinkled around me, but far away, on the rim of the earth.

Let go, I thought again, and suddenly it seemed to me the night wasn't so lonely, but full of life; rabbits crouched on the edges of the arc of my headlights, owls, deer, javelina. And I was headed for Dudley, for people I knew, for my house, which I'd been occupying like a stranger. It didn't need to be that way. I was headed home.

It was a little after 9:00 P.M. when I reached Dudley. Rain fell in little hissy-fit drops on my windshield as I drove up the hill to my house and pulled into the carport. The house was dark; I realized I should have left a light on. The car panted exhaustedly, but aside from that, everything seemed very quiet, not even enough rain to make a sound on my tin roof. Sunday night in Dudley. Where was Big Foot? After this long an absence, he should be waiting for me at the door, I thought.

I got out of the car and stood in the cool evening air, rubbing my shoulders to get the stiffness out. I picked up the Sunday paper, which was lying in the carport, then opened the kitchen door. I stopped, my hand still on the knob. Something felt wrong.

It was lighter outside than inside the house. Straining my eyes, I waited for them to adjust, till I could see past the kitchen counter, in through the dining room to the living room. I saw a dark shape silhouetted against the French doors, heard a creak, and they opened. Simultaneously, I reached for the kitchen light, flicked it on.

Stuart.

In an instant, his concern for Troy, anger about Erica—a slew of little half memories, impressions, unformed until now, flashed through my mind.

I screamed.

chapter twenty-five

STUART STOOD ON THE THRESHOLD OF the French doors, a shocked look on his face, as if I'd just slapped him. "Jesus Christ, Chloe," he said. "It's *me.*"

"How was I supposed to know that?" I said angrily. But I *had* known—Stupid, what was I thinking? *Stuart?*—my heart still thud-thudding in my chest as if it weren't yet convinced. I took a deep breath and walked farther into the kitchen, my knees shaky. I put the Sunday paper on the counter.

"Breaking and entering now?" I said to lighten things up, but my voice sounded wrong.

"The door wasn't locked. I just opened it and walked in." He came over to the counter and sat down on a stool. I smelled a whiff of burnt tobacco. His blond hair looked slightly damp. Of course, I thought, his truck wasn't outside; he must have walked over in the rain. "I was sitting out on your porch, smoking."

"In the dark?"

"You don't have to see to smoke. I thought if I turned on a light, you'd see it and get worried." He gave me a self-pitying look, inno-cence falsely accused. "You should lock your doors. Especially now, after . . ." He shrugged.

"I lock them when I'm home," I said. "And where's my cat?"

"I haven't seen any cat." He paused and looked me up and down.

"Where were you anyway? You look different, kind of, I don't know, like a . . . cowgirl."

My blue plaid shirt, jeans—clothes for seeing Kyle in. "I just needed to get away," I said evasively, angry at him for making me feel like an errant wife.

The kitchen light shone on his wire-rimmed glasses, glittered off his earring. Our last conversation about Erica nagged at me. My hands trembled ever so slightly. Hypervigilance. Nerves. I'd just driven a couple hundred miles or so and back in one day. Had hardly eaten a thing.

Stuart looked suddenly forlorn. "Mind if I smoke in here?"

For a second, I wanted to say no, punish him, but I got the ashtray off the top of the refrigerator, plunked it down. "Be my guest."

I rummaged through a cupboard until I found a box of saltines. "I still don't know what you're doing here."

Stuart lit up. "I called you and called you. You never said you were going anywhere. I was worried. I mean, that librarian's still missing."

"You didn't seem to care that she was missing yesterday."

"I was just pissed," he said.

I sat down at the counter with the saltines and ate one, then two more. Salty, hard to swallow, a stick-to-your-throat dryness. "What's it to you anyway?"

He looked defensive. "Like I said, I was concerned."

I got up again and ran myself a glass of water. De rigueur with saltines and hypervigilance. "How's Troy doing?" I asked.

"Okay, considering. He's met Mariah and Wally. I went with him; we had lunch at the Copper Queen." An accusing note crept into his voice. "You were *invited*."

"Are they going to take him? Adopt him or something?"

"Troy doesn't know if he wants that. Wally was a trooper, but Mariah got all teary-eyed. That woman needs counseling or something. She scared the hell out of Troy, telling him how he'd love L.A. He's always thought of her as the wicked aunt. I told him I'd see if he has any choice, any rights."

I felt sad. Poor Troy, nothing left of his former life. "Can he go back to the house? I mean, someone needs to clean up Erica's room before he does."

"He's still staying with me. Ed Masters showed up to question him about the room being trashed."

"Why? Troy was in jail when it happened. And he told you he doesn't know anything."

"The thing is, no one knows for sure when it happened. Ed asked me if I looked in Erica's room the day I was over there when Troy was arrested. He thinks Troy could have done it himself."

"What utter bullshit," I said angrily.

Stuart shrugged. "Of course it is."

"I mean, I *know* it's bullshit." I closed the box of saltines, got up so I wouldn't have to look at Stuart, and said, "*I* was in Erica's room after you left."

"You were?" said Stuart eagerly. "You'd testify to that?"

"If I have to," I said, walking to the door.

"What were you doing in. . . ." Stuart began.

Snooping, spying, going out of bounds. "Kitty, kitty, kitty," I called loudly, drowning out the rest of his question. I went past him, across to the open French doors. "Kitty, kitty, kitty."

In the living room, my message light was blinking.

"Messages!" I said brightly. I pressed the message button.

Stuart's voice. "Hi, Chloe. Guess who? I know it's early, but I thought we should talk. Call me when you get up. Bye."

Blip.

"Hi, Chloe," Stuart again, "well, it's ten A.M. Where are you? You're invited to lunch at the Queen with Troy, Wally, and Mariah. Want to give me a ring?"

Blip.

"Chloeeee, it's Lourdes, your neighbor. Big Foot's over here and he won't leave. I didn't want you to worry. I think he's angry about something."

"Thank God," I said.

"Hi, Chloe, me again, you know, Stuart? Well it's five P.M. My home number, in case you forgot, is five five five–two two two oh."

"That's right," called Stuart, "humiliate me."

"Hi, Chloe, Stuart Ross here; it's now eight-fifty. If you're there, pick up. Or I'm coming over. Bye."

"Chloe? Chloe, are you there? This is Frankie and it's eight-fifty-seven. We got a call-out, and I'd sure like you to go on this one. It's Dot Stone. She's okay but I'm going there now, so get on over as soon as you get this message."

I looked at my watch: 9:15. Frankie would have left from Willcox. If I hurried, I could get there almost as soon as she could.

"Dot Stone?" said Stuart.

"Stuart, shut up."

He got off the stool and started toward me. Instinctively, I backed away.

"This thing with Erica," he said urgently. "I know I reacted like a shit, but my ego was involved. Can you understand that? We need to *talk*."

For a moment, I stared at him. It wasn't that I was wholly innocent; I'd pawed shamelessly through his photos, but now just the sight of him filled me with a strange, mindless fatigue, my body still alert but my brain exhausted. "We need to *talk*." Erica had said something like that to me in the parking lot: ". . . let's get together sometime and talk." But I'd decided to be too busy, to punish her for being such good friends with my favorite brother.

Kyle had been too busy, too, going to the Sheriff's Posse Barbecue, sewing up his new job; I'd been too busy to stick around until he came home. Probably that was just as well, but what did Stuart want from me now—something small, unimportant? Maybe just a moment of intimacy, which we were all too busy to get around to?

I'd wanted to trust him. I almost had. Feeling safe in his house until I found the photograph. Stuart had lied to me once about how well he knew Erica. I could understand that—it was just ego and pride. But maybe he'd lied to me again, to cover up something more ominous.

Like what?

I couldn't take the chance until I knew more. No wonder I got dizzy sometime when I thought too much. Besides now there was Dot.

"Later," I said. "Where's my purse?"

chapter twenty-six

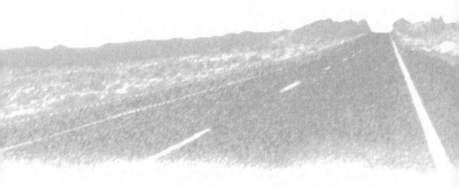

ALL THE LIGHTS WERE ON AT DOT'S HOUSE, as if she were having a party, and Frankie's pickup was parked in the driveway, along with Dot's station wagon, a deputy's car, and Ed's Geo. A dog barked warningly as I got out of my car. Fudd.

"Quiet, you!" a voice said.

I looked over to where it came from. The light was on in the screened porch and a sheriff's deputy was standing inside. I hurried over. He was young and Hispanic and very serious-looking. Right next to where he stood on the matting was a broken blue pottery cup and a large dark stain.

I swallowed, but the lump in my throat didn't go down. "Is that *blood*?"

He gave a short laugh, looking disgusted. "Cocoa. Dot was out here drinking cocoa and someone shot at her." He gestured at a couple of jagged holes in the screen. "Don't worry—he missed."

The front door was wide open, so I walked in. In the living room, Ed sat on the edge of a brown vinyl recliner, Dot and Frankie on a brown-and-yellow-flowered couch. Frankie, dressed in brilliant pink sweats, was holding Dot's hand and patting it, and Dot had her head back and her eyes closed. Her glasses lay on the coffee table, next to her shotgun.

"Look, Dot, Chloe's here," Frankie said.

Dot opened her eyes and looked at me, her eyes pale and unfocused. "I dropped down at the first shot," she said. "Fired off a few rounds from my knees." Her voice was querulous, old-womanish. "But I missed him."

"My God." I looked at her in astonishment. "It's lucky you had your shotgun with you."

I sat down on the couch beside her. She wore men's blue-striped pajamas, Daddy's probably, one sleeve stained with cocoa. The top fit her oddly, too square and bulging at the chest.

Frankie's eyes, rimmed with midnight blue mascara met mine. "Luck had nothing to do with it. And that's a bulletproof vest, she's wearing."

"Daddy's," said Dot with satisfaction. "From when he was a deputy back in '72. Knew I'd find a use for it sooner or later."

"Dot Stone, you're a damn fool," said Ed Masters sternly. It was cool in Dot's house, but his broad pink forehead was peppered with sweat. He wiped it with the sleeve of his navy blue cop windbreaker. "Acting like some kind of decoy is what you was doing."

"You sat out there on purpose," I said to Dot. "Hoping he'd shoot at you?"

Ed snorted. "You really wanted to help, you'd of called nine one one before you fired off that shotgun."

Dot rallied. She sat up straight and let go of Frankie's hand. She felt on the coffee table for her glasses and put them on. Her voice was firm. "I wanted to try and hit him first."

"But you didn't," said Ed, "so now he's long gone. And it's grass out there by the orchard. It's been trampled, but it don't take no footprints. We'll be back when it's light." He hefted himself up tiredly.

Dot glanced at him with scorn, then looked away, smoothing her pajama bottoms around her legs. Her hands were spotty and wrinkled and there were dark smudges on the knees of the pajama legs.

"Glad you could make it," she said to me, as if greeting me at an informal get-together among old friends. "I sure talked your head off about my kids the last time." She got up off the couch. "Here, let me show you some pictures, so you can put a face to those names."

I followed her to an old upright piano shoved against the opposite wall, covered with a bright Mexican blanket and crowded with framed photographs. "That's Ernest right there." She pointed to a high school class picture of Ernest, face blank and nearly obliterated by an air-brush. "And here's my Ruthie, and that's Henry."

Ed paced the room, looking out windows. "You know what people been saying, don't you, Dot?"

"What's that, Ed?" said Dot over her shoulder.

"That you know who shot that bookmobile lady. That you saw him real good."

"I already told you ten or twenty times, Ed," said Dot. "I *never*."

"Then why are they saying it?"

I looked at the pictures while they bickered. Henry was hand-some certainly, strong-jawed and clear-eyed, but Ernest didn't look bad, either, and Ruthie was a teenage dream. All three of them nice, clean, expressionless kids. I cursed whoever had invented the air-brush.

"I don't want you staying here tonight," said Ed. "We ain't got enough deputies to keep an eye on you. We're not leaving till you do. That's that, Dot Stone, and I won't listen to argument. You think I want some old lady shot dead on my conscience?"

"Ed, you got the worst way of putting things," said Frankie.

"Dot!" I said, attempting to shut them all up. "The one with all the kids out in front of Valley Union? What was it, Henry's senior class? And *Lucas* is in it, too."

"You better go with Ernest when he comes," said Frankie, "but don't you listen to Ed. You done real good, Dot. Why, they could have used you over in Vietnam."

"That's right," Dot said to me, "Henry and Lucas were the same graduating class. Excuse me, but I got to put on some clothes. And pack some things, but it's for one night only, Ed Masters." She walked across the living room.

"We'll see about—" Ed began.

I broke in, holding the picture of Henry's senior class aloft. "I've seen this guy before, too," I said, "At Lucas's. Isn't he Clyde? Clyde Daugherty."

Dot stopped in her tracks, just where the living room turned into a hall, and looked over at me. "I guess," she said. "No one wants to talk about Clyde now." The light glinted off her glasses, so I couldn't see her eyes, but I had the impression they were blank. Ed wiped his forehead in the heat.

A vehicle pulling up outside broke the silence. A door slammed. Ed coughed. "That'll be Ernest," he said. His voice was subdued.

Dot vanished down the hall. Ernest came in the door, wearing gray coveralls, his name embroidered in red on the bib. I half-expected to see a big bag of tools in his hand. He wasn't wearing his cap. Without it, he'd lost a certain grandeur, become a small, aging man, losing his hair.

"Goddamn it, Ed, didn't I tell you to have a couple of deputies looking out for her," he said belligerently. He looked nervous, distraught. He opened his hands, then closed them into fists.

Ed said patiently, "Ernest, we ain't got but one, and there's other crimes, too."

"What the hell we pay taxes for, then?" Ernest demanded loudly. "When we can't get no protection? This here is a matter of life and death. Life and death and . . ." He didn't seem to know how to continue.

Ed said, "Well, we pay 'em for the library district and we pay 'em for all that environmental stuff and for that new paved road over by Tombstone, so next time you come to vote, you might think about paying some more for law enforcement. Plus, your ma set herself up. Your ma's crazy, Ernest; you need to consider that."

Dot came in from the other room, dressed in her usual man's khaki pants and a bright red sweatshirt. The sweatshirt lent color to her face and made her look hearty. She was carrying an old brown hard suitcase with an ancient sticker on it that said SAN DIEGO.

Ernest looked at Dot worriedly. "Ma! Are you okay?" He walked over and tried to reach for the suitcase, but she held it away from him.

"I can carry it; there's nothing wrong with me. All I got in it's toothpaste, toothbrush and my pj's. I'm just going over for the night."

Ernest sighed. We'll talk about it on the way, okay?"

"If you think I'm going with you in that truck, you're dead wrong. I'm taking my car. You think I want to be way over there without any transportation?"

"Ed," I said, "I'd like to talk to you for a minute. It's important."

"Not now," he said impatiently. "I've got an investigation to run, Chloe. Give me a call tomorrow, or the next day."

"Frankie?" I said.

But Frankie had slipped out quietly, melted away into the night. I walked outside to a cacophony of pickups, cars, and a van, all trying to get away from me as fast they could. Even Fudd, in the back of Dot's station wagon, stuck his doggy head out the window as she drove off and barked nervously at me as I got in my car.

I headed after them down the dirt road, bumped into the wash, bumped back up again. Everyone so busy, like Ed, on their own little track. No one had listened to me, but I had the broader picture. More pieces of the jigsaw—that tired old image—trial lawyers used in their opening arguments to a jury. Erica's rape, Stuart, Lucas. And one more piece, which even I hadn't tried to fit in: the woman Larry had seen coming out of Nelson's house with Erica two months ago. *Two months ago.* And as far as I could figure out, it was just about two months ago when it had all started.

Sally Smith.

chapter twenty-seven

I THOUGHT OF SALLY SMITH AS I DROVE TO work the next morning. The leaves of the young cottonwoods were intensely yellow in the soft, cloudy light. I breathed in the rich smell of decay in the fall air and thought, I have to find her. Everyone else is too busy. And Nelson might know where she is.

I didn't have to be in court; I could check in, check out. I stopped in for my messages.

"You have a visitor," said Gigi happily, all decked out for Monday in a burnt orange dress with a big gold belt buckle. "I told her you weren't here yet, but she said she'd wait. Maria."

Shit. I didn't have any clients called Maria at the moment, but that didn't mean anything.

I went back outside to my separate entrance, and there she was, sitting on the steps outside my office, where Neva and Jude had sat on Friday. She was wearing a shapeless linen dress and thick-soled linen espadrilles with ankle ties, which made her feet look small and helpless. Her hair of many colors looked unbrushed, untended.

"Hi, Mariah," I said cautiously.

She stood up, stumbled, grabbed the iron railing for balance. "Could we talk?"

"Come on in."

I unlocked the door and she followed me into the waiting room. On the floor, the huggy bears that Volunteers carried in a tote bag to give out to victimized children spilled out from a black plastic bag. Handmade bears, a donation from the ladies of the Sierra Vista Senior Center.

"Excuse the mess," I said.

She sat down abruptly on the hideous sagging brown couch without comment. I sat down beside her. "How are you doing?"

"All right," she said in a wavery voice. "I wanted to ask you about the . . . the investigation. If they found out who . . ." Her mouth trembled. "Who . . ." She began to cry.

Blindly, she reached down, grabbed a huggy bear, pink gingham with a red bow, and blubbered into it, using it like a handkerchief to wipe her tears.

I went into my office, got a box of Kleenex, brought it back, and set it down beside her. She grabbed a handful. I waited, and after awhile, her sobs receded.

"I . . . I'm *sorry*," she said, her voice muffled through the Kleenex.

"Nothing to be sorry about," I said. "Cry as long as you want."

She shook her head, then blew her nose vehemently. "It's okay. I'm going to stop." Her voice was determined. She took a deep hiccuping breath and squeezed the bear. He was missing one eye. "It's *Wally*."

"Oh?"

She nodded, staring past me at the magazine rack, which was full of five-year-old *Ranger Rick*s, as well as ancient copies of *Sunset* and *Good Housekeeping*. "He's . . . he's *left* me."

"Left you? *Wally*?"

She nodded. "Yesterday afternoon, we were going to drive to the scene, so I could videotape it. I walked over to Main Street to get some things I needed, and when I came back, he was . . . Wally was *gone*." She dropped the bear. "I couldn't sleep all night. I called our house in L.A. this morning early, but no one answered."

"Why do you think he's left you?" I said. "Don't you mean he's missing?"

Mariah's eyes got round, as if this was a new idea. "I . . . I don't . . . He left a note. I mean, we *were* fighting. He kept saying there was nothing we could do here, unless someone was arrested. I mean, if they arrest someone, I want to videotape it . . . Anyway, he wanted to leave, take Troy with us, but Troy and I, we . . . we haven't really *bonded.* In the note, he said I would have to decide, that he couldn't do any more."

So good old reliable Wally had finally burned out.

"It's horrible without him," Mariah went on. "I keep remembering the last time. Erica and I were bickering the whole time, and then when she came back from that camping trip, she wouldn't even speak to me anymore. She went straight to her room and closed the door and wouldn't come out or even answer when I knocked. She stayed there the whole day."

In her room, traumatized, because on that camping trip she'd been brutally raped. Erica and her pride, too proud to tell her sister what had happened, too proud to let herself be seen as a victim.

"Finally, that evening," Mariah went on, "Wally and I just left. What else could we have done?"

"It doesn't sound like you had a choice," I said.

For a moment, she looked thoughtful; then she put the bear in a sitting position on the couch and stood up.

"I guess you have work to do," she said. "I don't want to take up all your time. Thank you for listening. Would you call me if they arrest anyone? I'll be at the Copper Queen."

I got up, too, walked her to the door, stood there while she started down the outside steps in her thick-soled espadrilles. She stopped, reached in her purse, pulled out her big sunglasses, and put them on. She looked back. "I told you she called me, didn't I? Just a few weeks ago?"

"Yes," I said.

"I know what you're thinking."

"Oh?"

"That when she finally called me, I should have called her back right away." She bowed her head, as if waiting for the judgment.

"You don't *have* to take on blame," I said. "There were years of anger between you two. It sounds to me as though she treated you very badly. Maybe you deserved to have her try harder than just one phone call."

Mariah put her hand on the iron railing by the steps. I couldn't see her eyes behind the sunglasses. "What *I* keep thinking is, because I didn't call her back, she won." Her mouth trembled. "She was always doing that . . . *winning.*"

I couldn't think of anything to say.

"Well." She shrugged. "Bye."

"Bye, Mariah," I said. She looked small and pale, fading into the beige background of the county attorney's offices, as if she were nothing but a big pair of sunglasses. If she turned her head away, she would vanish entirely. "Take care."

I went back to my office and called Nelson and Larry's. Nelson answered.

"Nelson," I said. "Larry told me that Sally Smith is one of your clients."

"Larry mentioned your conversation," he said. "Yes, she is."

"Do you know where she is?"

"Possibly."

"Please. I need to talk to her. It's very urgent."

There was a long silence. Then he sighed. "Maybe you should stop by here. I'll be around all day."

I hung up, called Gigi to tell her I'd be out for the day, and then locked up my office. Thoughts of my talk with Mariah were still nibbling at my mind. Mariah, and Wally, until now her faithful defender. Something was bothering me about that. What?

chapter twenty-eight

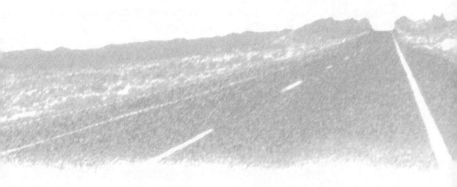

THE PINK HOUSE WITH THE TEAL TRIM LOOKED immaculate, as always, its perfection seemingly impervious to anything the outside world could do. As I parked in front, Larry came out the door, wearing old jeans and a long-sleeved pink shirt, his hair wonderfully tousled.

"Hi." His voice was rueful. "Guess I kind of lost it the other day."

"God," I said, "who could blame you?"

"Nelson's in there." He nodded toward the house. "I promised I'd take a walk—client confidentiality—but to tell the truth, I'm dying to be a fly on the wall. You'll have to come over sometime when he's gone and we'll talk our heads off. Not about that, of course." He smiled—a smile without guile, open, not trying anymore to charm, to seduce.

Nelson appeared at the front door.

Suddenly, Larry's mask was back on. He took some keys out of his pocket, tossed them in the air, caught them, and sauntered over to the red Ford Cherokee in the driveway.

"I thought you were taking a *walk,*" Nelson said.

Larry got in the Cherokee and leaned out the window. "Changed my mind," he said cheerily.

"Don't forget dinner," said Nelson. "Pork roast with *prunes.*"

Larry smiled. "It's hours and hours to dinner." His voice was flippant. He started the car.

Nelson looked after him worriedly as he drove off.

We went inside and I sat on the couch and Nelson on the chair slipcovered in white duck. He looked careworn, bags under his eyes, as if he'd thought too hard on his retreat.

"I had no idea Sally didn't tell anyone she was leaving," he said. "She stopped by on her way out of town and gave me a key to her place so I could water the plants."

"She didn't even tell her boss," I said.

Nelson nodded. "I called Neva back, told her Sally is okay."

"And the investigator thinks she's missing, too."

"She didn't like the investigator. I don't think he handled her very well." Nelson clasped and unclasped his hands. The light came through the gauzy curtains, filtered to a dreamy haze. *Here we are safe.* But we weren't. "He needs to understand how fragile she is."

"Well, he may have to talk to her again," I said. "Fragile or not, she shouldn't have just taken off. It's possible she knows more than she's told anyone."

"If so, I'm not aware of it."

"Nelson, look," I said. "I've already talked to her once. I know what she's like. But Larry told me Erica came to one of your groups, and that's how she met Sally."

"He shouldn't have told you that," said Nelson sadly.

"As a victim advocate, I'm bound by confidentiality as much as you are."

"Sally's been coming to groups for a long time; we finish one and go on to the next. She's comfortable in the group situation, but lately, I don't thinks she's growing." He sighed, an anxious man in a beautiful room. "Counselors learn techniques, how to deal with situations, but sometimes I think mental illness is like a virus. It adapts and changes to protect itself. Maybe you should talk to her. See if there's anything the investigator really needs to know. After all, you're experienced with victims. She's in Tucson."

"I can drive to Tucson. Now. Right away."

"Let me go in the other room and give her a call."

I leaned forward. "Nelson," I said, "when I saw her last, she was so frightened. *Scared to death.*"

He looked sad. "She's been that way ever since I met her."

Nelson went through the dining room into the kitchen and closed the door. It took awhile for him to come back. I waited in the beautiful room, so orderly and undisturbed. Surely, it required work, a joint effort to keep this room so serene, a joint effort to create it. I didn't think they'd called in a decorator. They must have worked on it for months, long evenings of planning, days of getting everything just right.

I thought of an H. G. Wells short story, "The Pearl of Love," its message that once a work of art has been completed, the only thing still required is to remove what has inspired it. All was not right in Larry and Nelson's work of art. Bickerings, undercurrents. What was it Larry had said, standing at the door of Erica's room, distraught, defenses down, "And *Nelson,* Nelson hated . . ."

Hated what?

Or whom? Erica? Because Larry had loved her? I looked at the closed door to the kitchen. There were other doors, too, all closed. Were the rooms behind them different, rooms that existed in chaos? Rooms as full of loss, as brutal in their own way as Erica's room had looked to me just two days ago?

Nelson returned, looking as though he'd engaged in mortal combat and emerged the victor, but underneath, worry and tension were palpable. "It's okay," he said. "She'll talk to you. I wrote down the directions to the house, and her phone number, too, in case you get lost. She *liked* you. You need to get going. I hear it's storming again in Tucson."

I drove out of Dudley, late morning, under cloudy skies with raincoat, umbrella, and my snub-nosed .38, which I'd tucked in the glove compartment. I didn't make a habit of carrying it, but Sally's paranoia had infected me. "He's going to kill me, too," she'd said.

The closer I got to Tucson, the darker the clouds became, the heavy air dense with moisture. I hit the Tucson traffic at about one o'clock, the wind rising as I passed the Kolb Road exit. By the time I got to Ina, clear on the other side of town, it was buffeting my car and whirling up trash by the roadside. The smell of rain, rich and herbaceous, filled my car. Suddenly, I was filled with a huge release of energy, endless and ever-increasing.

I exited at Ina, entering a noisy world of gas stations, fast-food places, and supermarkets, then turned north on a side street of lower-income adobe houses with red tile roofs. Kids were out in the street, their arms raised to the first pelter of raindrops. Then suddenly, the sky fell apart and the rain came hard and fast, so even the kids ran inside, screaming. Raindrops beat on my car, encasing me in an oddly soundless world. Looking through the rain-streaked windshield, I saw the houses get larger as I drove, and by the time I reached 509, the number Nelson had given me, they were solidly middle-class.

I parked, reached in the back, and retrieved my umbrella, but I left the raincoat. I got out of the car and opened the umbrella. Rain pelted down on the thin black nylon and water dripped down the spines onto my neck. Number 509 was surrounded by a high stucco wall with a fancy wrought-iron gate in the center. I pushed open the cool, wet gate and walked into the yard. Orange bird-of-paradise grew in profusion along the front of the house, and in the center of the yard was a desert willow, its orchidlike lavender blooms heavy with rain.

For a second, I paused. I'd left the gun in the car. I'd brought it—for what? To shoot at anyone who followed me. To kill, presumably, in defense of Sally Smith, victim. I wouldn't need it now, at this quiet middle-class house. I saw a child's tricycle in the corner, out in the rain, a Space Ranger toy perched on its seat. Relatives, of course. Neva had mentioned a sister. Sally had run to her relatives, and in a minute I would probably be meeting them.

Polite introductions, offers of coffee, kids underfoot, and worried looks all around.

I went up one step to the front door and pressed a round white doorbell, wondering if it worked. Even if it did, the rain was so noisy, would anyone hear? While I stood there, the rain stopped, as suddenly as it had begun, replaced by an eerie silence; just the rainwater dripping off the red tile roof, dripping off the blooms of the desert willow.

From somewhere, I heard music. Ethereal music. The Beach Boys.

I pressed the button again.

A thin little voice called out, "Who's there?"

"It's Chloe," I said loudly. "The victim advocate?"

"Wait a minute," the voice said.

Strange noises came from inside, clanks and rattles. Finally, the door opened.

The Beach Boys were louder now; "...in my room..." Their voices were so soothing.

I registered this in some part of my mind, but what I saw was something else. Standing as if in the very center of the Beach Boys harmony, so golden with childhood sunshine, was Sally Smith, and up about the middle of her chest was a gun—a serious gun, big and deadly, a .357 Magnum probably, and it was pointed at me.

chapter twenty-nine

I DIDN'T KNOW ENOUGH ABOUT .357 MAG-
nums to know if the safety was on, but the way she was holding it, she could break her wrist if she fired. Easily. Her wrists were so tiny, so fragile. She didn't look like she knew how to use it, and that made her doubly dangerous.

"Could you get rid of the gun?" I said.

"I'm sorry." She lowered it. "I just had to make sure it was really you. I didn't mean to scare you. Please come in."

I hesitated. "Maybe you should put that somewhere safe. It makes me nervous."

She looked down, holding the gun awkwardly, pointing it at the floor now. She was wearing a long beige dress printed with tiny brown teddy bears, and next to it the gun looked like a giant scorpion in an itty-bitty zoo. "Me, too. I don't know if I could actually *use* it."

"No," I said. "And from the way you were holding it, anyone would have been able to tell that you couldn't. They might have used it against you."

She blinked in shock. I could have bitten my tongue. At least it had given her the illusion of safety.

"Please, come inside," she said. "I'll put this away."

She locked the door after me, shooting the dead bolt home, putting on the chain. I followed her down a hall, stepping over strands of what looked like fishing line, tied to tin cans. "What's this?" I asked.

"Oh." She ducked her head and looked embarrassed. "It's my . . . alarm system. In case someone breaks in. I can hear it over the music."

We walked on pale blue carpeting into a large living room.

"Little surfer girl," sang the Beach Boys. The windows in the living room were strung up with more fishing line and cans in an intricate jumble, reminding me of a Rube Goldberg drawing. A small, very round striped tabby lay on the couch.

"That's Sugar," said Sally, sounding like a proud parent. "Sugar," she cooed, "this is Chloe."

Sugar stretched on the couch, claws out, and gave a bored pink yawn. Sally reached out to pet her with the hand that didn't have the gun, and the cat grabbed a finger, bit it playfully.

"Sally," I said firmly, "I think you should put the gun away before you do anything else. Where did you get a gun like that, anyway?"

"My brother-in-law. He has lots of guns," she said confidingly. "He keeps them in the bedroom, under lock and key. But I found the key, after they left. They went to Disneyland. Please sit down. I could get you some lemonade."

"That would be nice."

I sat next to Sugar on the huge couch, which was covered in a dull beige striped material. In one corner was a small organ, and over that hung a stitched sampler with the words *No Other Success Can Compensate for Failure in the Home.*

On the next table next to me, under a lamp shade decorated with little bobbles, a china kitten played with a ball of yarn. Two red velvet recliners and a beige-upholstered wing chair were grouped in a semi-circle. A bookcase lined the wall beside me and I leaned to look. *The Miracle of Forgiveness, The Autobiography of Praley P. Pratt, The Evening Manual 1995, The Discourses of Brigham Young.*

Mormon. Sally's sister was a Mormon, and I was at this moment sitting in a shrine, the living room, of a Mormon home.

Sally returned, carrying two glasses of lemonade. "Nelson said he told Neva I was okay. Poor Neva. It was wrong of me not to tell her. Her life is tragic enough anyway." She put the glasses on the coffee table and turned the Beach Boys down to a low hum.

"Neva's life is *tragic*?" I asked.

"She and . . . and Myron. You know Myron? Jude's brother? He sweeps up at the library. He and Neva were in love. Then he had this accident; that's why he's the way he is."

I paused, my hand on the glass of lemonade, my impressions of Neva, Jude, and Myron, turned topsy-turvy. The three of them, locked into some kind of inescapable triangle. It *was* tragic—but that was another story.

Sally sat on the couch. "I should have let her know. But all I could think of was getting away."

"Why?" I asked. "Why did you have to get away? Remember when we talked last? You said, 'He's going to kill me, too.' Who were you talking about?"

She reached for the lemonade, like a blind woman, feeling her way, then withdrew her hand and held it with the other, tightly, her knuckles turning white.

The Beach Boys hummed on like cosmic cicadas in the background. Sally took a deep breath. "The man, of course," she replied, her voice rising, "the man who killed Erica."

"But no one knows who did it," I said. "Do you?"

"No! How could you think . . . Of course I don't!" She was almost shouting. She clutched at a cushion. The cat leaped off the couch and crouched under the wing chair.

"Relax," I said. "You're safe, Sally. There's nothing here to hurt you."

She hugged herself, rocking slowly back and forth, eyes closed tightly. "She's real fine," whispered the Beach Boys from out of the golden past. I waited, let her rock herself back.

When she seemed stabilized, I said, "It's okay to be scared. Lots of people are scared about this. The thing is, Sally, we need to catch him."

She opened her eyes for just a second. "So?"

"I know a lot of things you don't realize I know," I said. "For instance, you and Erica had a talk after one of Nelson's counseling sessions. And I have a pretty good idea what you talked about. You talked about rape, didn't you? How Erica was raped once. And you were, too. You were, weren't you, Sally?" I hated myself. It was just a guess. What if I was wrong?

She opened her eyes, hands falling to her sides. "Nelson told you?" she whispered.

"No," I said.

"It was a few years ago. That's why I was going to group. To . . . to deal with it."

"Good," I said reassuringly. "It sounds like you're working on it, then."

She didn't looked convinced. "Well, I didn't deal with it very well when it happened. I didn't even call the police. It was like I was walking around but was in a coma. I was Mormon, you know, and I broke it off with the man I was engaged to. I wasn't a virgin anymore. My sister says the bishop would have said it was okay that it wasn't anything I did wrong. But then a month later, my father died. I . . . I had this idea that somehow Daddy knew about it and it killed him. I thought it was my fault, somehow."

She stopped and leaned over. "Sugar," she called, "Sugar, come here."

Sugar stared up at her with chilly eyes.

"Rape is terrible," I said. "Devastating. Of course it wasn't your fault."

"I know." She sighed. "I learned that in group. Nelson says I didn't get good intervention. He says if I had, I might have been okay. But Erica *dealt* with it. She was like a superstar, the way she dealt with it. I think that's why Nelson got her to come to group; he thought she could help me. But it was a new group, and a lot of people talked, and neither of us really got to say much. But afterward . . ." She paused.

"Afterward . . ." I prompted.

"Erica came up to me at the door and started a conversation. I really admired her. She was the kind of person I would have liked to be. Anyway, I hardly ever do this, but I asked her back to my house." She stopped. "Sugar?" she said. "Kitty, kitty."

Sugar backed away farther under the wing chair.

Sally went on. "Anyway, we went to my house and talked for

awhile; then she asked me if I was happy with my life. And I said that it wasn't a life exactly, but it was the best I could do. So she told me that when she was raped, she'd tried to come to terms with what had happened to her, tried to understand why someone would do a thing like that. 'I still can't forgive,' she said, 'but, believe it or not, some good came out of it.' See, she knew who did it, and in the end, she decided not to tell."

"She *knew* who did it?"

"Yes. She said not right away, but later."

Later, I thought, later she'd have wanted to protect Troy. *"Sally, did she tell you who it was?"*

"No," said Sally, fiercely. "She never did. And I certainly wasn't going to ask."

She got up, went to the wing chair, and dragged Sugar out. The cat hung limply as she carried her back to the couch. She said confidingly, "There's a hard part coming up. I really need Sugar."

She kissed the top of the cat's head.

"Then she told me exactly what had happened to her. And as she talked, I got more and more scared. I was actually *shaking*. I started to cry. She got me a glass of water and she sat there and waited. So finally, I told her."

Sally gave a long, shuddering breath. The cat leaped free and hid under the organ.

"Told her?"

"I figured it out when she was describing it. The details—there was a bandanna, a gun, the way . . ." She shuddered. *"Everything* was the same as what had happened to me. It was later I was raped, eight years ago, but it was the *same man."* She looked queasy suddenly, put her hand over her mouth. "Excuse me," she said, getting up.

The same man, I thought as I waited for Sally to come back. I'd been hoping Erica had confided in Sally, told her something Sally was afraid to tell, but I hadn't expected this. The Beach Boys switched off as I sat there; water drip-dripped from the eaves of the house.

Maybe, hearing Sally's story, Erica had started to remember more than she wanted to. The classic thing about delayed flashbacks. And she'd found out he'd raped someone else, might still be doing it. If only Sally had reported it, maybe Kyle could have reopened the case, caught the guy, because Erica said *she knew who it was.*

Sally came back, looking embarrassed, bringing with her a sour smell masked with the minty smell of toothpaste.

"I'm sorry," she said, sitting down.

"No," I protested. "Please. Don't be. Are you okay?"

She nodded.

For a moment, I wanted to yell, scream at her, Why didn't you find out who it was? Why didn't you tell in the first place? It's *your* fault that Erica's dead. Your fault. But I kept my peace.

Sally sighed. "Anyway, after I told her, she changed. She went far away, like she was thinking about something else. She was angry, too. Not at me. But angry. I didn't want them to know at the library. When she got the job, I didn't talk much to Erica there."

Eight years ago, I thought. Were there others, before and after? Scared to tell, totally traumatized, like Sally? Had some of them reported it but no one made a connection?

Sally reached over and picked up the lemonade, then put it back down again. "Then, of course, he killed her."

"It's a possibility," I said. "But how can you be sure?"

"Because." She took a deep breath. "I guess I have to tell. At least now, if he kills me, maybe he'll get caught." She closed her eyes. "Maybe I'm ready to die. You see, Erica came to my house one more time, Thursday night, the Thursday before she was murdered."

"Oh," I said.

"She came to my door about six o'clock. She said she couldn't come in but that she wanted me to know something. She told me she'd thought long and hard and she'd finally made a decision and she would try to leave me out of it."

Sally put her hand on her chest and took a long, deep breath. "I asked her, 'Leave me out of what?' Erica said, 'I survived, but you didn't. There has to be justice in the world, *this* world, not later. I'm going to make him pay. I swear, I'm going to make him pay.' "

Sally gave a gasp like a hiccup. "But she didn't. Don't you see?

He got to her first. Do I have to talk to that *investigator*? Do I really have to? You see it all the time . . . on TV—when they have witnesses, they don't really protect them; then they get killed, too. And what if no one believes me but it's in all the papers?"

I didn't have any easy answers for her.

For a moment, she stared at me in frustration; then without warning, she jumped up, fists clenched. "I can't stand it!" she screamed. "I just can't *stand* it! She's wrecked my life. Her. *Erica.* I thought she was so great, but look what she's done!"

"Sally," I said, "Sally, hold on."

She kicked at the edge of the wing chair, ignoring me. "The superstar. Didn't care what she did to other people. I can't eat! I can't even *sleep*!" She grabbed her hair, pulling at handfuls.

I stood up, too, wondering what I should do, but she backed away from me.

"I hate her!" she hissed, like a small feral kitten that's been cornered. "Hate, hate, hate her!"

"Sally—"

"And you," she spat out. "You're just the same. Wanting to know everything, not caring what happens. Well, you can just *leave.*"

"Sally, you're upset."

For a moment, she looked almost calm. "I'm fine." Her voice was a low, sibilant whisper now, from across the room. "I've got my alarm system; I've got my gun. I can take care of myself better than anyone else can. And I'm going to get my gun, right now."

I headed for the door, fast. She hadn't left me much choice.

chapter thirty

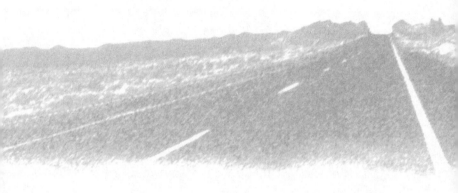

MAYBE SALLY'S ANGER NEEDED TO COME out. Maybe it would be good for her. I'd handled Sally badly, pushed her to tell me things, but I'd had to. And technically, Sally was safe, with her alarm system, her big bad gun. Besides, no one knew where she was, except for me and Nelson. But for how long was anyone safe? Troy, Sally, Dot.

As I drove over the Mule Mountains in the late afternoon, on my way back into Dudley, the storm had passed leaving behind it a chill in the air. It reminded me that soon the leaves would be gone from the cottonwoods, the Chinese elms, the cancer trees, gone from the rosebushes and the pomegranates. The quaint houses of Dudley would be exposed for what they were, little shacks built from scraps by poor people.

Come winter, I would have to get out my wool sweaters and heavy jacket from the crawl space in the attic, seal up the windows in my poorly insulated house. Still, it was Arizona; only a few days were really cold, and the sun shone nearly every day. Had Erica badly misjudged the lethality of her opponent, arranged a meeting at Olander Meadow, a nice private place to talk? That verged on insanity; Erica had been pigheaded, prideful, but not insane. She'd told Sally she was going to "make him pay." But how had she intended to do that?

There was still someone I needed to talk to. I had new information now, and maybe Lucas would tell me the truth this time.

I didn't want to think about it anymore, wanted to cocoon in my little house, cook up stews and soups, wear socks to bed, wanted it to be winter, everything over with. But instead, the worst was still ahead. I drove home, fed Big Foot, got a black cotton sweater from my closet.

Then a little voice in my head said, Forget this shit. Call Ed Masters and tell him everything you know. Let him do the investigating; that's what he's paid for. I *could* call him, check in, tell him some of what I knew, without involving Sally, or Lucas, either, not yet. I called the Willcox Sheriff's Department number and got Frankie.

"I need to talk to Ed Masters," I said.

"He's off today. I'm just about off myself, going to Safford with my grandkids."

"Give me his home phone number, then. It's important."

"What's going on?"

"It's a long story. It's all connected to a rape. Seventeen years ago."

Frankie clicked her tongue. "You're the *second* one to bring that up in two weeks."

"What?"

"Some women called week before last, wanting to know if we would have a police report on a rape that happened seventeen years ago. I told her it was probably destroyed but said she could call the main office. What's that got to do—"

"Never mind," I interrupted. "And give me Ed's number."

Erica, I thought as I hung up, she had to have been the one who called. It just reinforced everything. I punched in Ed's number.

"Dad's not here," said a teenage voice, sulky, withholding.

"When do you expect him?"

"Don't know."

Duty performed, I hung up, slightly relieved. But if I was going to do something as stupid as drive out to the valley, I should let someone know where I was going, whom I was going to talk to. That way, I thought, giggling to myself, an anxious little giggle, when they find my dead body, they'll know whom to question.

Tell someone who had some idea of what was going on. Stuart? I didn't know if I could trust him, wasn't sure. I bit my lip. Troy. I could trust Troy. He would be at Stuart's, home from school, but Stuart would still be at work, if I hurried.

I went back out to my car, pulled my snubby from the glove compartment. I knew it was loaded, but I checked it again; then I drove to Stuart's.

Erica's old pumpkin-colored car was parked under the chinaberry tree. Yellow leaves drifted down on me as I pushed open the gate, the fallen chinaberries treacherous under my feet as I walked up onto the porch.

I stopped. The door was open. I could hear voices.

"... *fucking idiot!*"

Pepper.

Then Troy: "I'm not an idiot. You could get your GED while she minds the baby. She'll do anything for me. She practically said so."

"She *says*. Until she's got you where she wants you, trapped in fucking suburbia."

"*L.A.*, Pepper, she lives in *L.A.* That's a really cool place to live. And she has money. Probably has a million bedrooms. We could say we used to be boyfriend/girlfriend but we're not anymore, see. That you have a hard life and you need to get away. She could fit you in. She loves children; she said so."

At this point, I should have knocked, but I didn't.

"You are fucking *dreaming*, man. You—"

"Wait," Troy interrupted. "I got it! We'll say the baby's *mine*. That's *it*. So the baby will kind of be like her grandchild. Then she won't be able to—"

I stamped on the porch floor loudly, then knocked on the door frame before more fraud could be perpetrated.

"If that's her, don't you fucking say *anything*, Troy."

Troy, in black baggy pants and a moth-eaten brown wool sweater, peered out at me through the screen. "It's only Chloe," he said over his shoulder.

"Only Chloe" smiled at him.

"Hi," he said. "Come on in. Did you hear about someone shooting up that old lady's house?"

"I heard all about it," I said.

Pepper was lying on one of the couches, wearing a man's tan corduroy sports jacket that looked like something Stuart would wear. A large Burger King sack sat among the full ashtrays on the enormous coffee table, along with a half-eaten Whopper and several bags of fries. Stuart's house, transformed into a teenage hangout. It didn't look that different.

"I wish I'd been there," said Troy fiercely. "With my twenty-two."

"But the cops took it." Pepper reached into a bag and ate a fry.

"Stuart got it back." Troy plopped down on the other couch.

Pepper squeezed a catsup packet into the fries bag. "Chloe, does Troy have to go with Mariah?"

"He should talk to a lawyer about that stuff. Troy . . ."

"I wish someone would adopt me," he said hopefully. "Someone I like. Maybe Stuart would. You could marry Stuart, so you'd be, like, this *respectable* couple."

"Forget it," I said. "I hardly know him. Troy, could we step out on the porch?"

He followed me out, looking interested.

"I want you to remember this," I said. "Don't tell anyone, not even Stuart, just remember, okay?"

"Stuart won't be home till later anyway," Troy said. "He has an AA meeting."

He didn't ask me to explain. And why should he? He was a teenager.

"I'm going out to the valley," I said, "to visit Lucas." Even as I said it, looking down at Troy, remembering something Troy had told me, an idea popped into my mind, one that had been lingering on the edge of consciousness for a while: a good idea, one that explained everything.

He looked up at me eagerly. "Right *now*? Can we go? Pepper would love to meet him."

"No. Another time. We'll all talk, I promise. Later," I said.

chapter thirty-one

A YOUNG WOMAN WAS JUST GETTING INTO a silver honda as I pulled up to Lucas's double-wide. When she saw me, she paused, her hand on the door. She wore a short jeans jacket, bleached out to the exact shade of her jeans—jeans so tight, you'd have to take a very deep breath to get into them—and cowboy boots that added a couple of inches to her legs. She was blond, impeccably groomed, and altogether snazzy.

I got out of my car and smiled, but she wasn't happy to see me. The air was chilly but it couldn't compare with the look she gave me. It was air-conditioned. I felt her eyes drilling into my back as I walked down the brick path to the front door, past the bed of petunias and marigolds. I heard her car door slam hard, the engine start up. I turned then and watched her go, gravel spinning out from under her tires.

I knocked.

Lucas answered the door right away, dressed in a plain white T-shirt and jeans. He wore one cowboy boot; the other he held in his hand.

"Miss Chloe!" For a fraction of a second, he glanced over my shoulder and down the road where the silver Honda had gone. "You come on in."

Then he smiled. His smile was as warm as Miss Jeans Jacket's glance was cold. And why not? I was the woman of his dreams, his one and only, the one he thought of each and every night before he said his prayers and went to bed. His smile said all this.

Never mind Miss Jeans Jacket; she was gone and I was here.

He hopped over to the leather chair, sat down, and pulled on his other cowboy boot. "Got any news?"

"No," I said. "Not really." I'd nursed the idea I'd formed on Stuart's porch, talking to Troy, thought about it on the way over. If I handled things right, Lucas would tell me what I needed to know. But I wasn't sure how to go about it. "But you might have something to tell *me.*"

His face was bland and blank. "Something to tell you? Not that I know of." He stood up and stomped on the floor with his boot. "I figure you already know about poor old Dot getting shot at. I thought you might be here to tell me they got a suspect, 'cause I saw her back in the valley this afternoon, driving by in that old station wagon. I thought she was staying with Ernest until things were safe."

"She's *home*?" I felt exasperated, but I put it aside. "I need to talk to you, Lucas."

"Sure. Look, I got to feed Gladys now. Come along, if you like."

"Gladys?"

"My horse. She's a filly. I named her Gladys after Elvis's mama. He really loved his mama. He never was the same after she died. You ever notice that?"

"I never kept tabs on Elvis," I said as I followed him to the door. He held it open for me, as if I were too precious to bear its weight personally. We walked to the back, then over to the fence and through a gate. The horse, dark brown and gleaming, was at the far edge of the paddock. She raised her head and snorted.

"Gladys," he called. "You beautiful thing, you. Come here, pretty."

The desert was a rich, majestic red-gold, the vegetation perfectly placed, as though Lucas lived on an estate landscaped by a master gardener. I trailed after as he went and turned on a faucet and began to fill Gladys's watering trough. The leftover clouds from the storm made for a beautiful sunset, a Michelangelo sunset, but without the angels.

"Lucas," I said, "you lied to me. You said you hadn't seen Erica for a long time, but she came to see you a few days before she was murdered."

"Ooops," he said.

Gladys came over and began to nuzzle at Lucas's shoulder. He patted her nose.

" 'Ooops'?" I said. "What does that mean?"

"It means I got to think about what you just said. Who told you that?"

"What difference does it make? It's true, isn't it?"

"Excuse me." He walked over to a shed and went inside, then came back out with a sack of feed and poured some into the other trough.

"Isn't it true?" I persisted. "That she came to see you less than two weeks ago?"

Lucas stroked above Gladys's nose sadly as she bent her head down to eat. Finally, he said. "Yeah, she did."

A breeze came up, carrying the rich smell of horse, as Lucas stroked Gladys. That's how he treats women too, I thought. Waters them with diet colas, tells them how pretty they are. Gentle as a breeze and about as reliable. Can you blame him? What does he have to offer that's solid?

"Did you tell Ed Masters that?" I asked him.

"Haven't seen Ed around. He's been pretty busy."

"I don't think you'd tell him if you did see him." I paused. *"I don't think you'd want him to know."*

He snorted. "Damn. You're about as crazy as Erica was. I got no idea what you're getting at."

"I think you do. She wanted to know how she could get hold of someone, didn't she, Lucas? An old friend of yours. Did she find him, or did you tell him and then he found *her*? Don't you see you could be protecting Erica's *murderer*?"

He looked at me. The evening light erased the lines on his face, giving it a kind of purity. The glass wall was completely gone now, his blue eyes clear and lucid. "I may be uneducated, but I'm not dumb," he said firmly. "If I knew who killed Erica, I'd be first in line to tell Ed Masters *and* anyone else who wanted to know."

"You knew Erica got raped, didn't you, a long time ago?"

He flinched. "Yeah, she told me that," he said after a minute.

"Well, I'm pretty sure it was the same person who killed her, Lucas. I didn't say you were dumb, but there're lots of emotional things tied up in this. Like friendship."

"Hold on," said Lucas. "I fell off the train. You lost me."

"You broke up with her right after Clyde came to visit you one time when Erica and Troy were here. Troy told me. It wasn't over this Patsy; it was because she told you Clyde had raped her, didn't she, Lucas? That's what happened to Clyde, he turned out to be meaner than anyone ever dreamed."

He laughed then, a good hearty laugh that seemed to go on and on while I waited patiently.

Finally, he stopped, wiping his eyes. "She *never.* You're way, way out in left field. We broke up over Patsy. Just like I told you."

"No," I said. "You can't accept that Clyde killed her, can you? That Clyde Daugherty, your old roping partner from the best days of your life, is a rapist and a murderer."

Lucas snorted through his nose. *"Damn,"* he said. "You *are* just like her. Jumping to conclusions, when you got nothing to go on at all. Clyde weren't a saint, and I'd be the first to tell you that, but he's *dead,* Chloe. Drove his old car on Highway Eighty, ninety miles an hour, straight off the road. He smashed up. People round here got real shook up about it. So whatever he done in his life, I guess he finally paid the bill. And he did it a good two weeks *before* she was murdered."

"Oh," I said. "Oh *shit.*"

"Come back over by the house; we can sit outside," said Lucas. "I guess now we do got to talk."

"What it was"—Lucas pulled a beer and a diet grape from a cooler on the ground beside him—"she wanted me to make a phone call for her. Acted real mysterious, said she had some things to say to someone."

"Oh?"

"I don't even have a damn phone, but she wanted me to go over, call from Mama's. Wouldn't tell me anything else unless I promised on my word to do it. I said she had to tell me first, and she kept saying, 'I just want someone to be worried at least, that's all I can do. You have to trust me.' We started to fight. She said I never had any faith in her."

"And?"

"Then she said, kind of thinking, 'Well, never mind. They'll never guess who it is, if I do it right.' And she stomped out."

"That's *all*? She didn't ever tell you who it was?" I was horribly disappointed. I popped open the diet soda and stared off at the mountains, feeling deflated. The sun was lower now, gold light fading to gray.

"I was planning on mentioning it to Ed, but I never could get ahold of him."

"You should have, right away," I said. "And told him about the rape, too."

"Damn." Lucas rubbed his chin. "That again. I don't see what her getting raped seventeen years ago has to do with anything."

"It does," I said. "She found out a couple of months ago that the same man did it again, to another woman. This woman isn't like Erica; she may never ever recover, Lucas. Erica told her the Thursday before she was murdered that she was going to confront him, make him pay. That's what the phone call must have been about."

"Son of a bitch." Lucas looked stunned. "Son of a *bitch*. Excuse me."

"I guess she didn't do it right." A note of accusation crept into my voice. "He must have recognized her voice."

"Damn." He kicked the side of the cooler. "That sorry, sick bastard. I thought she was wrong, got some idea in her head and wouldn't let go, the way she did." He crumpled his beer can and threw at an oil drum full of other cans, but it missed and bounced on to the dirt. He put his head in his hands. "She told me she had an idea who done it, back when we were seeing each other."

"Oh my God," I said.

"It was the voice that threw her. Didn't sound like him, but later, when she found the evidence, she thought, Well, he musta faked it."

"Wait," I said. "Start from the beginning."

Lucas sighed. "Her sister and brother-in-law was visiting her when it happened," he said, "she and her sister fighting all the time. A couple months after they left, she was cleaning the room where they'd stayed, and she found this receipt under the bed. It was from that western store in Sierra Vista—the receipt was for one cowboy hat, jeans, and a bandanna. That's what the guy was wearing, the rapist. I said to her, lots of guys dress like that in the Valley! Maybe not the bandanna so much but still."

Clear as day, I heard Wally saying to me at Erica's "I thought it was going to be like the Old West, cowboys and stuff. . . . I was going to buy an authentic cowboy outfit, and I ended up having to drive clear to Sierra Vista to get one."

"She thought he done it for revenge," Lucas went on, "to get even for her fighting with her sister."

"Wally," I said. My mouth was dry; I took the last swig of the diet grape, but it tasted like chemicals gone rotten.

And Wally was gone, who knews where. No one knew where. No one knew where, and Dot was home again. Suddenly from somewhere out in the desert came a whooping and a yelping like crazed children: coyotes. I shivered.

"And now someone's coming," Lucas said, craning his neck. "I swear it looks like Erica's car. How the hell would anyone—"

"Troy," I said. "Shit. I told him I was coming here." I stood up. "And you don't have a phone. I've got to go, Lucas. I need to talk to Dot, make a phone call. You keep Troy here, look out for him. *Don't let him leave.*"

chapter thirty-two

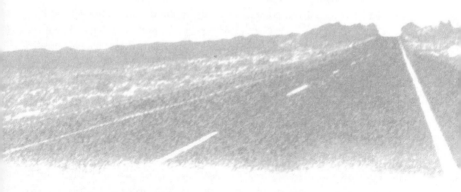

I TORE DOWN THE DIRT ROAD FROM Lucas's, turned right into the Junction. I had to get to a phone and I had to get to Dot. No one knew where Wally was. Dot was home again, and she was in danger. If what everyone said was wrong and Dot hadn't seen him clearly, Wally could just show up—he was so polite, so unassuming, I'd open my door to him.

The Junction was quiet, Monday night, one or two pickups parked at the bars, the Horseshoe Café closed. I reached in the glove compartment as I drove and got out my .38, the scenario working itself out in my mind.

It explained why Erica wouldn't make up with her sister, and also why she didn't tell. I'd heard other victims telling me about being raped by family members or loved ones of family members—how often they didn't tell. Protecting the ones they loved. Wrong and stupid maybe, but it happened all the time.

Wally could have heard the rumor about Dot seeing the man, people chatting about it at the Co-op, at the desk of the Copper Queen. After all, Erica was one of their own. Heard the rumor and knew he had to get rid of her. He was unaccounted for the night Dot was shot at and unaccounted for now, and until he was found, Dot wasn't safe. It all made sense, maybe a few pieces missing, but it did.

I whizzed through the outskirts of the Junction, sped down the highway, glad it was still light enough to see the turn to Dot's. Jackrabbits leaped as I hit the wash, bumped back out. I pulled into Dot's, spinning gravel. It was still light, but darkening fast.

But even as I pulled in, the place seemed empty, abandoned; no cars parked there. I got out of my car, gun in my hand. Then I realized what I was doing: standing there alone in the near dark at Dot Stone's house—a sitting duck.

But she had a phone. Could I get in? I went to the front door and found it slightly ajar. Why was that? Nervously, I went inside, saw the couch and the two recliners, saw Ernest, Henry, and Ruthie smiling blankly at me from under their graduation caps.

Why wasn't the door locked? Cautiously, I explored the house, peeking into two bedrooms—beds made up, a pile of library books on the bedside table in one of them—the bathroom, the kitchen. No one was here. I locked the front door and the kitchen door, found a phone book, and, squinting in the dim light, looked up the number for the Copper Queen. At least the phone had a lighted dial; I punched in the numbers and asked for Mariah Haskell.

"Hello?" Her voice was breathless with expectation. Wally, I thought, she's hoping it's Wally calling.

"Mariah," I said, "it's me, Chloe. Is Wally there?" I was certain of the answer.

Her voice was thick with disappointment. "No," she said, "I . . . I haven't even heard from him yet."

"Well, could you let me know if you do?" I gave her Dot's number. "Or if he shows up. Just call me here and let me know."

"Why?" she asked plaintively.

"He could be in danger."

She yelped. "What?"

"Just do it," I said, and hung up.

I sat on Dot's couch. Where was she? Why had the door been ajar, instead of locked? Could Lucas have been mistaken about seeing Dot's car? Maybe she was still at Ernest's, someone might have closed the door when they all left Sunday night and it hadn't caught. Wait. I had Ernest's card. I rummaged through my purse and found it. I could just barely make out the number.

"Hi," I said cheerily to the woman's voice that answered. "This is Chloe from the county attorney's. Could I speak to Dot?"

"She went back home," said the woman. She sounded exhausted. "Is anything wrong?"

"No, no," I said, not wanting to arouse any alarms at Ernest's house, where they paid their taxes and still didn't get protection. "Just wanted to say hi."

Then I sat in the silence of Dot Stone's house, my gun on the coffee table, waiting for Dot. It got too dark to see. My ears were straining so hard that I heard a clock ticking from one of the bedrooms, heard a truck going by out on the road, heard cars and pickups over in the Junction. I heard big semis going by on the freeway, all the way over in Willcox. I sat for what seemed like two, three hours. Then I looked at my watch. Fifteen minutes had gone by.

I got up and went into Dot's kitchen and opened the refrigerator. There was a jar of sun tea. It was old, had a film on the top.

I poured a glass and drank it—so strong, it seemed to gnaw away at the enamel on my teeth. Then I poured another. How was Sally doing in her fortress with the big gun? Sally. I went back to the living room and, straining to see in the moonlight that came through the window, punched in the number Nelson had given me. It rang and rang. No answer. I called again, thinking I must have done it wrong. Still no answer.

What had she done? Checked herself into a nice mental hospital, as Andy had suggested?

I went outside, debating if I should call the Tucson Police, have them look in on her. I peered down the road, hoping for the sight of Dot's headlights coming at me. There was nothing, just darkness at the end of the world.

Then suddenly, way far away, lights came on in a house. Hey, honey, let's get some light in here. Somehow, thinking of someone saying that made me feel lonely. Stuart, I thought. All this time, the muscles in my shoulders and my back had been bunched up with tension; now, at the thought of Stuart, they relaxed. He was out of the picture now. I *could* have him to dinner.

When this was over. Sally. Was she just not answering the phone, knowing there was no one on earth to talk to? Her faith in the whole world shot to hell?

And then it came to me: It made a kind of sick sense that Wally might have raped Erica in revenge, but then to fly back from L.A. and rape Sally, too? It was absurd. And this cowboy hat and bandanna stuff—everyone wore a cowboy hat in the valley. Some even wore bandannas. Sadly, I canceled Stuart's dinner invitation. I wasn't certain of anything anymore.

Except that my mouth was parched. I got my flashlight from my car and went back inside; I didn't want to turn on the lights. I poured more tea from the refrigerator. This wasn't wimp tea; it was Dot Stone tea. It should give me at least a minor dose of caffeine. I drank it while looking out the kitchen window. And then saw what I hadn't noticed before.

A gray car, parked at the back, a gray station wagon, rear end open and some sacks on the ground. Dot's car. All this time her car had been here. But where was she? The house was dead quiet; there wasn't a sound of any living creature in it. And then I noticed something else I hadn't noticed before. The dog. Fudd. Where was the *dog*?

Dead, I thought. Dot's dead. I didn't figure this out in time, and I still haven't, but most likely, Dot's dead.

I went back to the living room and called Ed Masters.

It rang once, twice, while I prayed someone would answer, and not the sulky teenager.

"Hello?"

"Ed." I plopped down on the couch in relief. "This is Chloe and I'm at Dot Stone's. You've got to get over here with a deputy. Dot's car is here and I can't find her anywhere."

"Hold on," said Ed, mouth full of something. Whatever it was that Ed ate. Peanut butter. Grits. "She's ain't at Ernest's?"

"No, she came home."

"Goddamn it," said Ed. "But if she ain't even there . . ."

"Her *car* is. She must be here somewhere. Ed, please." *Ed, you total asshole.* "You could be over here yourself in less than twenty minutes.

"It'll have to be a deputy." His voice was grudging. "We had a shooting over in Bowie just half an hour ago. It'll take awhile. Dot shows up, you two just sit tight, you hear? Wait for the deputy."

"Fine," I said, and hung up.

Then I clicked on my flashlight and systematically searched the house, going into the two bedrooms, opening the closet doors and shining the light inside. One bedroom closet had Dot's clothes; the other held what looked like Daddy's, still preserved. I looked under the beds, though they were low and you could hardly squeeze a person under them. A body. I felt sick.

I looked in the bathroom, pushed the shower curtain back. Yuck! A big black spider crouched by the drain. Over the shower rod hung a towel, damp. Why damp? How long did it take a towel to dry out here in the valley? Maybe a long time—there was moisture in the air. I looked in the closet in the front hall—full of windbreakers, and a bright yellow slicker.

I opened a narrow door in the kitchen and—wham!—something hit me on the arm. I struck out, then realized it was only an ironing board. I pushed it back up and slammed the door on it. There was no place else to look. It was a little old house and didn't have much room for any secrets. Though why not? Even something as small as a heart can hold many secrets. But there was still the car.

Dot might be at the wheel, slouched over, blood dripping from her forehead. You couldn't see inside the car from the kitchen window. I went out the kitchen door; an owl too-whooed into the night. Walked to where I could see the orchard, site of Daddy's demise. The moon was shining on the pecan trees, the trees belonging to Ernest, Ruthie, and Henry.

And back there in the trees somewhere was the place where you'd stand to shoot into the porch. Someone could be standing there now. I knew it made me a target, but I shone my flashlight briefly inside the car, then clicked it off. Nothing. The tailgate of the station wagon was open and the sacks lay on the ground. Potting soil, manure. Dot was probably going to put in a late-fall garden. Where would she keep the sacks? She wouldn't plan to have them lie out here all night.

I was afraid to turn the flashlight on again, but by now I could see fairly well in the dark. I stared at the back of the house and saw the little cellar, two doors that opened out and a set of steps. The doors were closed, a padlock on the hasp, but it was open.

I pulled the padlock off and opened the two doors. Something sailed past me, brushing at my hair. I jumped, almost screamed, combing at my head with my fingers. A bat glided off into the sky, swooping lazily, dark against the silver clouds. The place was full of life, spiders and owls and bats. A million more bats maybe right here in this little cellar. Because it was *little*. There'd just be room for the two sacks and that would be it.

Then I heard the gunshot.

Not close, but not that far away, either. I froze, dropped the flashlight, then grabbed it with the hand that didn't have the gun. *Get inside; lock the doors.* Where was the deputy? One could easily be here by now if he'd left right away. But he probably hadn't. I backed inside, locked the kitchen door, checked the front door.

I put the flashlight on the coffee table; then I sat on the couch, still clutching my gun. The hell with waiting for Ed's deputy. I was calling 911. I picked up the phone, punched in the number, put it to my ear. The phone was dead.

I'd never felt so alone in my life. What I should do is leave right now, I thought. Make a run for my car and drive away. *Sauve qui peut.* When had it gotten so cold? My mouth was trembling, trembling with the cold. I buttoned my black cotton sweater. I closed my eyes, wanting to sink into the dark as a kind of escape, waiting, waiting for Dot, waiting for the deputy.

Then I heard the noise, a kind of click and a shuffle, and opened my eyes again. Pointed my gun at nothing in the dark. And then there was light. Light, flooding the room. I blinked.

Dot Stone stood in the doorway that led to the kitchen, holding her shotgun, which was pointed down at the floor. "Chloe Newcombe, I just about shot you dead!"

chapter thirty-three

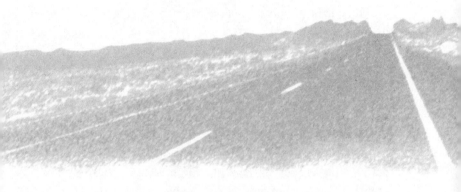

"DOT," I SAID. "THANK GOD. WHERE HAVE you been?" My heart was still pounding with shock.

She came farther into the room. Burrs clung to the bottoms of her khakis and her eyes were moist. "Someone shot my dog." Her voice was full of pain. "He came with me to the neighbors', and he stayed outside, sniffing around. We heard a shot, but we didn't think nothing of it. Then on the way back, I found him, dead in the creosote bushes."

I sat up straight, energized. "I heard the shot, too."

"There're people out here do that all the time," Dot said sadly. "Dog barks a lot and they get sick of it one day and up and shoot it." She sniffed. "But he was a good dog, just getting old."

She seemed a little out of it, befuddled with grief. I wanted to snap my fingers at her. Where was my one-woman vigilante when I needed her? "Dot, you don't *get* it. Who do you think shot him? The phone's dead, too. He must have cut the line. He's out there."

Dot shook her head as if to clear it, then opened her eyes wide and stood up straight, her expression suddenly fierce. "You're right. I guess I lost my head a little, seeing poor old Fudd." She patted her shotgun, looking at me. "Lucky you got a gun, too. You take the front windows and I'll take the back."

"It's okay," I said. "I made a phone call before the phone went out. I talked to Ed Masters."

She had already ducked into the kitchen. I called after her, "A deputy should be here any minute. I told Ed to send one out, said that your car was here and I couldn't find you."

Porch light, I thought. I should turn on the porch light. I went to the door, couldn't find the switch. "Dot?" No answer. *"Dot?"* I called again. I walked to the kitchen, but Dot wasn't there. Quickly, I checked the bedrooms, bathroom. She was gone.

And I knew where. Out to the pecan orchard. The deputy was coming. We could have stayed inside and waited for help. But Dot didn't want help—she was out to shoot the man who'd killed Erica, who'd shot her dog, too; out to shoot him dead "and then sleep all the night through." She was getting too old, senile. I clicked the safety off on my gun and started out there myself.

You couldn't see the kitchen door from the orchard. I dodged, keeping low until I reached the trees. The leaves whispered soothingly. The moon shone down. It was almost seductive. Careful not to let pecans crunch under my feet, I made my way from one tree to another, pausing frequently, listening for sounds.

Where to go? Then it came to me—Henry's tree. Henry would protect us both. Superstition, the last refuge of the helpless. I headed that way, moving from tree to tree. Just one tree to go. And then someone put a hand on my arm—softly, carefully.

Not carefully enough. I yelped.

Dot, standing behind the tree, right beside me.

Suddenly, a light exploded. Searing, painful light pointed right at my eyes. I closed my eyes against it, froze like a bunny rabbit in the headlights of a car.

"Drop the gun," a man's voice said.

I blinked, trying to see whose it was, but it didn't help.

"Drop it." Blindly, I did, and the light went away. That voice—I almost knew it. If only I could see.

"Now kick the gun, this way, over here." I kicked, watched the gun slither away. Now I could see—a bulky, solid form standing by the next tree over, a gun pointed right at me. Ed Masters.

"Oh shit," I said, my knees shaky with relief. "*Ed*. It's just me, Chloe. You told us to stay put, but Dot—" I stopped.

Where was his car? I should have heard it drive up. And Dot wasn't behind the tree where she'd been a few seconds ago, hadn't stepped out to greet her old third-grade pupil. She'd slipped away like some old lady spirit of the trees.

"But Dot what?" barked Ed. "Where the hell is she?"

What was he doing in the pecan orchard? Why was he still pointing the gun at me while the light moved back and forth, slowly, methodically, searching?

"I don't know where she is," I said. She'd slipped away. Slipped away at the sight of Ed. It was just me out here with Ed Masters. The primary investigator.

Why *was* he still pointing a gun at me? Little goose bumps rose along my arms and fear laid an icy hand on the back of my neck as a good reason slowly dawned. I made my voice conversational, a little concerned. "She never showed up. I'm worried about her. With this maniac running loose."

"Got to be here somewhere, 'cause her car is," said Ed matter-of-factly. "She's a damn fool, always was and always will be." He paused. I could see his face now, white in the moonlight. "For that matter, so are you. You been snooping around so much, I even thought about hauling you in—obstruction of justice."

"I've just been talking to the victims is all," I said, "helping them with their grief."

Maybe we were just standing out here in the moonlight, Ed and I, while he pointed a gun at me and gave me a lecture.

"Yeah?" The light moved back and forth still, but he didn't take his eyes off me. "Little more than that, I'd say. I talked to Frankie."

I was confused. What did Frankie have to do with anything? "So?"

"Saw her at the Circle K on her way out of town. Told me you was talking about some damn rape happened seventeen years ago. 'Remember,' she said to me, 'I told you about the other one calling.' Second time it was brought up, she said, in two weeks."

I swallowed. "Frankie said that?"

Ed's eyes gleamed at me, opaque as stone. He spat at the ground. "Then she called me up, saying things."

"Who? *Frankie?*"

"The bitch. The bitch with the hair. Saying everybody knew about me. How would I like my wife and kids to find out? I knew who she was." His voice growled out of the darkness, like thunder at a distance, the light still moving back and forth.

"Who?" I asked desperately.

"You *know* who."

"No," I said. "No, I don't." What was he going to do? Shoot me? Actually shoot me? And no deputy was coming. Where was Dot? She'd left me here, in danger of my life. Its possibilities stretched out in front of me like an impossible dream, Stuart to dinner, chicken mole. Let me live, I prayed. I'll be good; I'll be happy. Prayed to whom, to what? The *I Ching*?

"Sitting back there in the damn high school auditorium, staring at me," Ed went on, "all high-and-mighty, at the DARE speech I gave them kids."

That was it. Sitting in the auditorium, hearing his voice, that must have been when Erica had figured it out. Maybe he'd talked to them about his own kids, eight of them, and as a mother, thinking of Troy, too, she'd let it go until she'd talked to Sally.

"Then," said Ed indignantly, "they busted her kid. I stopped by to see some of the guys and heard her going on and on, out in the lobby of the police station. Snuck a peek to see who it was. So I *knew* her voice when she called up. And all along," said Ed, his voice rising, "*all along,* she was feeding her own kid drugs. Did you know that?"

He doesn't know, I thought, who Troy really is, never put it together. Thank God he doesn't know.

"She deserved to die," I said firmly. "She wasn't a good mother."

Erica, whom I'd last seen lying in the grass, copper hair bright in the sun, blood staining her pink dress deep red. It could happen to me now.

There was a silence. For a moment, absurdly, I thought I'd convinced him I was on his side.

Then he moved the light, shone it down between the trees.

"Okay," he said. "We're going back to the house and wait for Dot. You walk ahead, stay in the light."

My legs were so weak, I didn't know if I could walk at all. I started shakily down the path of the light, ducking under an unpruned branch.

Ed said from behind me, "Don't do anything funny now; I'll shoot first, think later."

He can't shoot me yet, I thought. He thinks Dot might hear the shot and get away. He needs Dot to be here. My senses had sharpened, reacting to my fear. I could smell the pecans, now rotting. One step, two steps. Heard a leaf fall and hit the ground. Three steps, four steps. Heard a whoosh.

Then I heard the scream.

The scream turned to a bellow; it seemed to go on and on, horrifying, obliterating everything. For a second, I thought I was the one screaming, that Ed had shot me. The sound was so intense, it seemed to exist in my own psyche. I turned as this was going through my head.

Ed was on the ground, in the leaves, moaning, and blood, blood everywhere, dark, dark in the moonlight—

"Chloe, get his gun."

For a minute, I couldn't think. What? Where? Then I saw it, just by his arm. I kicked it away, grabbed for it, fumbling in the leaves, picked it up. "Dot," I said then. "You *shot* him?

Dot stood there, holding something heavy and jagged in her hand. What was it?

"Couldn't shoot for fear of hitting you," she said. "I got him with this." She held it aloft, long-handled, ancient, medieval. Something Father Time might carry. "Daddy's old pruning saw. Lying right where he dropped it."

Ed raised himself briefly, fell back. Blood poured from his shoulder and all down his arm. Long rivers of blood, black pools in the leaves.

"Dot Stone," he said. His voice was weak, dazed. "You was my third-grade schoolteacher."

"I know it." She sounded disgusted. "I saw you out there, with poor Erica's body; I saw you, Ed Masters, and I ran. But I thought, I'm going to kill that man for what he done to her. Can't trust the law to do it. So I waited, waited for a chance, whispered to people that I'd seen you, so you'd come to get me. Kill you fair and square in self-defense. You were always a bully."

Dot lowered the saw, close to Ed. "Could just about prune off a head with this."

I shuddered.

Ed bellowed out, "Dot!"

She looked down at him; then she stepped back. "But I can't." Suddenly, her voice was tired. "Still see that little boy, skinny back then, eating paste. His ma didn't take good care of him, gave him those frosted flakes with soda pop on them, 'stead of milk, for breakfast, and she never took him to the dentist. Had green mold on his—"

"If you don't kill him, I will," a voice said.

Troy, the famous Troy, standing by a pecan tree. He held a gun in his hand, the .22, and tears were streaming down his face.

"I heard what she said," he told Ed in a choked voice. "I heard. You killed my mom, you . . . you big fat pig. And you tried to blame me. I hate you." His voice was thick and muffled with tears. "I hate you more than I hate anything in the whole wide world. I hope you burn in hell forever and ever."

"Troy," I said, *"no."*

From somewhere over by the house, I heard a snuffle and a snort. A horse. "You came with Lucas, didn't you?" I said to Troy, trying to distract him. "Where is he?"

Troy sniffed and blinked his eyes. He wasn't crying now. "In the front of the house. But we don't need him."

"Lucas!" I shouted.

"I can take care of this," said Troy, his voice firm now. He clicked the safety off.

I moved faster than I ever knew I could, hitting Troy, knocking the gun aside. It fired anyway, at nothing, the bullet ricocheting off the trees. Troy stood empty-handed, looking confused, as though he were just waking up from a bad dream. I had saved Troy, the famous Troy. Saved him from the kind of guilt that could haunt him forever. He would still have the nightmares, but in them, he'd be innocent.

At least maybe it was some kind of redemption.